Chloë Ashby is an author and arts critic. Since graduating from the Courtauld Institute of Art, she has written for publications such as the *Times*, *TLS*, *Guardian*, *FT Life & Arts*, *Spectator* and *frieze*. She is the author of *Colours of Art: The Story of Art in 80 Palettes*, a *Times* best book of 2022. She lives in London.

Wet Paint was her debut novel and *Second Self* is her second.

Praise for *Second Self*

'A magnificent novel about big decisions, social pressures, complex questions and finding clarity in the face of uncertainty'
i Paper

'This is a beautifully nuanced portrait of a woman at a cross-roads. Hard recommend'
Marie Claire

'Tender and acutely observed ... *Second Self* is a moving exploration of the choices that shape a life'
Mail on Sunday

'A poignant and beautifully written second novel exploring the decisions we may find ourselves having to make'
Glamour

'An elegantly subtle novel about motherhood, marriage and choice – I'm sure it will resonate with many'
Claire Powell, author of *At the Table*

'*Second Self* asks what happens when two people change separately as well as together'
Abigail Bergstrom, author of *What a Shame*

'There's a beguiling simplicity to Chloë's considered, timeless and elegiac prose'
Huma Qureshi, author of
Things We Do Not Tell the People We Love

'*Second Self* is written in almost hypnotically perfect prose . . . I can't wait to read all of Chloë's work'
Kate Sawyer, author of *The Stranding*

'Ashby handles her material lightly and atmospherically. It feels like reading the secret thoughts of a dear friend'
Rowan Hisayo Buchanan, author of *The Sleep Watcher*

'At times meditative, at times heartbreaking, but throughout compassionate and nuanced'
Jenny Mustard, author of *Okay Days*

Praise for *Wet Paint*

'A skilful, absorbing novel that is so much about seeing and being seen'

Spectator

'What marks Ashby out as a distinctive voice is the warmth and compassion with which she depicts her characters and their milieu'

Observer

'*Wet Paint* is a clever, gripping novel in which art and life reflect on and imitate one another'

Times Literary Supplement

'A blistering story of one girl's attempts to outmanoeuvre past trauma, loss and rejection only to find her life descending into chaos'

Stylist

'A realistic and elegant portrait of a young woman beginning to recover herself from bereavement'

Irish Times

'In this poised, heartfelt debut, Ashby paints a raw, richly detailed portrait of untethered youth, friendship and suppressed grief'

Olivia Sudjic, author of *Asylum Road*

'This isn't a book you read, but a book you step into. Chloë Ashby has created a mesmerising and energetic world of grief, art and self-discovery'

Emma Gannon, author of *Olive*

'*Wet Paint* is a searing exploration of grief, friendship and what it is to grow up. It made me laugh but also cry. I will think about this book for a long time'

Annie Lord, author of *Notes on Heartbreak*

'A courageous and unwinding exploration of female pain. Dark, funny and hopeful, it's a remarkable story'

Abigail Bergstrom, author of *What a Shame*

'Delicate, powerful and honest all at once. This is an unforgettable novel, and I'll read anything Chloë Ashby writes'

Lucia Osborne-Crowley, author of *My Body Keeps Your Secrets*

SECOND SELF

CHLOË ASHBY

First published in Great Britain in 2023 by Trapeze,
This paperback edition published in 2024 by Trapeze,
an imprint of The Orion Publishing Group Ltd
Carmelite House, 50 Victoria Embankment,
London EC4Y 0DZ

An Hachette UK company

1 3 5 7 9 10 8 6 4 2

A CIP catalogue record for this book is
available from the British Library.

ISBN (Mass Market Paperback) 978 1 398703056
ISBN (eBook) 978 1 3987 0306 3
ISBN (Audio) 978 1 3987 0307 0

The Adrienne Rich epigraph quote is taken from *Of Woman Born: Motherhood as Experience and Institution* with permission from the publisher, W.W. Norton.

Typeset by Born Group
Printed and bound in Great Britain by Clays Ltd, Elcograf S.p.A.

MIX
Paper from
responsible sources
FSC® C104740

www.orionbooks.co.uk

To my mother and her mother

SECOND SELF

SECOND SELF

'It is an unfortunate physical reality of the material nature of paintings that these objects are vulnerable to change and damage as a consequence of exposure to a variety of damaging causes'

– *The National Gallery*

'The body has been made so problematic for women that it has often seemed easier to shrug it off and travel as a disembodied spirit'

– *Adrienne Rich*

Noah had told me early on that he didn't want children. I can still see the look on his face as he said it, lips rolling in on one another, eyes tapering. He was bracing himself for me to say it was a deal-breaker, the way other women had done before. That's fine, I remember replying, laughing, I'm not exactly yearning for motherhood. He asked me if I was sure, and when I said yes, relief flooded his face. I stopped laughing, because he was serious and so was I. We went on with our day, and the days after that. The days turned to weeks, months, years.

We met when I was twenty-five and he was thirty-six. By now, we'd been together for ten years and married for eight. We'd established a routine, a way of living. With only ourselves to worry about, we could afford to be selfish, prioritising our relationship, our work – that was the way we liked it. During the week, we were out more often than we were in. Weekends were quiet and free. We rarely ate dinner before eight o'clock, and we always drank wine. Sunday mornings were spent in bed, reading the papers, and doing other more intimate things.

My period being late should at least have been a nuisance. An unwelcome surprise, like rain without an umbrella, or off milk on cereal. The one and only time it had been this late before, it had been more than that.

I blinked open my eyes and let my gaze brush over my fellow commuters. A young guy in a shiny new suit. An older woman bundled up in a bobble hat and scarf, nose-deep in a book. Some teenagers drinking cans of Coke on their way to school. Behind them, the passenger alarm: 'Lift flap and pull handle.' Still drawing a blank, I considered the possibility that I was simply tired and in need of a jumpstart.

My period was late, and so was my mother. It was twenty past one and I was sitting in the café at the National Gallery. I'd accepted a job at the museum a couple of months before Noah and I got married, a small ceremony at the local town hall followed by tonnes of sharing plates at a restaurant we loved right nearby. When we met, I was finishing my postgraduate diploma in conservation, exploring the techniques and materials of artists from the Middle Ages to the twenty-first century, learning how to identify signs of deterioration and conduct both remedial treatments and emergency interventions.

As soon as the minute hand began to lean to the right, I felt an itch of nerves on my forearms, because she was never not on time. I snuffed it out with thoughts of sandwich fillings. We were both keen on the poached salmon one, with ochre mayonnaise and peppery watercress that caught in the cracks between our teeth; before saying goodbye, we'd direct each other's little-fingernail towards the most conspicuous pieces of green. I left my coat on the back of my chair and slid two of those sandwiches onto a plastic tray, then after a split-second hesitation – my mind flickering to the box of untouched tampons in my bag – ordered two small glasses of white wine. By the time I was back at our table, like a shell her chair remained empty.

I called her mobile and it rang before going to voicemail, so she couldn't be stuck on the Tube without signal. Maybe she was walking, and it was buried deep in the belly of her handbag, so she hadn't heard it ring or felt it vibrate. Maybe she'd arrived early and decided to visit the permanent collection before instead of after lunch, as she usually did, and lost track of time. The itch crept up my arms towards my chest. I glanced again at the clock, the long hand advancing, and drank some wine. The self-reproach that made itself known in my reddening face took me by surprise.

When the table started to tremble, and the word 'Home' appeared on the illuminated screen of my phone, I almost knocked over my glass. 'Mum?'

'Cathy, darling, sorry I missed your call – I've been on the phone with the council all morning.'

'You're in Norfolk?'

A gentle laugh. 'Yes.'

'We're supposed to be having lunch.' I tried not to let the disappointment leak into my voice.

'Today?'

'Now.'

'Now?' I heard the jangle of beads as she slipped on the red-rimmed reading glasses that were a regular feature around her neck. Next, the licking of forefinger and thumb, and the leafing of pages – she'd always kept a diary by the phone, filled with writing that sloped to the right. 'Oh my god.'

I pictured her cheeks, pinched with guilt.

'I can't believe it.'

I drank some more wine, forcibly opening my throat when, involuntarily, it threatened to close up. I watched with interest as my free hand went to touch my stomach, then I tilted my head back and felt the cool liquid slip down inside me.

'I'm so sorry, darling.'

'It's OK.'

'It's not OK.' Her voice cracked. 'I've never missed your birthday.'

5

'Honestly, don't worry about it, Mum. Is everything all right at home?'

'Oh, everything's fine, it's just this new proposal for an offshore windfarm.' My mother was one of the few inhabitants in her local area to care more about clean electricity than the skyline. 'It could power almost five hundred *thousand* homes, isn't that incredible?'

'Incredible.'

'It is, and you can just imagine the response from some of this lot.'

I peeled open the clear plastic packaging of my sandwich as she started rebuking the naysayers.

'They're objecting because of the birds.'

'The birds?'

'The birds!'

Apparently, there was a risk of them colliding with the rotor blades.

'Anyway, enough of that.' The jangle of beads, followed by the turning of another page. 'Do you have lunch plans on Tuesday?'

'Hang on,' I said, moving my phone away from my ear and in front of my face. I could vaguely hear her talking into the receiver as I checked my calendar. I nodded to no one in particular, then: 'No plans.'

'Well, keep it free – it's on me.'

'Will do.' I glanced at the clock one last time and told her I should probably go.

'Happy birthday, darling.'

'Thanks, Mum.'

*

Frank was waiting for me inside the staff entrance. When he saw me, he raised a hand in greeting. He'd started at the museum around the same time as me. At some point during my first week, or it could have been the second, we were summoned by HR and instructed to stand next to one another and smile for an awkward double portrait that we later learned was circulated internally. We'd been friends ever since.

'Good lunch?' His voice was deep, the kind of deep you would attach to a large man with broad shoulders and big feet (like me, Frank had to stand on a stool to reach the solutions we kept on the studio's top shelf, right above the paintbrushes and pots of ground pigments). It was also coarse from sucking on skinny cigarettes that he rolled at high speed with liquorice-flavoured paper. Apparently, his partner, a kind and supportive Scotsman called Douglas, had tried to help him quit for years before giving in and taking up smoking himself.

'It was fine, thanks.'

He arched a single grey eyebrow, quite capable of reading me by now. 'Well, I have something for you.' I was trying to work out how word of my birthday could have got out when he added: 'It's ready.'

My lips curled up at the corners, any lingering disappointment about being stood up by my mother dispelled. 'The beach scene?' I whispered.

He nodded at a speed that told me he, too, was excited, though for different reasons. I was looking forward to working on the somewhat unexceptional *View of Scheveningen Sands* because it reminded me of home, while Frank had a thing for Dutch Golden Age paintings. He appreciated the departure from biblical themes and the focus on daily life. The tabletop arrangements, portraits, domestic interiors, landscapes. This one was nicely done in a muted palette of inexpensive browns, greys, yellows and blues, but admittedly nothing special. It had only come to me because the room where it hung was being renovated.

'Shall we?' Instead of opening one of the double doors, he gripped both handles and pushed them wide. As he did so, his mouth broke into a grin. There was something boyish about his features, which were all a tad too big for his face, as if he were still growing into them in his fifties. When he told me that one of the reasons he liked the decidedly secular subjects of the Dutch was because he'd been force-fed Catholicism as a child, his eyes had flashed left and right – the way they do whenever he lets me in on a secret.

I followed him down another set of stairs to the lower conservation studios, the sound of museumgoers muffled, the temperature a degree or two lower, or at least that's always how it feels. It might have something to do with the dusky-blue walls, and the chunky white lights hanging in front of them, vaguely resembling floating icebergs.

'Here are our findings,' said Frank, passing me a plastic folder of printed notes, the results of various investigations, including analysis under ultraviolet light. He was in the scientific department but often helped out with structural work, as dextrous with canvas and wood as he was with rolling papers. 'Also on the server, of course.'

'Of course,' I said, smiling first at his professionalism and then at the way he was eagerly rocking back and forth on his heels. I held the folder snugly to my chest as I approached the painting, which was resting on an easel in the corner.

The beach stretched out beneath a clouded sky; together with the heavy coats and boots of the men, women and children gathered on the shore, it told the viewer it was a gusty winter's day. On the left, a couple of old fishing boats rested against the grassy dunes, and further along a few more had been pulled up onto the sand, fresh from the waves.

'So, there's the split in the lower wood panel – that's one issue – and then there's the discoloured varnish.'

'Right.' The entire scene had a sallow tinge to it from where the natural resin varnish, applied to protect the paint, had darkened over time.

'Obviously there's only so much we can tell at the moment,' he added, following my gaze. 'We'll do some more investigations after your initial clean.'

'Mm-hm.' Like a camera lens on autofocus, my eyes zoomed in and started scanning the surface for losses. The sky was muddy with overpaint, probably from an earlier restoration. So was the sea.

'I'll leave you to it then,' he said, talking to me but looking at the painting. 'Will I see you at Mara's leaving drinks?'

I wondered aloud why the waves ran perpendicular to the beach in places, instead of parallel with it.

'Catherine?'

'Sorry?'

'Mara?'

'Oh, sure.'

As his footsteps receded along the corridor, I heard him chuckling. I closed my eyes and tried to breathe in the salty sea air.

*

I had no intention of attending Mara's leaving drinks, and Frank knew it. I was just too distracted to make a legitimate excuse. I spent the afternoon reading about my Dutch marine painter, Hendrick van Anthonissen, and if it hadn't been for Noah, I'd have continued sifting through books and journals late into the evening. Hendrick and I would be spending the next few months together, and before I started on his painting, I wanted to know all about him – his career as an artist, his life in Amsterdam, everything in between.

But I also wanted to meet my husband, who had booked us a table at my favourite restaurant. My husband, or my man friend – Noah had jokingly suggested I call him the latter when I'd told him I kept stumbling over his new marital label, and, to his dismay, it had stuck. I collected my things and headed for the exit, tapping out a message telling him I was on my way. I listened to a voicemail from Anna, my best friend since school, wishing me a 'happy fucking birthday!' and demanding we get together at the weekend.

As I emerged from the staff entrance, the cold air nipped at my bare ankles – Noah had given up on telling me, his face creasing with faux-concern, that I seemed to have forgotten my socks. After a December that had felt more like autumn than winter, January had been bitterly cold, and now so was February.

The Christmas tree in Trafalgar Square was long gone, leaving the stone lions guarding nothing but Nelson. Still, the concrete patch stretching out in front of the National Gallery was teeming. Tourists were pointing their cameras at buskers strumming guitars beneath lamp-posts, their low-rent version of a spotlit stage. A grey-haired man was humming to himself as he made art on the ground with coloured chalk. Unlike the framed pieces in the museum, this would be washed away by morning. Giving it a cursory glance as she passed by was a woman of about my age with a small baby strapped to her chest. I looked away and wrapped my scarf around my neck.

As I walked to the restaurant with my bag slung over my shoulder, I could feel the box of tampons gently but persistently poking my side. Noah was sitting at our table when I arrived. I saw him through the misty window, in conversation with one of the waiters, talking – as usual – with his hands as much as his mouth. He clapped and the waiter laughed. I couldn't help smiling as I opened the door and felt a warm flush of air. I shed my coat, and with it any thought of my cycle.

'Happy birthday, my love,' he said, standing to greet me with a kiss surrounded by his winter beard, an annual addition to our household. 'Here.' He held out his hands, well versed at reviving my fingers, with their poor circulation. 'I'm sorry I had to slip out early this morning,' he said, rubbing them warm. He'd planned to bring me breakfast in bed – 'proper coffee and almond croissants', he'd said, fresh from the sweet-smelling bakery around the corner from the flat – but a departmental meeting had intervened.

'Don't worry, Tom kept me company.'

'Oh good, I'm glad – I had a word with him before I left, you see.'

I shook my head, even as I felt my cheeks rise. He liked to think that he and our black-and-white rescue cat had a mutual understanding.

He carried on the joke for another minute or two, as he always did. 'I asked him to go and get some more milk, and he obliged, but then he was starving hungry . . .'

'As usual.'

'. . . as usual, and he couldn't wait until he got back to the flat. He tried his best to be careful, but the bottle was just so heavy, and when he tipped it up . . .' He bit his lip with disappointment. 'There were milky paw prints all along the pavement.'

I laughed.

'So, how was your day?'

I was halfway through telling him about the seascape when two glasses of champagne arrived, golden yellow in glasses shaped like tears. I cocked my head.

'What?' he asked, reaching out to receive them and handing me one.

'Come on, it's not exactly an important birthday.'

'Every birthday is important, especially your thirty-fifth,' said Noah, raising his glass to clink mine, looking me in the eye. 'I would know.'

'Oh, that's right, for a moment I forgot how old you are.'

He reached his spare hand under the table and gave my thigh a half-squeeze, half-pinch. 'Age is beauty, babe.'

'Well, that I believe.'

His darker than dark hair was threaded with grey, but it was still full and thick. When he smiled, the kind of lines that add character to a face sprung up around the corners of his mouth and eyes. He wore them well, the extra eleven years he had on me. With him, I was happy to accept the deeply unfair disparity between men and women when it comes to ageing.

'So,' he said, 'what are we having?'

We turned our attention to our menus, and shortly after the waiter reappeared. He and Noah picked up where they left off, half laughing, half despairing about the US president's latest outrage, while I weighed up the pros and cons of ravioli versus spaghetti.

After we'd ordered, Noah asked about lunch with my mother. 'Did you and Janey have fun?'

I swallowed my final sip of champagne and felt the tiny bubbles fizz against the sides of my throat. 'She didn't make it, actually.'

'Oh?'

'She forgot.'

He paused. 'Lunch or your birthday?'

I tried a little too hard to put on a smile. 'Both.'

'Wow.'

'Yes, well, there's a lot going on at home. Which is good, obviously.' Ever since my father's heart had unexpectedly given out, she'd been keeping herself busy, helping to manage the local nature reserve, volunteering at beach cleans. I didn't blame her, living in the same house, with the same things – an inhabited reliquary. Still, there were times when I couldn't help but take it personally. My mother, who used to be the one to call, who if anything should have been more available, had become absorbed in other things. The one thing that had kept *me* going after Dad was the thought that she needed me.

'Anyway, we've rearranged,' I said, waving away his sympathy and steering the conversation back around to his meeting. 'How did it go?'

'Oh, fine, there's some reshuffling going on – a couple of promotions coming up over the next few months, apparently, but we'll see.'

Noah had worked in the same university department for the entire time I'd known him. He spent his days researching and writing about diplomacy, nationalism, and conflict past and present, as well as teaching. He cared as much about his students and their futures as he did his own work, encouraging them to apply for internships and then jobs, joining them on marches. His ability to sit and immerse himself in a text, no matter what was going on around him, was one of my favourite things about him. He would probably have said the same about me and paintings.

'Well, I would promote you,' I said, hooking an ankle around his.

'That's good enough for me.'

Our mains arrived, followed by a double portion of tiramisu adorned with a single candle. Noah sang to me, quietly to begin with, then loud enough for the tables on either side of us to hear. My cheeks were burning, but that didn't deter him – we both knew that I secretly loved being serenaded on my birthday. When he was done, I blew him a kiss, and the waiter brought us complimentary shots of limoncello.

On the Tube home, he told me there was a birthday present waiting for me in the bedroom.

I gave him a look, and he laughed.

It turned out there was a parcel tucked away in his bedside table. I asked if I could wait and open it the following morning and have my other gift first.

'Your other gift?' he asked, pulling me towards him hungrily.

His lips tasted of lemon sherbet.

After, I went to the loo, and there it was – as they say, better late than never. I stared at the swatch of red until my vision blurred, then I shook my head and looked away. When I stood up and went to wash my hands, I realised I was trembling. I gripped the edge of the sink to try to steady myself, but the tremors started up again as soon as I loosened my hold. I gazed at my reflection in the mirror and tried to work out whether I'd had too much wine, or whether it was something else. Again, I willed my gut feeling into action. Again, it played dead.

Had you ever imagined the two of us together, Noah asked me, lying in bed the morning after the first time we'd slept together, our limbs entwined beneath the duvet. My head was resting on his steadily rising and falling chest, and his index finger was drawing faint circles around my hip. In truth, I hadn't – I'd always thought of him as Anna's – but I didn't want him to interpret my loyalty as indifference, so I lied and told him I had. And you? He told me he had, too. For a while it made me wonder if he still pictured himself with other women.

That was how we met – he and Anna had been dating. It would have been a dodgy move on my part if she hadn't been the one to suggest that he and I get together. By this point, she'd been introduced to her now-husband, though she maintains there was no overlap and that Caleb had nothing to do with her dumping Noah. Still, she traded in a brilliant if slightly scruffy lecturer in international relations for a hot young music producer with his own record label.

It was Anna who'd pursued Noah in the first place. They'd met through a mutual friend who also worked in the war studies department. Back then, when we were in our early twenties, she'd been charmed by him being a decade older and having more than one book to his credit. He was as kind and supportive then as he is now, two qualities she'd long been craving – she would laugh when asked about it, make some joke about Freud and her 'daddy issues'. Maybe I was craving those qualities too. Though I loved my father dearly – he was the only man I'd ever loved before Noah – it was my mother I missed if we ever went more than a week without speaking.

I followed up with Anna a couple of days after my birthday. Caleb was away that weekend, so she suggested we spend the Sunday together. After my morning run, I caught the overground from Hackney Central to Kentish Town, where they'd lived for roughly the same amount of time that Noah and I had been in London Fields. We got lucky, Anna would tell friends, when they commented on the size of the house, and the garden, and the shed that Caleb had converted into a home studio. She'd stretch her lips into an apology as she added, It seems our house price has been the one good thing to come out of us leaving the EU! In fact, they'd paid just under the asking price, and the seesaw of Brexit negotiations had only just begun.

I arrived at the recently brightened brick façade and climbed the steep stone steps to the front door, the letterbox of which was stuffed with weekend papers. The bell emitted a two-pitched 'ding-dong'. A moment later, the click of a lock and the glossy black door swung open.

'Cathy, hello!' Anna had Theo on her hip. My unofficial godson.

She ushered me into their honey-coloured hallway, and I took off my coat and hung it on the rack while she closed the door behind me and freed the papers from the letterbox's grip. I considered kicking off my shoes, wary of the leafy mulch that had gathered on the pavements after a night of heavy rain, but decided instead to give them a quick wipe on the doormat. Anna didn't care about that kind of thing.

After she'd lowered a babbling Theo to the floor, paved with reclaimed tiles, we hugged, and I breathed in the sweet scent of her woody perfume muddled with baby skin, soft and clean.

'It's *so* good to see you,' she said, clinging on tight like we were floating in the middle of the ocean and I was her rubber ring. 'And not just because I haven't spoken to anyone above the age of two since Caleb left on Friday morning.'

'It's good to see you, too,' I said, laughing. 'Both of you. In fact, I might have something in here for a certain small friend of mine.'

Theo's coffee-coloured eyes ballooned as I knelt beside him and began to rootle around in my bag. He'd inherited them from Caleb, together with his thick black hair; even with a buzz cut, Caleb's was glossy and dark. Theo's skin, a warm brown, was a blend of his mum and dad's.

'Um, you're the one who's supposed to be receiving gifts today,' said Anna, tapping me with her toes.

I reminded her that I got a good discount in the museum shop and handed him a colouring book of paintings by famous artists. He opened it onto a pot of sunflowers.

'Oh Theo, isn't that kind of your fairy godmother? Are you going to give her a big kiss to say thank you?'

Still holding onto his book, he reached out his pudgy arms.

Anna and Caleb had a cleaner who came every Monday, and yet, whenever I visited at the weekend, their beautiful home looked like it had been burgled. The blue table in the hall became a landing station for bags, post, keys. Pairs of shoes lined the hall, and that day a small, foldable umbrella that had been left to dry half-closed resembled a crouching spider. As I made my way to the kitchen at the back of the house, overlooking the garden, I glanced into the living room and could barely make out the sofa beneath the soft toys and magazines. It would have driven me mad, and Noah madder, but they weren't fazed by it. I suppose they knew that, in a couple of days, order would be restored.

While Anna put Theo down for a nap, and I waited for the kettle to boil, I returned various bits and pieces to the kitchen cupboards, painted a soothing sage green, and wiped the counter clean, scrubbing extra hard at a sticky patch by the sink. When the whistle sounded, I made two mugs of milky tea, Anna's sweetened with sugar. I brought them over to the table, pollinated with crumbs, and smiled as I noticed a bunch of irises wrapped in brown paper and an envelope with my name on it.

I was loading the dishwasher when Anna wafted in and plonked herself down in the chair closest to the window. She was wearing a thick woolly jumper that made her legs, clad in stretchy black leggings, look extra-long and dainty. Toes with strawberry-red nails. She'd agreed to live in a period property on the condition that Caleb would pay for underfloor heating. Reminded of it, I decided to slip off my shoes after all.

'Thank you, lovely,' she said, cradling the wrong mug in her hands. 'This is just what I need.'

'Sugar's in this one,' I said, joining her and handing her the other mug.

'Ah, even better.'

'And thank *you*,' I said, smiling as I brushed my fingertips against the violet-blue petals.

'I know you like them.' She held her hands, hot from the mug, over mine, her rings glinting in the winter daylight leaking through the window. Beneath hers, my own fingers were bare except for a plain gold band. Noah had suggested we pick out an engagement ring together after he'd proposed, but at the time I hadn't felt I needed one, and when he'd got his own plain gold band, I liked that we matched.

I took a sip of tea and pressed the soles of my feet against the warm wooden floor. 'So, where did you say Caleb was again?'

'Oh, they're shooting a video for that Willesden indie group I told you about.'

'Very cool.'

She drank some tea and licked her lips, which were cracked from the cold. As she leant back on her chair and reached into the drawer of a large dresser for a mini tin of Vaseline, she said she had something to tell me, actually.

'What is it?'

She smiled like she used to when we were younger and she was harbouring a secret, lips curled, eyes crinkled. Like when she had her first kiss or got straight As in her exams, or when she was accepted to study English at university, which she did before her law conversion. She and Noah shared a love of literature, though she never talked as animatedly about it as he did. I liked to read too; I just didn't always pick up on their references. Every Christmas I asked Noah to choose a couple of the well-thumbed classics lining the shelves in our bedroom for me. He would take great care in his selection and tell me why he thought I would like something or find it interesting or moving or funny. As I read, say, *Pride and Prejudice*, I would mentally bookmark phrases and descriptions I wanted to share with him, like 'A lady's imagination is very rapid; it jumps from admiration to love, from love to matrimony in a moment.' In that instance he nodded, solemn, and replied, It's true, fortunately.

Anna rubbed her lips together, shiny and wet-looking. She was still smiling.

'So?' I asked.

'I think I might be pregnant.'

I remember this moment distinctly. My breath snagging. Clinging onto my mug, though the china was thin and the tea piping hot against my palms. At the time I felt like I'd been winded but looking back I think a more accurate description would be that I'd caught the tip of a gentle breeze. A taste of how simple life could be. How light and nimble. How easy. No different from saying yes or no to a spoonful of sugar in your tea.

'Well? Are you happy for me?' She was laughing.

I laughed in return and felt myself blush. 'Of course, just surprised.' I put down my mug on the table and we hugged. 'Congratulations!'

'I haven't told Caleb yet,' she said, holding me tight again.

'What do you mean?' I pulled away and looked her in the eye. 'When did you find out?'

'Well, I haven't yet.' She bit her lip, eyes still smiling. 'I just realised I'm late.'

'Wow.' I let out a breath of air as I said it. 'How late?'

'Two or three weeks.'

'Were you trying?' The question was out of my mouth before I had time to properly consider it. I scrunched my toes inside my socks.

Anna answered with the same coy smile. 'We weren't *not* trying.'

I felt clammy. Maybe it was the tea. She often spoke about her sex life with Caleb, how good it was, how *healthy* it was. I wondered whether she used to talk to me in the same way about Noah, but I couldn't remember. I was living with her at the time, south of the river, in a small flat with paper-thin walls. I could see the two of us sitting on the sofa after he'd stayed over for the first time, me leaning towards her, listening, her mouth moving at speed, but I couldn't hear what she was saying. I'm relieved that, although sights and smells tend to stick in my mind, I find sounds to be less adhesive.

'I feel gross.'

'Sick?'

'Sick. Tired. Generally grotty.'

I nodded sympathetically while simultaneously trying to figure out if I'd felt that way when my own period was late.

'Hey, don't worry, I'm happy too!'

I quickly rearranged my face, which must have changed without me realising.

'Mum's over the fucking moon.'

'Oh, you spoke to her already?'

She nodded, swallowing a mouthful of tea. 'She rang just before you arrived, and I told her that I suspected it at least.'

I nodded back, wondering when they'd started talking again. Anna regularly went through what she jokingly called periods of 'drying out' from her mum. She'd always been openly envious of my ability to spend unlimited amounts of time with my own mother. I contemplated telling her that she'd forgotten my birthday, then decided against it.

'Hey, how about Lemonia for lunch?' she suggested, two lines appearing between her eyebrows, eyes searching mine.

I snapped out of the wicked spiral I was on the brink of succumbing to – the one where Anna's life decisions implicitly challenged my own – and said, 'You're always disappointed with what you have there.'

'But you love it,' she said, squeezing my arm. 'Besides, we're celebrating!'

I smiled. 'Of course – I really am so happy for you.'

She tapped her forehead with her palm. 'I mean your birthday!'

'Oh, that,' I said, half laughing. 'OK, let me just nip to the loo.'

I could tell from the soft glow of our two first-floor windows that Noah had switched the ceiling lights off and the floor lamp on. It was something we did every evening in winter to make the flat feel cosier than it was. I crossed the road and hooked my keys out of my bag.

On the stairs I caught the scent of fried onions and garlic. The smell got stronger when I opened our door, and sure enough, in the kitchen I found Noah standing over a sizzling pan, some chopped mushrooms and a packet of rice beside him on the wooden counter. In the dining room, also the living room, I could see candles glimmering on the table, which was already laid for dinner. Smooth-sounding jazz was playing on the radio, and Noah was humming along. Beside him was a glass of red wine.

'Hello you,' he said. 'Happy with risotto?'

I helped myself to a glass and sidled up beside him. 'More than.'

When we first met, I liked that he was interested in food, mainly because I wasn't. If not for him, I'd have made do with a combination of hot buttered toast and one-pot meals. After a while, I became a convert.

'Did you have a good day with Anna?'

'I did, thanks.'

He tumbled in the mushrooms then dipped his head down to look me in the eye. 'All OK?'

He was too accustomed to the tone of my voice, could detect even the slightest dip. I made a conscious effort to smile and said, 'Anna thinks she's pregnant.'

'Wow, that's great news.' He raised his hands in the air as he said it.

I felt myself stiffen, just a little.

'She's always wanted two.'

'How do you . . .' I stopped mid-sentence. There was no use in me asking a question we both already knew the answer to.

His eyebrows twitched, almost imperceptibly, as he continued: 'And now Theo will have a friend.'

I laughed. 'I don't think Theo is going to have any trouble making friends.'

'You know what I mean.'

Noah and his brother Daniel had always been close, and when their parents died shortly after we got married, they became even closer. We saw Daniel and his wife, Griz, roughly every other week; even though it could take up to an hour to travel between us on public transport, either they would come to ours or, more often than not, they'd host us at their house in Golders Green. Their youngest, Allie, had taken to making place names every time we went for dinner to ensure that she and I would be sitting next to one another. Her favourite subject at school was art and she'd told me more than once that she wanted to work in a museum, just like me. I'd never considered that I'd been hard done by, being an only child, until I saw her together with her brother, Nick, and her older sister, Lizzie. I'd always thought of my father, my mother and me as a small but nicely formed family unit. Three sides of a triangle.

'She wants a girl,' I said, sipping my wine.

'I'm sure she does.'

I wriggled out from under his arm and asked him to pass me the tallest glass vase on the top shelf, too high for me to reach without standing on a chair. I unwrapped the irises and laid them out on the counter lining the other side of our narrow kitchen with my back to Noah. As I snipped at the ends, Tom weaved in and out of my legs and purred, trying to trick me into thinking he hadn't already been fed. Quietly, I scooped a small handful of extra pellets out of the bag kept in the cupboard beneath the sink. When, less quietly, I dropped them into his metal bowl, Noah made the kind of sound that accompanies raised eyebrows. I pretended not to notice and continued with my arrangement.

Anna had always known that she wanted to be a mother. Inexplicably, I'd always viewed it as extracurricular – something you did if you had the time and energy to spare in between holding down a relationship and a career. It was one of the things Noah and I had in common that he and Anna didn't. We were better suited, a natural fit, really. She

24

said so herself, and not just because she wanted children and he didn't. She wasn't all that interested in hearing about his students, or particularly excited when he had something published – a piece in an academic journal or a chapter in an anthology. Likewise, his eyes glazed over whenever she talked about the law. She was bright, on her way to becoming a barrister, one of the most promising pupils in the chambers, before she got pregnant with Theo.

It's not that I hadn't considered it. Every so often I would become quietly preoccupied with searching for something outside myself, something bigger. My mind would idly drift, stray thoughts of responsibility and care slipping in and out of my consciousness. Just occasionally, I felt I ought to be more selfless, that I had more to give. I was happy with Noah, and doing well at work, so an extracurricular was surely viable. Sometimes the notion coincided with my cycle, which made sense, I thought – probably it was hormonal. Sometimes it was sparked by an announcement on social media. Occasionally, it came out of nowhere. Whatever the source, it never lasted.

'Hey, I have to keep stirring this, so can you please come over here?'

I put the vase on the table and my birthday card from Anna on the mantelpiece. I felt a chill and sighed at the fireplace, which, like the one in our bedroom, was purely decorative.

'Is everything all right?' he asked, as I walked back towards him, lifted his arm away from his side and slipped in between.

When I couldn't figure out why it wouldn't be, I smiled and said, 'Of course.'

'Are you sure? You look very deep in thought.'

'I'm sure.'

Almost a foot taller than me, he kissed me on my crown, and began to push the rice around the pan.

The following week, I was due to meet my mother for our rearranged lunch. Same time, same place. I'd texted her the night before to remind her, and she'd replied telling me she'd already booked her train ticket and couldn't wait to see me.

In the museum café, the same table I'd been sitting at the week before was free, so I took it again – hoping that was where the déjà vu would end. My eyes were moving towards the clock when they landed on my mother, wrapped in a winter coat the shade of stewed plums and a velvet scarf I'd always liked. She smiled at me, and I smiled back, my heart rate quickening the way it did whenever I hadn't seen her for a few weeks.

'Cathy, darling.'

I was up and about to slide out from behind the table when she leant across it and enveloped me in a hug, her hair, thin and wispy like feathers, tickling the side of my face. Her looks were another thing I'd inherited from her: we had the same dark eyebrows, straight nose, and big eyes that I'd always felt were slightly on the googly side. Dimples that revealed themselves as we spoke. Other than the fact that she wore more make-up than I did, the only physical differences between us were those wrought by time.

'I'm sorry again,' she said, still holding onto my arms.

'About what?'

Finally letting go, she reached into her bag and pulled out a neatly wrapped present. 'Your birthday.'

I felt my forgotten disappointment rise, then noticed the glisten in her eyes, hazel with fewer flecks of green than mine. 'Oh, honestly, don't worry about it, Mum. As I said to Noah, it wasn't exactly an important one.'

'Tsk, every birthday is important.'

I liked the way they agreed on things. If he'd been here, they would have exchanged knowing glances, maybe touched hands.

'I just got caught up in all that windfarm business,' she said, shedding layers and sitting down opposite me. She rolled up her too-long sleeves to reveal two bony wrists. 'Peggy's been telling me that I need to take a step back, trust people will come to their senses.'

Peggy was more a friend than a cleaner. She lived next door to my mother, who still paid her to tidy the house once a week, and was often around when I phoned, the pair of them sharing a pot of tea. When I was a child, she would pick me up from school when neither of my parents could. She kept a packet of fruity sweets in the glove compartment of her car, and on our way home we would see who could make one last the longest. When my mother said her name, I ran my tongue over my teeth, remembering the sugary feeling that would settle on them during the winding journey.

She shook her head, her beaded earrings, which matched her glasses chain, rattling against her lobes. 'Anyway, never again.'

I smiled. 'Never again.'

'Well, go on, open it!'

I started with the envelope. On the front of the card was a black-and-white photo of a little girl standing in front of a candled cake, her eyes closed, her cheeks puffed as she prepared to blow them out. I thanked my mother and turned my attention to the violet wrapping paper. Inside: a sketchbook. The same gift every year.

'I hope you like it,' she said, reaching out to graze the black leather cover with her fingertips. 'You must say if you ever want something different.'

I flicked through the blank pages, full of promise. 'I love it.'

She smiled at me from across the table.

'So, glass of wine? Salmon sandwich?' I asked.

'I'll go,' she said, reaching back into her bag for her purse. 'This one's on me, remember.'

'I do – thanks, Mum.' As I waited, I wrote my name in the front of the sketchbook, the black ink stark against the creamy white page, the start of something.

She returned with our usual, plus a piece of Victoria sponge to share. 'We can't have you going without cake.'

'Mm, if you insist.'

'Tell me what's going on with you,' she said, as we started tucking in.

Between mouthfuls, I told her about Hendrick and the beach scene, and my birthday dinner with Noah. After a brief pause, I also told her about Anna.

'What wonderful news.' She held my gaze while tilting her head, aware of my reflex to compare my own life with that of my best friend.

I smiled and nodded. I was happy for her.

She did the same.

After we'd finished eating, I walked her through the shop towards the permanent collection, the pair of us turning back and waving to one another, more than once, before making my way back to work.

March

Before I wanted to preserve art, I wanted to make it. From an early age, I enjoyed the sense of freedom contained within a blank sheet of paper. Like lots of children, for birthdays and Christmases I was given flat, rectangular metal tins of colouring pencils and plastic briefcases filled with felt tips. There were paints in white trays that arrived looking like hard-boiled sweets, and after they'd been stroked with a wet brush, glistened like they'd been sucked. At home in Norfolk, on the long, flat beaches, sand was my medium. Where it met the sea, I scooped it up, wet and runny, and dribbled it out between my fingers into towers. The dry, soft grains closer to the dunes I sprinkled in neat lines across pebbles and along the length of my father's hairy legs.

He would describe himself as creatively challenged, but my mother had an artistic streak. Typically, it manifested itself in the garden, which despite teetering on wild-looking was carefully maintained. In spring, it burst into life with frothy blue forget-me-nots, primroses in soft shades of pink and cream, and yellow and white narcissi. In winter, in and among the sombre palette of the evergreen foliage were snowdrops, bright pansies, buttery honeysuckle, climbing clematis.

I think now that it was me and my sense of science that put a stopper in my dream of becoming an artist. When I look back at myself as a seventeen-year-old, I see a curiously neat and ordered girl with poised fingers and a thirst for knowledge. I wanted to do more than create art; I wanted to understand it, to take care of it. Still, I continued to sketch. Pencils and charcoal replaced the rainbow of colours. The subject matter had changed over time, too. My father's leather boots, the laces a tangle. Half-filled glasses of water, some dashed with viscous whirls of oil. Noah's ears. Raindrops wriggling down windowpanes. Tom with a full snow-white belly. Noah's eyebrows. Waves, churning. One thing that had remained a constant source of inspiration was my mother's hands, her fingers growing crooked with time, the skin loosening its hold, crinkling like tissue paper. When I look down at my own fingers now, I'm glad to see that a couple of mine curve towards one another. Inheritance is about the body as well as possessions.

It had been one of the coldest winters on record. So said the BBC's new weather presenter, blowing hot air into his palms and rubbing them together, standing in front of a video of a snowy scene. On my morning run, my own hands were toasty inside a pair of gloves whose finger pads, Noah had told me, rubbing his own palms together with excitement, would work on a touch screen. He'd given them to me at Christmas, along with a dozen other small gifts, including a hand-tied bundle of pencils and a red diary. Every year, we agreed, no stockings; every year, we failed. We did try, though. Noah's most recent effort: presenting my presents to me in a plastic Tesco bag. I had raised an eyebrow, and he had held his hands up and said, What, I don't see a stocking? Thankfully I too had been resourceful, and presented mine to him in Tom's travel crate.

It had rained during the night, then the temperature had dropped. That morning, as I ran, the towpath was icy, as slippery as an eel. I ran on the narrow verge, the real grass crunching like fake grass beneath my feet. My nose was running, and probably pink. Eyes leaking, cold air coaxing out tears with no need to spill.

I continued past King's Cross to Camden; at Kentish Town Road, not all that far from Anna and Caleb's, I turned around. When I reached the northern fringes of London Fields, I wasn't quite ready to start my day, so I walked around the block, breathing deeply. I was enjoying the feeling of beads of sweat trickling down my back when a couple with a pram walked by and the pram started wailing.

Back at the flat, I peeled off my running clothes. I was in the shower when Noah appeared from our bedroom with bird's-nest hair and bleary eyes.

'Good run?' he asked, raising his voice so I could hear him over the chute of water.

'Slippery run,' I replied, scrunching my eyes shut as I tipped my head back.

'God, Cathy, please don't go disappearing into the canal.'

At least I think that's what he said. Water and shampoo were muffling my ears. I pictured a half-submerged bicycle wheel, empty crisp packets and floating plastic wrappers amid the duckweed, a rusty shopping trolley. Occasionally

I would see folk in waders fishing things out during maintenance jobs. Mud-stained scraps of clothing and chunks of outdated technology.

When I opened my eyes, Noah was stepping into the shower to join me. I reached out my arms and wrapped them around his waist, pulling him towards me.

He'd received a decent advance for his last book – on new perspectives in diplomacy – and we'd celebrated, the adults that we were, by renovating the bathroom. Or excavating the bathroom: the search for the wooden floorboards we were sure we'd find beneath our milky-tea-coloured carpet wasn't entirely successful; we'd settled for white tiles. Still, here we were. Squared-off sink, walls painted – sceptically, at least on my part – a very pale pink. Now we had a rain shower big enough for both of us to stand under. Our morning ritual used to be less sexy, more squeeze.

'Maybe you should give the towpath a break for the time being.' Right on cue, he twisted the dial to add more hot water.

I could feel my already red face getting redder.

'Run around Victoria Park instead?' he suggested.

'You're honestly worried I'm going to slip and fall in?'

'Well, it would be a shame, wouldn't it?' He shook his head at my offering of the shower gel and started massaging my shoulders, one at a time, firmly. 'I mean, who would I wash with?'

'Oh, I'm sure you'd find someone.' I tipped my head back again to rinse my conditioner.

He stopped massaging and slipped his hands down my front and between my legs.

'You do know I'm going to be late for work?' I asked, trying not to smile.

'Well then, what's a little later.'

I half-heartedly resisted, and then I didn't.

When we started dating, Noah often referred to my work as 'restoration' rather than 'conservation'. I would patiently correct him and explain that it wasn't my job to return an artwork to its exact original state or a particular moment in time – pre-damage, say – but simply to put the brakes on its ageing process. He would smile and say he'd lucked out, that I could wave my magic wand at him whenever I was ready. I would smile back and say that, sadly, the deterioration of both artworks and boyfriends is inevitable.

Once, sitting on the sofa, he asked me what kind of interventions I would carry out on him. I turned towards him and, like a plastic surgeon, traced the features of his face. Thick, dark eyebrows; oval eyes with big, brown pupils. Gently, I brushed the tip of my finger through his eyelashes, naturally curled and fuller than mine. I ran that same finger across the bridge of his nose and along his lips, pressed together in what I'd come to recognise as his more mischievous smile, then parted as he nipped at me with his teeth. Next, I held out each of his hands, always a little rough, in need of moisturiser, and traversed the creases running like rivulets along the fronts and backs.

When I was done, I sank back into the sofa. He inspected his hands, then stood up and looked in the mirror. He poked and prodded at his face and told me he didn't see a difference – he wanted his money back. If I refused, he would write a nasty review on Amazon.

I laughed.

Tripadvisor?

The thing is, I said, if my efforts are invisible, it means I'm doing something right.

He looked unconvinced.

There is one other thing, I said.

What's that?

I wouldn't change a thing.

It was time to remove the old and overzealous layer of varnish on the seascape. I'd already completed the initial clean, eliminating any dirt from the paint film using small cotton swabs dipped in deionised water. The colours hadn't changed, but the surface had a fresh sheen to it. Now that I was beginning to apply the solvents, it was like peeling back a layer of hazy film.

'Wow, would you look at that?'

Frank had stopped by on his lunch break to check on my progress. We'd be collaborating for the next five or six months, as long as it took, with my work pausing now and then for him to run scientific tests. He'd mentioned that he and Douglas were going out the night before, so I searched his face for the tell-tale signs of a hangover. As usual with Frank, there were none.

I'd started with a patch in the lower-left corner of the canvas, where the type of wooden fence erected to stop dunes from 'walking' bordered a grassy verge. I'd followed the fence a little way along, then moved upwards, towards the straggling group of people peering down at the beach from high up on the dunes. Who knew what they were peering at – a far-off ship, maybe, swelling clouds, empty air?

'Well, it looks a lot brighter, for one thing,' said Frank, pointing to the sky, which after cleaning had turned from yellowish green to bluish white. I followed his gaze as it slid down to the grassy dunes. 'And more realistic now that you can properly see all those highlights and shadows.' When he turned his attention to the church tower, his gaze hooked on the tip of the spire, the point of which seemed sharper and polished to a shine.

'I'm glad you approve,' I said, dipping my head at him and standing back to get a better look myself. My shoulders were stiff from spending the day hunched over the panel, and when I raised my arms towards the ceiling to stretch them out, my fingers interlinked, there was an audible crack. A couple of years earlier Noah had tried to persuade me to buy one of those foam cushion supports, and had held up his hands in defence when I'd reminded him how old I was. Now I was beginning to wonder whether it was time to place an order.

Frank cleared his throat, probably out of habit, though perhaps to remind me why he was here.

'Sorry,' I said, letting my arms rest back down by my sides. 'Want to take some paint samples now?'

'No, you're all right, just keep doing what you're doing.' He held out a flat palm, which I tapped with my own. 'I'll come back in the morning.'

He did, and the morning after that. By the third morning, I'd reached the sea. Like the sky, it was visibly disfigured from a build-up of varnish and overpaint. The paint handling where the waves ran perpendicular to the beach was rough and patchy. I dipped a cotton swab in the solvent mixture and touched it along the horizon line, working from left to right.

I was about halfway when it happened. Again, more recent restorations began to dissolve along with the discoloured varnish. Roughly in the middle of the line where the sea and sky met, dark specks started to appear. I kept at it, moving the swab in concentric circles, and soon the specks formed a rough human figure. A human figure hovering on the horizon. Walking on water.

Once more, I could feel a stiffness settling across my shoulders, but this time I found myself unable to look or move away. I replaced the stained cotton swab with a clean new one and carefully turned my attention to the patch immediately to the figure's right. Steadily, a triangle began to emerge, a shade darker than the figure. I was following its curve skywards when someone appeared by my side – the lingering scent of smoke and liquorice let me know that it was Frank.

'How goes it?'

I could tell from the tone of his voice – flat, even – that he wasn't seeing what I was seeing. The rustle of paper suggested he was reading, probably the culture section. He and Douglas liked to keep on top of what was showing at the theatre; I got all my recommendations from him.

'Frank?'

'Hm?'

Still reading.

'I think I might have found something.'

More rustling.

'Frank?'

'What on earth?' He was leaning forward, his face almost level with mine, the paper fallen to the floor.

At last, I put down the swab and sat back to get a better look.

For a few seconds, neither of us said anything, our eyes taking it in. The seconds turned to minutes and still we stayed silent, each of us turning over in our mind the possible outcomes and what it could mean.

Then: 'Frank?'

'Yes?'

'There weren't windsurfers in the sixteen hundreds, were there?'

I looked at my phone as I walked to the Tube. I had one email from my mother floating the idea of us spending the May bank holiday weekend in Norfolk to coincide with her seventieth birthday, another from Noah about an invitation to have dinner at Daniel and Griz's place next week (*Yes, no, maybe?*), and three WhatsApps from Anna.

The latest: *Just checking you're getting my messages . . .? xx*

Before that: *We won't be late, just having dinner down the road with one of Caleb's colleagues and his dull wife, lol. Trust me, I would get out of it if I could!*

And before that: *Hello, I don't suppose you're free this evening, are you? Babysitter bailed. ARGH. And she waited until now to tell me, why???*

Noah was out that night – a monthly pub quiz with colleagues – and I was looking forward to having the flat to myself. I'd planned to put on my pyjamas and watch one of those personal trauma documentaries that I love and he hates. For dinner, I'd thought I might treat myself to a takeaway.

I could see that Anna was online, watching, waiting. She would be able to see that I'd finally picked up her messages, those fickle ticks turning from grey to blue. While I was staring at the screen, a fourth message landed: *I'll put a bottle of wine in the fridge AND order you some Ottolenghi (please?)*

I paused at the top of the stairs that spilled down to the Tube, deliberating, then realised I was blocking the way of blinkered commuters and quickly joined the descent. I supposed having Anna and Caleb's house to myself wouldn't be all that different from being home alone. The pyjamas might have to wait, but that I could cope with. I actually fancied something a bit greasier than Ottolenghi, but I couldn't complain. And Theo was such an easy kid. The last time I'd babysat, he hadn't made a noise all night – to the extent that I'd felt the need to check on him every twenty minutes, just in case.

I started typing: *Sorry, yes, I'm free*

Anna: *Thank you!!*

Me: *Be there in about forty-five minutes x*

Anna: *WINE IS IN THE FRIDGE*

Theo was already in bed. Literally.

'We've just started putting him down in his bed rather than the cot,' explained Anna, quietly, holding her hand to her chest and smiling, a cocktail of happy and sad. 'He's had a couple of tumbles, but fingers crossed he'll sleep through tonight.'

'Wow, he's growing up.'

'He sure is,' said Caleb, less quietly, walking down the hall in black jeans and a sleek grey shirt and giving me a kiss on each cheek. 'Cathy, hi, sorry you've been roped into this.'

When he and Anna first got together, I was sceptical – of his good looks, his expensive, white-soled trainers, and the amount of time he spent alone in his studio with beautiful young women. But I was wrong. Caleb's kind and caring and, to be honest, just the right amount of cool. When I'd told Anna I thought so, she'd pretended to be disappointed: Wait, so you don't think he's a player, not even a little bit?

'No need to be sorry, it's my pleasure,' I said, laughing as he raised his eyebrows. 'I mean it.' Turning back to Anna, I told her not to worry. 'If Theo wakes up, we'll be fine. You know, I'm pretty good at doing the voices in his storybooks.'

'Thanks,' she said, shaking her head as if she was, in fact, erasing her concern. In its place, she applied some rosy lipstick.

'Hey, I hear my wife told you the good news?' As Caleb grinned, his ears lifted a smidge. One was pierced with a tiny gold stud.

I glanced at Anna, or rather her reflection; she was looking into the large, round mirror by the door, and when she caught my eye, she smiled and nodded while rubbing her lips together.

'She did,' I said. 'Congratulations!'

It turned out a test had swiftly confirmed Anna's hunch.

'I take it you guys haven't changed your minds?' asked Caleb.

Anna laughed out loud, then quickly covered her mouth with her hand, eyes flashing towards the stairs, wood painted white with a stripy blue runner. When Theo didn't make a squeak, she returned her lipstick to her handbag and her attention to Caleb. 'Oh, yeah right, you know they're not interested.'

Her words nicked my skin, sharp and pointed like barbed wire.

'That's not true,' I said, before I could stop myself, my self-doubt rearing up at her decisiveness. I tried to keep hold of my voice, which, to my embarrassment, was shaking

39

slightly; I clumsily cleared my throat and continued, hoping they hadn't noticed. 'We love hanging out with Theo, and Dan and Griz's kids. Both of us.'

'Of course, I didn't mean that,' she said, still smiling, but with a faintly furrowed brow. In comparison with mine, her voice was steady and self-assured. 'I just meant you don't want children of your own, especially Noah. Imagine!'

The nicks dug a little deeper. I rubbed my arms. I'm not sure what bothered me more, what she said or the certainty with which she said it. We'd all spoken about children before, so it's not like it was a secret that Noah and I didn't want them. Maybe it was the fact that she'd had these conversations with him herself, back when they were together. I felt my face redden – after eight years of marriage, I should have moved on from how we met. I tucked my hair behind my ears and surreptitiously, I hoped, touched my fingers to my flushed cheeks.

Oblivious, Caleb swore under his breath. 'Wine. I'll grab a bottle from the rack, then we should make a move.'

As he went stomping off towards the kitchen, Anna shushed him. 'For fuck's sake, you'll wake up Theo!' Then she turned to me, without a hint of a smile: 'I'm sorry, Cathy, is everything all right? I really didn't mean—'

'It's fine,' I said, still feeling flushed. I realised I hadn't taken off my coat and added, 'I think I'm just overheating!'

She clearly wasn't convinced, even when I started to unbutton my coat, my fingers fumbling over the buttons, because she didn't stop talking. 'Did I say something wrong?'

I looked down at the tiled floor then back up at her eyes, which like indicators were flicking left and right, searching mine for some form of explanation. Still grappling with it myself, I waved away her question with a flick of my wrist. 'Ignore me, please.'

'Have you spoken any more about having children?' she probed. She knew me too well, could sense something was off balance. 'Has something changed?'

I opened my mouth to tell her about the false alarm, if I could even call it that, and to describe how it had made me feel, or not feel. The way it had taken my vague want for something bigger and made me wonder whether that something bigger could be a baby. 'I—'

'Right, ready?' Caleb was by her side, bottle in hand. He looked at her, looking at me.

'Yes, you two should go,' I said, clapping my hands together as if to pronounce the conversation over. Now it was my turn to glance nervously towards the stairs.

Anna tilted her head to one side, asking – like my mother, without asking – if I was sure.

This time when I looked away, I didn't look back at her. 'Have fun,' I said, shrugging off my coat and slinging it onto a spare hook on the rack beside a small person's puffer jacket.

Caleb said they would do their best, and Anna, still sounding concerned, added that they wouldn't be late.

I had just swallowed my first forkful of grilled aubergine and saffrony yoghurt when I heard a dull thud followed by a sharp cry. I rested the white takeaway box on the coffee table alongside a glass vase of daffodils that looked like they only had one or two days left, their petals slightly curled and beginning to crisp at the edges. I paused my TV show on domestic violence and hurried up the stairs and onto the landing. Straight ahead, Anna and Caleb's room was dark, while around the corner, on the right, a wedge of dull light emerged from Theo's door, slightly ajar. Inside, a constellation of yellow glow-in-the-dark stars on the ceiling and a blue-green night light in the shape of a dinosaur plugged into a socket by its tail. Our very own northern lights.

I found him curled on the beige carpet, his face a mix of snot and tears. I scooped him up and sat on the edge of his bed with him on my knee, rocking gently from side to side, stroking his fuzzy black hair. 'Oh Theo, what happened?' I asked. 'Did you fall out of bed?'

He didn't answer, but his crying did become less urgent. A few minutes later, his breathing had steadied, and after a few minutes more, he was quiet, drifting back to sleep with his free hand clutching my jumper and his face nuzzled into my shoulder. I sat there for some time, listening to him, looking around his room. There was a shelf filled with children's books, at least half a dozen of which I'd bought myself, and a wicker basket of stuffed animals, including a fluffy white rabbit that Anna had picked up during one of several baby-related shopping trips I'd joined her on before he was born. At the time she didn't have any other friends who were mothers, so I was the default companion for the job.

Since having Theo, she'd fallen in with a bunch of 'mum friends', and now she would be making more – women who spoke the language of motherhood, whose schedules were more closely aligned with hers. I'd noticed that some of my other friends had become less available since they'd had children, but not Anna. Perhaps, I thought, it was a transition that, for some, happened only with the arrival of their second child, or third, or fourth.

Slowly, I unfurled Theo's small brown fingers and rested him back down on the mattress, pulling the duvet up and over his shoulders. I kissed him on the forehead then crept out of the room, leaving the door open just a crack, like it was before.

Back downstairs, sitting on Anna and Caleb's sofa, surrounded by their belongings, was – I think – the first time I actively envisaged what kind of mother I would be. I thought about my own childhood, and my relationship with my mother, the days we spent together at home, in the garden, on the beach. The days when she would lie patiently on a towel waiting for me to bury her in sand, which took some time when I refused to use a spade and the grains slipped so easily through my fingers. When we'd search the vegetable patch for the snails that had been hungrily chomping holes in her lettuce. We always told each other everything, often to my father's dismay – he didn't think, for example, that a nine-year-old needed to know that he'd lost his job as a grain merchant and we were short of money.

I closed my eyes and tried to picture myself with a baby, but when I did, the baby either wasn't real – instead, it was one of those china dolls with tight ringlets and glass eyes – or it was missing entirely. I could vaguely muster up an image of myself with a small child, but again, something wasn't right; like a video that needed to be left to buffer, the image was blurry. I tried to push the thought to the back of my mind, but it kept creeping forward, demanding my time and attention. Visions flashed in front of my eyes of me happy, sad, devoid of energy, centreless, complete.

By the time Anna and Caleb got home, I'd hardly touched my food and the TV show was still on pause, a woman's tired face on the wide screen. Theo had fallen out of bed again, and again I'd picked him up and rocked him until he'd drifted back to sleep, then tucked him in beneath the duvet. Anna thanked me for taking such good care of him. When Caleb opened the fridge to get some cold water, he discovered the bottle of wine they'd put in there earlier, undrunk. He joked that I must be coming down with something.

I headed home with my leftovers on my knee and an unfamiliar ache inside me.

The day Theo was born, Noah and I were at my parents' house in Norfolk. It was October, and as we'd left behind the glass and concrete of the city and slid deeper into the countryside, I'd noticed the sepia and russet tones of the trees. The hedgerows had shed their summer growth. Freshly ploughed fields had an earthy finish. I remember thinking that we should try to make that journey with every change of season.

We'd arrived the night before and were sitting down to a cooked breakfast of scrambled eggs and bacon that my father had proudly 'rustled up' when Caleb called to say Anna was having contractions. The doctor suspected it would be at least a few hours until she was properly in labour, and in fact, it wasn't until late that night that he called again to say she'd given birth to a boy. I looked across the bed at Noah, who was holding a book and also his breath. I smiled and nodded, and he sighed with relief. I tried to continue smiling as I listened to Caleb telling me there had been a complication – something to do with Anna's placenta – and an emergency C-section. The hospital planned to keep them in for a few days to monitor both her and the baby. We could visit if we liked. Something in Caleb's voice, softer than usual, with protracted pauses, told me Anna wanted me there. I hung up and, without discussion, Noah and I agreed we would leave first thing in the morning.

I must have been stealing glances at him in the car because he said there was no need to worry. When he took hold of my hand and pressed it firmly to his lips, I knew he wasn't just talking about Anna and the baby. A week or so after he'd first told me that he didn't want children, he'd told me the reason. He'd been married before, when he was fifteen years younger, to a French woman he'd met during his undergraduate course. Soon after they graduated there was a wedding, and a few weeks after that she was pregnant. It didn't matter that it was an accident; she took the test and crescent smiles stretched wide across their cheeks. They shared the good news with their friends and family and rented a two-bed flat with a small balcony.

I turned to face the window as I tried to imagine how it must have felt. Giving birth to a baby girl who had, inexplicably, died in the womb two months before the due date. Undoing the plans already made around her. Feeling the emptiness where she'd once been. My fingers found the window switch, and wind began buffeting at the car. Noah opened his own window a crack, and the beat softened.

They'd tried to work through it, but once their grief had latched onto them, it refused to loosen its hold. Gradually, it filed down their points of contact and picked apart the feelings, thoughts, opinions that had brought them together. It was what the loss did to their relationship, Noah said, rather than the loss itself, that had sparked a change inside him. After, she'd packed up her things and moved back to her family home in France, and he'd returned to Warwick to do a PhD. To begin with, they'd kept in touch, but as time went on the communication had crumbled. She was the person he'd planned to spend his life with.

I never met her, but I had googled her. She was a novelist and, though she didn't have social media, her books had been published widely enough for there to have been reviews and interviews in newspapers and magazines. The one time I'd typed her name into my browser and pressed return, I'd clicked on the first link – her Wikipedia page. I'd read briefly about her childhood and her education in France and the UK. The part about her career was the longest, with details of the first novel she wrote in her twenties, and the ones that followed, the criticism, the prizes. Below that, at the very end, was a short section on her personal life, composed of just three sentences. It was enough. I'd learned that she was remarried, that she lived in Paris, and that she and her husband had two daughters.

I couldn't ask Noah about it without admitting to my online sleuthing, and he never mentioned it. But every now and then, I would find myself wondering whether he knew, and driving to visit Anna, Caleb and the baby was one of those occasions. When we arrived, I asked if he would prefer to wait in the car – he'd hated hospitals ever since – and calmly, he shook his head. But as we walked up to the busy entrance and along extended corridors smelling of linoleum and marked with multi-coloured lines and arrows, I felt his fingers tighten around my own. I told him, It's OK, I'm here.

Eventually, we found the maternity ward, and a nurse directed us to Anna. She was lying in bed with a small bundle in a clear cot beside her; I remember thinking the cot looked like a shopping trolley. When Anna saw us, she opened her mouth to say hello and immediately began to cry. When the same thing happened again, Caleb explained that she was having trouble getting words out. He kissed her on the forehead, then got up from the armchair pushed against the other side of the bed and gestured for me to sit. I squeezed Noah's hand and he squeezed mine back.

'Does anyone want coffee?' he asked.

'Good idea,' said Caleb, lightly knocking him on the shoulder in greeting. 'I'll show you where the machine is.'

I sat down in the chair and marvelled at my friend. 'How are you feeling?'

She cried some more, and in between sobs and bouts of laughter she told me she was frightened.

I glanced again at the delicate bundle beside her, with a little brown face and hair that was thick and dark, even at just a day old. His eyes were closed, peaceful. When I listened carefully, I could hear him breathing.

'I know, he doesn't look particularly frightening,' she laughed, explaining that she was more frightened about doing something wrong. 'I just can't get him to feed, and I don't know why. What's going to happen when we take him home?' she asked, her voice rising. 'What if I can't get him to go to sleep?'

I smiled and brushed her chestnut hair away from her face and told her to look again at him sleeping by her side. 'You'll be great,' I said, my heart as full as it had ever been. 'And whenever you need me, I'll be there.'

It was the weekend after I babysat that Noah and I had dinner with Daniel and Griz. Noah had been in the middle of marking some papers when we left the flat and his mind

47

was still mulling over an essay on gendering global politics as we passed through the turnstiles to catch the overground to Camden, from where we would take the Northern line to Golders Green. He tried to pass through his turnstile two or three times before the attendant told him, politely if patronisingly, Take a step back, Sir, and give the machine a minute. Noah apologised and did as he suggested, all the while retaining a furrowed brow and a fixed stare, thinking deeply. Worried he might trip, I held onto his arm as we walked up the stairs.

It was a cold but clear evening with the kind of tie-dye sky that makes me long for Norfolk – somehow the sky always seems bigger there, the Earth topped with an extra-large technicolour blanket. The days were growing longer, the light gaining in strength and lasting until around six-thirty; in the morning the clocks would change, giving us an extra hour until sunset. As the train peeled away from the platform, I found myself twisting in my seat to get a better look at the ragged rooftops casting a striking silhouette against the pink and blue. Feathery plumes of smoke spouted from chimneys, softening the spiked aerials beside them. I was twisting a little further to see what someone had planted in their roof garden, my thoughts pleasantly turning to my mother, when Noah returned to the present.

'I love you,' he said, taking my hand in his.

I twisted back around.

At the other end, it was a short walk to Daniel and Griz's place, a semi-detached house – part exposed brick, part smooth stucco painted white – set back behind a small, rounded hedge on a road that curved around and down towards the Heath. Noah and Daniel grew up in a house just a few streets away, in what was a typical northwest-London Jewish family, Noah had told me. He also said that growing up surrounded by other Jewish families had meant that he and his brother were, for better or worse, mostly sheltered from anti-Semitism. We hadn't been together long when I asked if his interest in security and development stemmed from what had happened to his grandparents' generation. He told me he'd never thought about it. After we watched a documentary on the Holocaust and I broached the subject again, he admitted that as a child he'd become fascinated by stories about fleeing from the Nazis. I think the adjective he used to describe that fascination was morbid.

We arrived and used the knocker.

After a few seconds, eleven-year-old Lizzie, Daniel and Griz's eldest, opened the door.

'Lizzie, look at you,' cried Noah, 'you're almost as tall as Cathy!'

She laughed and so did I. My height, or lack thereof, was a running joke. That and my childlike hands and feet. Noah always said he was amazed that I was living an adult life with shoes that were a size three and a half.

He stepped forward and enveloped her in a hug. 'Been swimming?' He tugged at her wet hair, which was pulled back into a ponytail.

Swimming was Lizzie's thing. It was more than a hobby – she was good, great even. We'd been to watch her in a handful of races, all of which she'd won. As I leant in to hug her hello, I considered that the thing I liked best about pools was the smell of chlorine, the chemicals reminding me of work.

'Yes,' she said, 'and now I'm starving.'

'Well, let's see how long it takes for your dad to bring out tonight's food,' said Noah.

Ever since Griz had signed him up for a cookery course a while back, Daniel had assumed the role of head chef in their family kitchen. He was talented, and *very* thorough.

'Oh, I did it, by the way,' said Lizzie. 'I tried telling him you two don't count as guests.'

'And?'

'He said that was no reason not to make an effort.'

'Well, it was worth a shot.'

I smiled at their camaraderie.

'Where are your brother and sister, then?'

'Uncle Noah!'

Right on cue, Nick appeared at Lizzie's side, swiftly followed by seven-year-old Allie.

'Hi there, you two!'

More hugging. Though Nick was in awe of Noah, he was at that awkward age when touching a woman was hell on earth, and as soon as he was in my arms he stiffened like a piece of cardboard. Allie, on the other hand, held on tight. When I went to stand up, she latched onto my necklace, her blue eyes bulging.

'I like this,' she said, twirling the single natural pearl between her fingers.

'Thank you, sweetie. Your uncle gave it to me.'

She gasped, in the dramatic way she'd taken to doing lately, and told me how lucky I was, that it was soooooooooo pretty.

I looked up at Noah, who was smiling. 'You're right, Al, my wife's one lucky lady.'

When he'd given it to me, however many years earlier, he'd said that the least he could do if we couldn't live by the sea was to bring the sea to me. Of course, if I wanted to stay at the National Gallery, I really had to live here. But there were museums up and down the coast, and I went through a brief period of wanting to trade London in for a town suffused with sea air. Margate, maybe. Or St Ives, though that was far from home. Noah was vaguely open to the idea, but my wanting was never strong enough for me to push it. Eventually, like a fever, it subsided. I'd learned to live with my lingering curiosity.

'OK, enough hellos, kids, give your uncle and auntie some room to breathe,' Griz said as she appeared, shooing them off down the hall, the red tiles barely visible beneath kicked-off school shoes and trainers and discarded sports bags.

As they rounded the bend into the kitchen, the biggest room in the house, with a light-filled conservatory tacked onto the back, Allie yelled out, 'Ouch, Nick!' Lizzie told them both to stop it.

It was no wonder that Lizzie was outgrowing me – Griz was the same height as Noah. She was slender too, with the kind of long legs I often think are wasted on non-runners. In the beginning, I was intimidated by her beauty – that and her being Jewish, a natural fit in the family. Though Noah was no longer observant, Daniel and Griz were still active in the community, as were the kids. When I'd said as much to Noah, he'd assured me, with a glint in his eye, that I would feel more comfortable if I paid less attention to her classical features and more attention to her fashion sense.

She turned to me, pompoms dangling from the bottom of her jumper, and gave me a kiss. 'Cathy, hi.'

'Hello, Griz,' I said, smiling.

I'd followed Noah's advice, but that wasn't the only reason Griz and I got on. I was interested in her role as a civil servant and admired her ability to balance her home life and her career thanks to music lessons, after-school clubs, and summer camps. She was one of those rare women who made the idea of having it all look less like a myth, though of course keeping her children busy so that she could work cost money.

'Thanks for having us again,' I added, taking off my coat. 'I'm sorry, I'm sure it was our turn.'

'Oh, you know how Daniel loves to cook.'

Noah laughed.

It was around half-past eight when we sat down at the table and, much to Lizzie's relief, dinner was served. About an hour earlier, when everyone apart from Daniel had been sitting and chatting (and waiting) in the living room, Noah had gone to get a fresh wine glass and covertly snuck a bag of crisps out from the kitchen under his shirt. When, like a magician, he'd pulled it out, Allie had squealed, and Nick, a little heavy-handedly, had covered her mouth. Lizzie, who had been playing the piano at Griz's suggestion, had ended the argument that ensued by threatening to eat the entire bag herself.

Daniel stood at the head of the table, which was made from the same dark wood as the old-fashioned dresser pushed up against the wall. He was the spitting image of Noah, just younger and, that evening, in a black-and-white striped apron that fell to the knee. He had the same thick dark hair, his as yet unsalted, and matching eyebrows, eyes the same shape and shade of brown. But beyond his looks, even his mannerisms were familiar. The way he gestured for us to go ahead and help ourselves to some herby couscous while he served the chicken with artichokes and lemons. He, too, talked with his hands.

'So, Cathy, Noah says you're working on something new?' he asked.

'I am,' I replied, holding the bowl as Allie scooped a generous portion of couscous onto her plate, and a small portion onto the table. 'A seventeenth-century Dutch seascape.'

'The artist?'

Daniel had taken a module in art history while studying for his history degree, and when we first met, he'd delighted in deftly navigating the subject, showing Noah that we most likely had more in common than he and I did. That, of course, and our ages. We both graduated the same year, a decade later than Noah.

'Hendrick van Anthonissen.'

'Of course.'

I looked up from my plate to see if he was smiling – Hendrick was hardly a household name – but he was slicing a piece of chicken straight-faced. Before returning my gaze to my own food, it collided with Noah, who, on the other hand, was wobbling his head in mock surprise. Lizzie must have noticed because she started to laugh. After completing his degree, Daniel had gone on to become an actuary.

'It's exciting, actually,' I said, trying to avert any more mockery, 'I've just finished removing the varnish, and I've found something.'

'Something?'

'A figure and beside it a sort of triangle.'

'Oh, that *is* exciting.'

53

'It could be,' I said, smiling and shrugging my shoulders, not wanting to get ahead of myself. 'I mean, these tonal paintings are usually quite predictable. But it is strange.'

'What do you think it is?'

'I don't know . . . I mean, I thought it might be a fin, but the others are sceptical, to say the least. I'm waiting for the results from the scientific department, but if it's not contemporary with the painting, I might be able to do some careful digging.'

'Which is when a steady hand is of the essence,' said Daniel, looking at Allie.

I started rattling my cutlery, which made her giggle.

We ate and chatted, about everything from our weeks to the sudden death of a famous DJ. Mealtimes with Daniel and Griz often descended into heated discussions about whatever item was currently top of the news. Daniel liked to challenge the children to think about things critically, to consider other perspectives, something Noah said his father had always done with them.

'It's hard to feel sorry for someone so rich and famous,' Daniel commented, glancing around the table to see who would take the bait.

He would often throw in provocative comments, and Lizzie and Nick thrived off the debates that followed. That night Nick constructed a compelling counterargument, and satisfied with his son, Daniel reached across the table and gave him a high-five. Accustomed to tuning out at times like these, Allie hummed happily to herself as she picked at the bone of her drumstick.

When dessert was served – honey cake with plums – talk turned to a lighter subject. Griz's youngest sister, Sandra, had just given birth to her first baby.

'She went into labour in the back of an Uber!' Griz said it laughingly, though the look in her eyes suggested she was less amused than giddy with relief. 'Here.' She passed around her phone so we could all see the photos, including one of the driver, a pale-faced twenty-something. 'Daniel tells me Anna and Caleb are expecting another?' she said, as I flicked through images of a squashy baby, bald as a lightbulb.

'Yes,' I replied, glancing at Noah and wondering when that had come up in conversation between him and his brother. 'Their second.' There was a moment's pause, and I felt the need to fill it. I smiled as I added, 'It's wonderful.'

Griz tilted her head to one side and smiled back. Then she asked, in a way that suggested I'd just let something slip, 'Are you two still set against it? We haven't spoken about it in a while, so maybe . . .'

'What's that?' asked Noah, mid-mouthful.

'Starting a family!'

He laughed and I wish I had, too. But when I opened my mouth, there wasn't any sound. Instead, I tried to keep hold of my smile as I silently rolled the words around on my tongue: starting a family. As if we weren't one already.

I passed the phone to Nick, who passed it straight to Lizzie, and clasped my hands together on my knee, trying to figure out why these kinds of comments were coming up again, and why my reactions weren't chiming with Noah's. We'd both laughed them off in the past – they came up a lot when we got married, when I turned thirty, when friends' bellies swelled. We'd found it funny at best, boring at worst. When female friends cooed over how good Noah was with kids, which he was, he'd whisper in my ear that maybe he should mix things up a bit – let them sample his wine, teach them to swear, stay up late with them watching unsuitable films. In time, the people we chose to surround ourselves with seemed to have accepted that procreation wasn't the plan for us. And now?

'But Uncle Noah and Auntie Cathy already have a family.' Allie. I felt my eyes sting.

'Yes, sweetie, they're absolutely a part of our family,' said Griz. 'I just wonder if they might be getting a little bit tempted to have a family of their own.' As she said it, she looked at me, eyebrows raised a smidge, conspiratorially.

I locked eyes with Noah, who was finishing his piece of cake, unfazed. He gave me a relaxed smile that said, I've got this, and told her no, we still didn't intend to have kids. 'We've talked about this,' he reminded her, coolly. 'It's not for us.'

I watched Griz turn back to me, ready to laugh and roll her eyes – *men* – then quickly press her lips together. She looked at Daniel, who opened his palms as if to say, Well, obviously.

Noah smiled at me from across the table, looking for some back-up maybe, a bit of give.

I forced another smile in return, though I felt my lips tremble. 'That's right,' I said, pushing on, hoping the trembling wasn't visible. 'We really are happy just us.' As soon as I'd said it, I wished I'd left out the 'just us' and wondered what it meant, the fact that I hadn't.

'Oh, of course,' said Griz, nodding and smiling, a tad too hard, trying to make up for what she now realised had been a blunder. 'As you should be – happy, I mean.'

Polite smiles ensued.

Allie's own lip wobbled as she asked if we still liked her and Nick and Lizzie.

Noah reached for her hand and explained that, of course, we loved them. 'In fact,' he said, sincerely, 'we love you three so much that it's almost like having children of our own.'

I could have sworn I felt my heart crack.

'But—'

Before she had a chance to reply, I pushed my chair back and away from the table, its legs scraping against the wooden floor and making everyone turn to look. 'Sorry,' I laughed, or at least I tried to laugh, 'don't mind me.'

The downstairs loo was the smallest room in the house, tucked away beneath the stairs. My heart was thumping hard against my chest – not cracked after all – as I struggled with the latch. I sat down and stared at the framed photos of the children on the walls, in school uniform and sports kit and home clothes, lined up with their friends – other people's children. There were pictures that had been taken every year of all the cousins, lined up in a row from oldest to youngest. Griz was one of five, which partly explained her preoccupation with producing offspring.

I could hear muffled voices leaching through the walls from the dining room but not the topic of conversation. Was it still the apparently gaping hole in my life with Noah, or had the talk moved on to plans for the weekend? I bit my lip and tried to get a hold of myself. But it was too late – I could feel tears of frustration prickling in my eyes and knew I would be better off letting them fall than trying to contain them and having a spillage back at the table. Frustration both at the situation and at my reaction to it, the fact I could no longer seem to simply laugh along.

I looked up at the photo directly ahead of me: Lizzie and Nick sitting on an old peach-coloured sofa, their feet hovering inches above the carpet, with baby Allie plonked between them, small with staring eyes, blue and still. We were here that day, and moments after the photo was taken, Griz had given me Allie to hold. Another photo showed Allie snuggled against my front, koala-like, and Noah with his arm around me. I remember the subject line of the email Griz sent me the next morning, with the photo attached: *Family portrait!* Before I'd even opened the email, I'd showed it to Noah, and the two of us had shared a private smile – the kind we shared whenever new parents encouraged us to procreate.

Sitting there on the loo, I tried to smile that same smile. No luck.

Noah must have noticed my puffy eyes when I reappeared. He didn't say anything while we were all sitting around the table, and neither did anyone else, though Griz clearly felt she'd put her foot in it. She kept stealing glances at me and, whenever I caught her eye, smiling apologetically. I smiled back, quietly grateful.

As soon as we'd slid onto the back seat of our Uber, Noah put his arm around me and asked me to talk to him. When I didn't respond, he started singing: 'Talk to me, baby.'

I laughed and told him I was just tired, which was partly true. Work had been full-on and, apart from a couple of days in Norfolk over Christmas, we hadn't been away since the autumn.

'Well, that we can fix,' he said, squeezing my shoulder and kissing the top of my head.

I reached my own arm across his front and clung on to his waist, a second seatbelt.

58

April

We'd only been together for two months when I got pregnant. I was twenty-five and Noah was thirty-six. One morning, when it was just us, I told Anna – casually, between mouthfuls of cereal – that my period was late. How long, did she think, before I had to worry? She grabbed my hand and marched me out of the kitchen and into my room. Get dressed, she said, we need to get you a test.

Anna's mother had put the fear of god into her about getting pregnant when she brought home her first boyfriend, Sam, with the lanky legs, aged fourteen. She'd also taken her to the doctor, who'd put her on the pill. She'd swallowed it ever since, which meant her periods were regular – definitely to the day, pretty much to the hour. It was Anna who'd recommended I try it, which I did for a while at university. Then I read an article about several women coming off it and seeing an improvement in their mental health. I was struggling with what I would describe as low-level anxiety at the time, a gentle but insidious simmering beneath my skin. Now, when I call that feeling to mind, I think of a pot gently boiling on a hob; the water isn't bubbling over but if you turn up the heat by just one more notch, you could be in danger. I'd decided that I too would be better off without it, and I explained this to Anna as we walked up the road to the nearest pharmacy. She rolled her eyes and told me that simmering feeling was normal when you had a hefty student loan to pay off and, as of yet, no promise of job stability and an income.

The door to the pharmacy dinged merrily as it swung open. I kept close behind Anna as she strode confidently towards the pregnancy tests. Standing in front of them, I froze, arms stiff by my sides. Anna, meanwhile, diligently studied the different brands. As my gaze drifted along the plastic shelves lining the walls from floor to ceiling, it occurred to me that the space had been badly curated. Who had decided that it was a good idea to place the pregnancy tests between the different-coloured condoms and squeezy bottles of flavoured lube and the baby lotions and nappy-rash creams? The last thing I wanted to think about was sex and babies.

At the till, I didn't realise I was tapping a rhythm on the counter with my fingernails until Anna gently rested her hand on top of mine.

'Why don't we just nip across to Starbucks?' she suggested with a gentle but take-charge tone. 'You can do it there – less time to think about it.' She linked her arm through mine and ushered me towards the zebra crossing before I had a chance to reply.

We had to buy something to get the code to the bathroom, so Anna ordered a vanilla latte, then the two of us went in together. While I peed on the little plastic stick, and a little on my fingers, she sipped her sweet, milky coffee. I'm sure an 'mmm' escaped from her lips.

When I was done, I held out the stick at arm's length from our faces, and we waited, and waited, so long that I remember my arm started to feel heavy. When two small pink lines appeared, and failed to disappear when I shook the stick, hard, I turned back around to face the loo, sensing that I was about to be sick.

At the beginning of April I came home from work to fresh pasta with pesto, one of Noah's specialities, and, he told me, a surprise. He picked up his phone and tapped the screen, and a few seconds later my own phone pinged. I opened my emails and clicked on the most recent unopened message. The subject line: 'Fancy spending Easter with your man friend in Italy?' Attached were two plane tickets.

'Really?' I asked, grinning.

'Really,' he insisted, with a grin that matched mine. 'And I got the promotion.'

I crossed the room and threw my arms around him. 'When did you find out?'

'They announced all the changes happening within the department today.'

'I'm so proud of you.' We hugged some more, then I nipped upstairs and retrieved the bottle of champagne I'd been stowing at the back of my wardrobe.

'And you say *I'm* over the top,' he said, trying not to smile.

I kissed him and put the bottle in the freezer for a quick blast, then I asked if anyone was disappointed.

'Not that I know of, but I did get out of there pretty quick this afternoon just in case.' He laughed and I did, too. 'There is one other thing—'

'There's more?!'

'Well, wait.' He bit his lip. 'I've also been invited to take part in an exchange. They want me to go and teach a semester in New York at the end of the year.'

'Wow.'

'I know.'

'What an opportunity.'

'You think so?' He looked at me with the same face he pulled whenever he was reading, brow crinkled. 'Because I can always postpone.'

'Noah.'

'You don't quite seem yourself at the moment.'

I said his name again, this time followed by a question mark.

'Yes?'

'Please don't worry about me. I love you, and I know you. This is something you've always wanted.'

I'd spent three months in Florence before starting university, studying art history and learning Italian. I went by myself but quickly found my group. There were late nights in sweaty clubs and more than a couple of adult sleepovers. Early on in our relationship, I made the drunken mistake of telling Noah it was my wildest time. He laughed, and to begin with I was indignant. What? It was! When he laughed some more, I realised how ridiculous it sounded. I'd been back since, but this would be our first trip there together.

'It's about time I get to know your wild side,' he said, as we boarded the plane. He was no longer laughing, but I could tell he was smiling from the lilt of his usually well-modulated voice.

'Very funny,' I replied, playfully swatting the back of his thighs as we climbed the unsettlingly shaky metal steps, and taking the same deep breaths I took whenever I was about to be ferried up and into the sky. 'No, I would much rather we spend our time eating good food and visiting museums.'

'If you say so,' he said, taking hold of my hand as we entered the plane. He knew that I wasn't especially fond of flying and could do with some comic relief. 'Just let the wild Cathy know that, if she changes her mind, she's welcome to join us.'

He'd booked us into a *pensione* in Sant'Ambrogio, a neighbourhood to the northeast of Santa Croce. After pressing the buzzer, then trying the number on the website, then pressing the buzzer again, the heavy door popped inelegantly out of its socket. On the other side was a square courtyard dotted with round tables and filigree chairs in matching shades of pistachio green. There were more terracotta pots than plants and two pigeons trying and failing to bathe in a dried-up water fountain. The sun was shining, its rays skipping across the stone building that closed the courtyard in on three sides. Wisteria crept up and across the façade, and roses had been trained to grow up a wooden trellis.

'*Buongiorno!*'

The gravelly voice made me jump. I spun around and came face to face with the owner, a buxom woman with long red hair piled on top of her head like a bundle of yarn. It was tinged violet, not unlike the blooming wisteria. Her face was ruled with narrow lines, and I was busy trying to guess her age when we locked eyes.

'*Buongiorno!*' Noah replied for us both, belatedly, giving me a look that told me he'd been waiting for me to do the talking, and continuing in broken Italian, '*Mi chiamo Noah e . . .*'

'*Il mio nome è Cathy.*'

'*Va bene,*' she said, glancing at her watch, then giving it a shake. '*Vieni, vieni.*'

We followed her into the reception, a small space at the foot of the stairs, the walls covered with old family photos, mostly black and white and in plain frames. She tapped at her keyboard and leafed through a diary filled with spidery script in pencil and ink, and after a few minutes she handed me a small brass key attached to a heavy metal keyring.

Our room was upstairs, the first door on the left. It was simply furnished, with eggshell-white walls and wooden floors, a big wooden wardrobe, and a nice writing desk. As I unzipped my bag, Noah unlatched and opened the windows, which overlooked the street, stereotypically lined with mopeds. I was reaching for my sandals when he pulled me towards him and said he liked it when I talked Italian. I talked Italian some more – not fluently, but not badly – and twenty minutes later, the two of us lying on the bed, our clothes discarded around us, he said we should come to Florence more often.

After three days of cold persistent rain, he reconsidered.

Though Noah had been to Florence before, he wanted me to act as his guide and take him to my favourite places in the city, which I did, gladly. I was also glad that the constant drizzle meant museums were top of his list, too. We started with the Uffizi, where we stood for some time in front of Botticelli's decorative canvases and mimicked the grave expressions of the duke and duchess in Piero's celebrated diptych. It had been cold waiting outside in the queue, and as we walked between the artworks Noah blew warm air onto my fingers.

We visited too many churches to count and hurried past the Duomo more than once, huddled under a cheap umbrella we'd picked up from a man selling fistfuls on a street corner. I told Noah the story of Ghiberti's gilded bronze doors to the octagonal Baptistery, which Michelangelo considered so perfect they could be the gates of paradise. He tried and failed to make it through a dirty joke about my own gates of paradise. Our laughter reverberated against the slabs of green and white marble.

Once, sometimes twice, a day we went in search of a *gelateria*, and Noah soon agreed that ice cream tastes as good in the rain as it does in the sunshine. We had soups and sandwiches for lunch – he even tried *trippa alla Fiorentina* – and after aperitivo hour we ate pasta and more pasta, washed down with carafes of Chianti. We left the cheap umbrella behind in one trattoria or another and returned to the *pensione* sopping.

On the third afternoon, when the sun made a brief appearance, we crossed the Arno, a ribbon of blue running through the coffee-coloured city, and sauntered through the Boboli Gardens. Reminded of how much my mother had loved their layout when she and my father had come to visit me all those years ago, with the grottos and green expanses and fountains, I decided to give her a ring.

'Hello?'

'Hi Mum, it's me.' I sat down on the end of a stone bench and watched Noah continue through the canopy of trees, the dappled light throwing shapes onto his back.

'Darling, what a lovely surprise.'

I smiled. It was something she often said, despite the regularity with which I called.

'I just wanted to wish you a happy Easter,' I said. 'I'm sorry we're not there.' After Noah had presented me with the plane tickets, I'd spoken to my mother, and she'd told me not to worry about her and that she was looking forward to seeing us in May.

'Oh, that's kind, and happy Easter to you, too. Are you doing anything nice?'

'We're in the Boboli Gardens, which made me think of you.' When she didn't respond, I looked at my screen to check we hadn't been cut off. 'Mum, did you hear me?' I thought perhaps there was a delay, and sure enough, after a few more seconds had passed:

'The Boboli Gardens, of course. I remember your father and I visiting with you. He left his hat behind on a bench.'

'I'd forgotten that,' I said, laughing. My mother had ticked him off and then made him bend his knees so she could reach to rub some sun cream onto the top of his head, where there was a bald spot. 'I'm sitting on one of those benches right now, so I'll make sure I do a thorough check before moving on.'

'Oh gosh, do.'

I smiled at how earnest she sounded.

'Well, send my love to Noah.'

'I will, and I'm sure he sends his back to you.'

I caught up with him and when he asked how she was, still smiling, I said she was well.

That night, like students, we sat on the stone steps of the great Franciscan basilica of Santa Croce drinking cheap red wine late into the evening – though, as I said to Noah, it wasn't nearly as cheap as the bottles I used to drink. When he quoted a line from *A Room with a View*, something about the black-and-white façade 'surpassing ugliness', I told him to shush. He laughed and raised his voice, waving his arms around theatrically: 'But how like a barn! And how very cold!' He'd been rereading it and suggested that we make like Lucy Honeychurch and George Emerson and head to Fiesole, the small hillside town overlooking the valley, the next morning before heading back to the airport. Instead, we had a lie-in and nursed our pounding heads, and he lamented the fact that the older he got the more vigorous his hangovers had become.

By the end of our trip, my cheeks ached from the smiles and the laughter, and my stomach felt full, and not just because of all the eating and drinking. At checkout, the owner – Beatrice was her name – asked me how long Noah and I had been together. I said it had been about ten years and she held my hand and told me what we had was special. On the plane home, there was a crying baby. When I closed my eyes and tried to picture the same weekend with a small child in tow, the image became overcrowded. No, not just overcrowded, but sticky and arduous and loud. I reopened them and looked at Noah, who was almost finished with Forster, the final few pages tucked neatly under his thumb. I smiled and rested my head on his shoulder.

I'd arranged to meet up with Anna and Theo for a morning on Hampstead Heath. Still recovering from my Italian diet, and craving the exercise, I decided to cycle. The air was cold, and the backs of parked cars were topped with a thin film of frost, like they'd been covered with lightweight quilts over-night and hadn't yet thrown them off and climbed out of bed.

When I reached the great park's southern fringes, my heart was racing and I could feel that beneath my woollen jumper my top was clinging to my back. Anna had sent me their location, a pinpoint in the middle of a square-shaped patch of green, so I locked my bike to a railing along with a load of others and walked across the grass to meet them.

The new spring growth was in full swing, with cow parsley and bluebells, and fresh green leaves sprouting from the mighty oak trees. I spotted Anna and Theo before they spotted me. She was crouching down behind him, holding tight around his middle, pointing at something. When I got closer, I saw it was a pair of ducks – a drake with an emerald-green head and his brown speckled partner. I also heard Theo quacking, and I quacked in return.

Anna glanced over her shoulder: 'Theo, look who it is!'

All at once, the three of us hugged hello, Theo squeezed in the middle. We found ourselves a bench, the paint peeling in places, and Anna asked me about Florence.

'It was perfect,' I said, talking her through our days and nights away, describing the food and the wine and the art. 'God, I love it there.'

She smiled and tipped her head back, as if to say, I knew it. I must have looked confused, because she went on to explain: 'He was worried – because obviously you don't like surprises – but I assured him this was the kind of surprise you *would* like.'

'It was your idea?' My throat caught as I said it. I turned to look at Theo, hoping she hadn't noticed the frown lines

I could feel puckering between my eyebrows. Instinctively, I tried to iron them out with the pad of my index finger.

'Oh no, it was all him,' she said, shaking her head. 'I was just a sounding board.'

Relief? I think that was the cool feeling that flowed through me, mingled with irritation – at both Anna's involvement and my childish reaction to it. I opened my mouth to ask when they'd spoken, but thankfully she beat me to it.

'So, tell me how work's going.'

It was always the first thing she wanted to know, which made me wonder whether she missed her own job. She never said as much, and whenever I asked if she was considering going back, she would shrug her shoulders and say, Maybe, but it's not the right time. If she went back now, she would be on maternity leave again in less than a year.

'Work's great, thanks.' I was compensating, I could feel it, making the most of the one thing I had in my life that she didn't have in hers. I took a breath and continued as I should have begun. 'I mean, it's great, but it's also long and slow, as usual.'

'The beach scene?'

She'd always been a sponge when it came to absorbing information. 'Exactly.'

'Well,' she said, 'lucky you're the most patient person I know.'

I smiled. 'I don't know about that.'

After I'd filled her in on my progress, and we'd caught on camera Theo's attempts to catch a duck in his bare hands, she asked, 'And how *is* Noah?'

'He's well. Busy teaching, and he'll be even busier probably, with this promotion. He's also waiting to hear back about a book proposal, which reminds me—'

'More champagne in the wardrobe?'

69

I laughed. 'More champagne in the wardrobe.'

'That's great, though. What's this one about?'

'It's to do with how the US became involved in Vietnam.'

'Phew, sounds heavy,' she said, before adding, as if he might be listening, 'and of course super interesting.'

I laughed again. Neither of us had an entirely firm grasp of the critical approaches and methodologies that cropped up in Noah's writing. 'What about Caleb, did you say he's away again this weekend?'

'No, he's around,' she replied, rubbing her eyes. She swept her hands up into her chestnut hair, winding it around her finger and into a bun at the back of her head. She felt her wrist for a hair tie and, failing to find one, let her locks fall loose again.

I offered her mine, and she waved it away.

'We're out this evening, actually.' She touched the inner corners of her eyes with each middle finger as she said it.

'Are you feeling OK, Anna?'

'Is it that obvious?'

'No, not at all! You just look a little tired.'

'I'm definitely feeling the effects of this one more,' she said, peering down at her belly, which was still pancake-flat. 'Of course, Caleb has too much on to notice. He was so thrilled when I told him, though,' she added, her eyes shining. 'He almost cried. What a girl, hey?'

I smiled.

'Anyway, I just feel a bit sick, zapped of energy, sore tits – you know how it is.' She looked at me. 'Sorry, I didn't mean—'

'Oh god, don't worry. It sounds tough. How about a short walk?' I offered, suddenly aware of the cold sweat drying on my back. 'Then coffee and cake.'

'Let's do it,' she said, standing up and calling Theo's name.

He waddled over with a twig in each hand.

'Here, let me do that,' I said, scooping him up and slipping him into his buggy. 'Say bye-bye to the ducks, Theo.'

He waved with his twigs.

After we'd walked to Parliament Hill and looked out over the London skyline, the buildings sprouting from the streets like bulbs in earthy beds, we headed back to my bike. I wheeled it along the side of the road while Anna pushed Theo beside me on the pavement, and we soon found a café, its window still decorated with blown eggs painted in pastel shades of rose and mint.

Inside, we took turns eyeing up the freshly baked goods lining the wooden counter, then both ordered the carrot cake. As two generous slices arrived at our table, along with a murky juice for Anna and a cappuccino for me, I don't know why, but I blurted out what had happened at dinner with Daniel and Griz. As I laughingly told her about my meltdown, she eyed me suspiciously over her glass of what looked like pond water.

'Does that mean you *do* want kids?' she asked, fishing a cheese sandwich out of her bag and unpeeling the cling film. It was already cut in half, but she broke each piece in half again, then passed a quarter to Theo, who gripped it and turned around to face a small dog whose owner was waiting for a coffee to go. 'Cathy?'

'What do you mean?'

'Well, it obviously upset you, Noah saying kids still weren't on the cards.'

I stabbed a hunk of sponge with my fork and shoved it into my mouth, wishing I hadn't brought it up and hoping that chewing would save me from having to answer. I pointed to my mouth and smiled, chewing slower, slower, slower . . . until I had to swallow. It's not like we hadn't spoken about this before. When Noah told Anna he didn't want children. When he told me the same thing shortly after we started dating. Anna and I had talked at length about what it would mean for me to commit to never becoming a mother. She'd urged me to consider it properly before agreeing to anything, and I'd reminded her that there was no contract involved and laughed as I'd used the words 'legally binding'. But that was years earlier. The subject hadn't come up since our marriage – presumably because she'd accepted as given that we wouldn't have children. I looked up and saw that she was watching me. 'Oh, it caught me off guard, that's all.'

She didn't look away.

'I shouldn't have said anything.'

'Are you sure? Maybe you should talk to him, tell him how you're feeling. Just because he wasn't interested then—'

'It's not him,' I said, bristling at the fact that she assumed it was Noah who steered our relationship. That I must be squashing my maternal wants and needs to keep him happy. The man of the house. 'I mean, it is. But it's me, too. Really, we're fine.'

'OK—'

'We're happy.'

'If you're sure.'

Sensing a lump form in my throat, I brought another forkful of sponge to my lips. As I swallowed it down and licked at the icing sticking to the sides of my mouth, I tried to cling onto the feeling of fullness I'd had in Florence. The feeling of us being complete. The feeling I'd had until my almost-missed period. 'I'm sure,' I said, smiling, though my mouth felt strange now, numb maybe, the way it does after the dentist has pumped it full of novocaine. Thankful, at least, that I wasn't drooling, I tried to change the subject: 'Quite warm now, isn't it?'

Anna put her head in her hands.

'What?'

'Just tell me it's not because of the pissing planet.'

When a mutual friend had got pregnant with her *fourth* child, I'd made a throwaway comment about the fact that she clearly wasn't considering carbon emissions.

'It's not because of the planet,' I said, laughing. 'But really, would that be the worst reason? You know one child contributes sixty thousand tonnes of carbon dioxide into the atmosphere?'

'Did you hear that, Theo?'

The first quarter of his sandwich had gone, I suspect to the small dog, which was wagging its stumpy tail, and now he was busy pulling the sliced cheese from the second quarter.

'You better hold your breath, mister.'

'Anna, that's not what I mean!'

'Quick, Theo, one final gulp!'

'Anna!'

We both laughed.

'I know that's not it,' she said, wiping her eyes. 'Besides, I know you still get your takeaway coffee in a paper cup.'

'Guilty.'

'As long as you're happy, that this is still what you want?'

I went to fill my mouth with cake again, but the plate was empty. When I reached for my cappuccino, she slid my mug away from me.

'You know you're allowed to change your mind, Cathy,' she said. 'We're not getting any younger.'

This time I rolled my eyes like my teenage self would have done.

'It's true! I wish it wasn't, trust me, but it is. You have to think about these things.' She put her hand on mine and looked me in the eye. When I didn't respond, she started telling me about a single friend of hers who had frozen her eggs just last week.

I wanted to slip my hand out from under hers and back onto my knee, or at least I thought I did. It didn't budge. 'But I'm not single,' I said, quietly.

'Well, maybe that's even more of a reason. Just think about it, OK?'

I didn't nod, exactly, but there was some sort of head movement.

'Men can afford to hang around,' she said. 'We can't.'

'Gone!' Theo held up two pieces of bread, robbed of their filling.

Noah was horizontal on the sofa when I got back to the flat. He had his laptop balanced on his chest and was catching up on the football. He calls himself a Tottenham fan, but I think his compulsion to watch every game is less about Spurs and more about his dad. When Noah and Daniel were kids, he took them to the stadium twice a month to soak up the atmosphere of a live match. When we met, Noah had all but stopped following it, then his dad died, and he started talking about his love of the game as if it had always been there.

'Hello, you,' he said, as I leant forward over the end of the sofa to give him an upside-down kiss. 'Did you two have fun?'

74

'Three.'

'What?'

'Us three,' I said, smiling. 'Theo was there.'

'Of course, how could I forget the little man.'

'Actually, I suppose it's four – us four – with the baby.'

'OK, let's rewind.' He rolled his shoulders back, wincing when one of them clicked. 'Did you four have fun?'

'Watch it, we don't want you putting your back out now, do we?' I laughed and so did he. 'We did, thanks.'

I sat down in one of the two armchairs opposite and told him about the Heath, how beautiful and fresh it was looking. He suggested we go back the following weekend if I didn't mind a repeat visit. Maybe Sunday afternoon? I said I would love to. I told him about the coffee shop and how Anna was finding pregnancy harder the second time around.

'I guess it's worth it.'

Slowly, I felt the emotions I'd managed to quell since saying goodbye to Anna and Theo ripple inside me. 'You think so?'

He laughed. 'Of course.'

Before I had time to think, I'd asked, 'So, having children is a good thing?'

'What do you mean?' The tone of my voice must have changed because, although he was still smiling, he was no longer laughing. This time, when he spoke, his eyes locked with mine, rather than flickering between them and his screen. 'Cathy?'

I turned towards the window, trying to get a hold of myself, but it was too late, the emotions swelling. 'I don't know, what about us?' When I turned back around, I noticed he'd stopped smiling now, too. I kept talking. Uncontrollably. Like I'd pulled a plug out of a bath. I tried to smile through

75

it, to keep it light-hearted, even as I said, too soon, without considering whether it was what I really wanted, 'What if we had a baby?'

Slowly, he moved his laptop from his chest to the coffee table, home to a tidy scattering of books. Then he swung his feet around and onto the floor. 'Cathy—'

'You love hanging out with Theo, and Lizzie and Nick and Allie.' The words kept coming, tripping over one another in their haste, even as I tried to make them stop.

He stood up and walked towards me, reaching for my hand.

'Why not, Noah?' Without warning, my eyes had pooled with tears. 'I'm sorry, I know why, I'm not even sure that I . . . I just . . .'

'Hey.' He wrapped his arms around me, firm and steady like the roots of a tree, and held me. For a minute or two, neither of us spoke. Then he asked: 'How long have you been feeling like this?'

I felt a tear spill over a lower lid and dribble down my cheek. 'I don't know, I don't know what I'm feeling.'

'Is it because of Anna?'

I closed my eyes and breathed in his woody scent. I opened my mouth to say that I didn't think it was, to tell him about the feelings and the memories that had resurfaced since my period was late. But something was holding me back, physically, pulling tight around my waist.

'Cathy?'

I stopped struggling. 'Maybe.'

He stroked my hair and kissed my lips.

'I just wish people would stop asking us about it,' I said, quietly, a ribbon of guilt twisting inside me. It wasn't fair of me to put this on Caleb and Griz, on him.

'I know,' he said, still stroking. 'I'm sorry.'

The ribbon twisted a little tighter. 'Please don't be sorry.'

He shook his head. 'I know it's not the same, me saying I don't want children and you saying you don't want children. It should be, but it's not. And for that I'm sorry.'

He was right, of course. If a man doesn't have a child, people don't think of his life as incomplete. They don't assume he's harbouring some innate longing or talk of regret and back-up plans and a lack of meaning. His happiness isn't bound up in family. There's no social obligation.

'Do you ever have moments of doubt?' I asked, my breathing steady again. 'Moments when you're with Daniel and Griz and you wonder, even just for a moment, what it would feel like to be a parent?'

'Honestly?'

'Honestly.'

'I don't, Cathy. You're all I need.'

All those years before, after I'd peed on a stick at Starbucks, I wasn't in any doubt about what I would do – perhaps it was my 'gut feeling', but at the time it felt even more physical than the bodily sensation my mother had described to me when I was a child. I was only just learning how to look after myself. I'd worked hard to get into university, and now I was working hard to get a good job when I came out the other end. I had a plan, and me getting pregnant wasn't a part of it. I just hoped Noah would feel the same.

Walking back to the flat with Anna, the positive test wrapped in a wad of blue paper towels in her bag, I could feel myself shaking. I didn't say anything, but Anna must have sensed it, or seen it, because she linked her arm through mine and quietly guided me along the pavement, past strangers chatting and laughing and generally going about their day.

Back in our kitchen – which was also our hallway, dining room, living room – she told me to sit down while she made me a cup of tea. After putting it in front of me, along with a packet of chocolate biscuits, two of which she'd nervously nibbled while waiting for the kettle to boil, she sat down opposite and asked if I wanted to call Noah.

I didn't hesitate, which I think surprised her – or at least that's what I remember thinking when she coughed and said a piece of biscuit had gone down the wrong way. In an instant, I'd pulled my phone from my pocket and started typing.

Still sputtering, she leapt to her feet. 'You're not telling him over text, are you?'

I laughed, or I tried to laugh. I'm not sure any sound came out.

At the whoosh of my message sending, she clapped her hand to her mouth. 'Fuck.'

'Don't worry,' I said, waving the phone in front of her face. 'I've just asked him to come round.'

It was the weekend, and my message sounded mildly urgent, so he came within the hour.

Anna answered the door and led him to the table, where I was still sitting, cradling my tea, now tepid and with a thin layer of skin. One look at me and he knew something was wrong. Later, he told me he'd never seen me that pale, that it was as though even my freckles – another feature I'd inherited from my mother – had faded from my face. He held my hands in his and I told him. I managed not to cry until, tentatively, he asked me what I wanted to do. I remember searching his eyes for some sort of clue, and when I couldn't find one, telling him, in a small voice that didn't sound like mine, that I wasn't ready to be a mother. He held me close and told me everything would be all right, that he understood. Taken aback by how easily he'd accepted my decision, I asked him what he wanted, but he wouldn't say until he was sure of my own feelings. Eventually he told me he hadn't wanted to sway me, and that if I'd said I wanted to keep it we would have made it work.

The main thing I remember about the clinic was the smell – like everything and everyone in there had been doused in disinfectant. We sat side by side in the waiting room, not talking, but together, his arm around me. When the nurse called my name, Noah turned to me and asked, one final time, Are you sure? I nodded. He wasn't allowed to come in with me, but he was there waiting to take me back to his place when it was over. He made me dinner – cheese on toast, my favourite whenever I'm unwell – and we went to bed early, our bodies touching. It was the following week that we spoke about children and how he felt about the future.

It's funny – or not, really – but when we went to Florence for that long weekend, we walked past the *Ospedale degli Innocenti*, the Hospital of the Innocents. I paused, wondering whether to go in, recalling what I'd learned about it as a student. It had a seventeenth-century hatch, sort of like a hole in the wall, where parents could abandon unwanted babies without being judged or seen. For a moment, I imagined all those babies as children, and my own baby among them – a girl, just like the daughter Noah had lost. She had my hazel eyes and wispy hair, and Noah's ears, sticking out slightly. She had his laugh, loud and, like a cold, catching.

79

Noticing me hesitate, Noah asked if I wanted to go inside. I decided against it. It's silly, stupid even, but I let myself imagine walking in and people turning to look – they could tell what I'd done, that I'd got rid of our almost-baby. I visualised a sort of aura outlining my body, an unholy halo, marking me out as someone who'd selfishly denied another human life. Other than Noah and Anna, I'd never told anyone what had happened, not even my mother, to whom I tell everything. I don't know why. That same vague sense of guilt, perhaps. I wondered if Noah also felt it.

Having agreed with Noah that it was probably Anna's pregnancy that had thrown me, I tried to believe it, and to banish the whole idea of motherhood. I began each day with a half-hour run along the canal, before launching myself into the seascape.

It worked, until, again, I was thrown by my period. As I walked through Trafalgar Square, I wondered how many of the hundreds of women around me were bleeding – a peculiar thought, maybe, but it wasn't the first time it had occurred to me. Perhaps it was prompted by those adverts for sanitary pads and tampons that, lo and behold, onlookers would never know were there, their wearers smiling and stretching and swimming. It turned into a challenge: could I tell if another woman was ovulating from her damp brow or rosy cheeks? I was busy sizing up a woman in a shaggy black coat when my thoughts were interrupted.

'Catherine, everything OK?'

Frank was standing in front of me, an almost-spent roll-up pressed between his lips. He hooked his pass out of his pocket and looped it around his neck. He'd had a haircut, his greyish white hair a thin covering.

'Frank, hi. Yes, sorry, I was miles away.'

'Well, we better get you a strong coffee,' he said, clearing his throat. 'Big day.'

It seemed only fitting that, as the lining of my uterus was shedding, I was due to start chipping away at the overpaint. On the wood panel, as inside my body, old tissue had to be broken down before there could be any real hope of regeneration. Frank's scientific analysis had revealed that the overpaint wasn't contemporary to the painting, and after infrared and X-ray imaging, we'd decided to take a closer look at what it might be hiding. Quiet murmurings of anticipation could be heard throughout the conservation department.

'Right, coffee. Can I get you one too?' I asked, as he disposed of his battered stub and we entered the building. He would never say yes, but I would always offer.

'Not for me, thanks,' he replied, as he continued towards the stairs. 'You go ahead, though.'

I kept at my game of who's on her period as I walked to the café and waited in line, only ceasing when I reached the studios, where it was just me and Frank. Unsurprisingly, no food or drink is allowed around the art, so rather than waiting for it to cool down, I swallowed my coffee when it was still scorching hot. The burning sensation at the back of my throat was soothed when I saw the seascape, blustery and cold.

'Better?' asked Frank.

I nodded in confirmation, then smiled when I saw that he'd neatly lined up my solvent solution and a small surgical scalpel on the table beside the easel.

He pressed up onto his toes and his eyes flashed towards the painting, a combination of nervous and excited.

'Hey, why don't you stick around?'

'No, I should probably do some work,' he said, with a mock eye-roll. 'But I'll come back and see how you're getting on before lunch.'

'OK, then, wish me luck.'

A double-tap of his chest – *courage* – and, after stealing one more glance at the painting, he was gone.

The thin layer concealing the floating figure and whatever was beside it had dissolved while I was removing the varnish, but both still needed fully uncovering. The rough patch of overpaint below was thick and hard. It would require time and patience, which was presumably what had led the past restorer – who Frank guessed had worked on the painting in the nineteenth century – to abandon his removal of the alteration and simply cover what he'd unearthed back up again.

I pulled up a stool and slipped my optivisor onto my head, then I took a deep breath and slowly and carefully started to chip away at the overpaint. I worked on a small patch at a time, starting with the dark triangular shape by the floating figure. With a couple of bits that snagged, I made an initial incision with the scalpel and then, like a scab, picked at it with my fingers. Before moving onto the next patch, I took the solution and cleaned off the residual thin layer of white lead.

As I chipped and dabbed, chipped and dabbed, my mind started to drift. My womb was pulsing, and I couldn't help thinking about what Anna had said in the café, that time was running out with my own bodily shedding. I don't know, maybe it had something to do with my suspicion that the artwork in front of me was no longer functioning as intended. If that were the case, I felt fairly confident that I could fix it. And me? How long before my body was past the point of repair?

I hadn't moved from my seated position up close in front of the painting when Frank reappeared almost three hours later. He was saying something, but his voice sounded muffled, as if he was standing far away on the beach.

A little louder: 'I'm no expert, but I'm starting to think you might be right about that being a fin.'

I rolled my stool back from the easel, and there it was, curved and coppery green. I twisted in my seat to meet his gaze, a smile tugging at my mouth.

By the time the fin was fully formed, my period was over. Another month had passed, and my next cycle was about to begin. Frank and I met with the curator and discussed what should be done, and the three of us decided – the air thick with excitement – that we should respect the original intention of the artist and uncover what we agreed was most likely a beached whale. That would explain the crowd then.

The quiet murmurings in conservation rose in volume and soon spilled over into the other museum departments. It wasn't long until my colleagues in education, press and sales stopped me in the corridor and asked how, what, why? I told them what I'd told the curator. The whale had probably been concealed in the eighteenth or early nineteenth century to suit changing sensibilities. Perhaps its presence offended its new owner. Perhaps the painting was deemed more marketable without the stench of death.

That evening, as I reluctantly turned down the lights and left the whale buried beneath the paint, waiting for another day, I felt something like liquid guilt pool in the pit of my stomach. My body might not be functioning as intended – but as intended by whom? I'd never subscribed to the notion that women have a biological instinct to have children, and standing in the studio in the dark, I experienced a moment of clarity: even if I did, it wouldn't make a difference. What mattered was that Noah and I had made a promise to one another. Like Hendrick, we had original intentions, and I had to respect that.

May

I was eleven when my mother and I reported a sperm whale washed up on the beach. It wasn't the first to take a wrong turn from the Atlantic into the shallow waters of the North Sea – on the hunt for food, probably – and there have been others on shores up and down the country since. We were walking across the sand playing our third or fourth round of I Spy when I saw something resembling a tarpaulin or a fishing boat, beetle-like with its belly in the air, a flock of gulls above. My mother said that was strange; it hadn't been there the day before when she and my father had been out. As we came closer, we were able to make out a small flipper, pointing towards the sky, and a softly forked tail.

I don't know whether it was the vastness of it, but for a moment my body felt rigid with fear. My mother said we should ring the coastguard, and before she'd finished asking me to do so I was running home to use the landline. I ran and I ran, up over the dunes and through the marshes, even though I couldn't feel my legs. The coastguard came quickly; before I was back on the beach, my heart hammering, he'd arrived, and a group of men and women who specialised in marine life rescue weren't far behind. Soon some other locals and a couple of tourists had gathered. One of them pointed a camera lens at the whale's open mouth, which had been closed a few minutes earlier. I narrowed my eyes.

I also begged the coastguard to do something. 'Listen, it's still breathing.' As I said it, I held out my hand to hush the onlookers. 'Can't you help it?'

The coastguard said that, sadly, there was nothing to be done. The whale was simply too big and heavy to lift or roll. He turned to the tourists and added, in a whisper that wasn't meant for my ears, 'Besides, the process of decay has already begun.'

Decay. I repeated the word, quietly, under my breath. Only then did I notice the smell, like old flower water.

As more people gathered, the whale's breath quickened. My own breath quickened in response.

Taking hold of my hand, my mother suggested, 'Perhaps we can make it more comfortable?'

After consulting the others, the coastguard told us we could try to keep it wet. Buckets were produced and we scuttled back and forth from the sea, saltwater sloshing against our legs. What remained we poured over the toppled whale's grey-blue skin, as rubbery as the wellies on our feet. For a while, it seemed to help. Its breathing slowed. But as time went on, like a flat tyre, the twitching body before us gradually began to sink in on itself.

A man in the crowd with a toady face said we ought to let nature take its course.

I turned to him, my own face as angry as a fist, and demanded, 'How would you like it?'

My mother's cheeks burned, though I couldn't tell whether she was cross with him or embarrassed by me.

Half an hour later, the whale was dead, its internal organs collapsed and ground to a halt under its own weight. It was a young male, we were told. To try to lift our spirits, a kind but misguided woman from the rescue team told us that by removing swatches of muscle and blood, as well as teeth, we could learn more about these mysterious mammals.

The beach was cordoned off for the necropsy, and quietly my mother and I made our way back to the house. When we arrived, my father asked what was going on – he'd tried to ask me before, after I'd hung up the phone, but I'd told him there wasn't time. As my mother explained to him about the whale, the feelings that had been swelling inside me since we first saw it lying there on the shoreline burst, not loudly or violently, but in a way that was soft and quiet. I think part of the reason I remember that moment so clearly is because it was the first time I'd cried without making a sound. By the time my parents noticed, I could feel the tears spilling off my cheeks and onto the floor. My mother held out her arms and told me these things happen.

I'd never witnessed death before.

Noah couldn't stand the train to Norfolk, which was long and languid and often cancelled at the last minute, so we decided to drive when my mother's seventieth birthday weekend finally arrived. The week before I still hadn't settled on what to give her and, in the end, accepting the fact that she already owned most things she could want or need, I bought her a voucher for a night away at a posh but not stuffy hotel near Bury St Edmunds. The voucher was for two, so I would suggest we go together. A mother-daughter outing. Noah smiled when I told him.

I'd never owned a car; growing up in Norfolk I'd made do borrowing my parents' and I hadn't needed one since moving to London. Noah had a hatchback; the same one he'd had when we first met. Once shiny and new, it was now showing signs of age, with sputtering windscreen wipers and several scratches – mostly crooked white lines, like someone had run a key across the black paintwork. I once jokingly asked him what he'd done to piss off his ex-girlfriend, then when I thought of his first wife and their baby girl, I held my breath. He laughed and said, You.

We didn't have free parking on our street in London Fields, but an old school friend of Noah's had a garage nearby and let us keep the car in one of his unused spaces for a nominal fee. With our bags packed, and a bottle of wine on the kitchen counter for the neighbour who'd volunteered to feed Tom while we were away, we walked ten minutes to get there. The sun was warm on my face, but not hot, making me long for the oven-like heat only ever on offer abroad. Outside a greasy spoon that smelled of fried onions, I stopped to take off my jacket in a bid to soak as much vitamin D into my skin as possible.

Driving in London makes me nervous, but it didn't faze Noah. He slipped into the driving seat and turned on the radio as he steered his way out onto the street, the news sounding from the tinny speakers. I pulled up Google Maps on my phone and the well-spoken woman whom we referred to as Moira began to spew out directions. After we'd heard the latest on Brexit and listened to Trump trying to justify stripping funds from clinics providing abortion services, I suggested some music. The last words I heard before they were replaced by tunes were lifted from his final presidential debate against Hillary two years earlier: 'rip the baby out of the womb of the mother'.

Home was the house I'd grown up in, on a quiet and not particularly popular stretch of the north Norfolk coast. It took ten minutes to walk across the marshes to the sea, the ground soft underfoot. From a narrow, arched window in an awkward corner at the top of the stairs, you could keep an eye on the tide's ebb and flow. As a small child, I would clamber onto the white wooden bench my father had installed below that window, press my nose up against the glass, my breath turning white, and wonder at the water being a living thing.

My parents had moved there just after they got married. Together with a part-time carpenter friend, they had fitted built-in cupboards in the kitchen, which over the course of my life had changed from plain wood to off-white to wine red and, by this point, olive green. In the garden, my mother had salvaged an old vegetable patch – she was particularly proud of her two-toned courgettes – and planted fresh bulbs in the muddy beds.

Like the creepers she'd trained to twist and turn along the garden wall, the house was tangled up with memories happy and sad. The previous owner had given birth on the carpeted bathroom floor (unplanned), which prompted my mother to have a planned home birth with me; luckily the midwife called for an ambulance when I arrived looking like the newest member of the Simpsons family. My father had his heart attack in the living room; they'd just finished dinner and were debating which new BBC drama to watch when my mother went to make some tea and the blood stopped pumping to his heart. After that, her brother, Duncan, who lives in the States and rarely visits, suggested she put the house on the market and find somewhere smaller, more manageable. She told him she could manage just fine where she was. To me, she said she'd never believed the business in the wedding vows about 'till death do us part'.

She was peering into the post box when we arrived. Despite the crunch of gravel beneath the wheels, she didn't hear us – or at least if she did, she didn't turn around. Noah gently tapped his palm against the middle of the wheel and the car emitted a toot. She brought one hand to her forehead to shade her eyes and with the other, clasping a bunch of white and brown envelopes, she waved – slowly at first, then wildly when she realised it was us.

'Darling!' She opened my door before I had a chance to unbuckle my seatbelt. She'd had her hair done – I could tell from the extra volume – and as she bent down to get a better look at me, I caught the familiar whiff of her locally made lavender perfume. 'Did you have an OK drive?'

When I leant in to give her a kiss and a hug, she held on for what felt like longer than normal. She let go and I told her that, yes, it was pretty easy. 'Just the usual traffic around Norwich.'

'Janey, happy birthday weekend to you.' Noah was kissing her now, once on each cheek, and she was telling him to hush.

'I haven't told the neighbours! Apart from Peggy, of course.'

'Why not, Mum? It's your seventieth!'

'Shh! I don't want them making a fuss.'

'Well,' I said, wrapping my arm around her shoulders, which had become bonier with age, 'we're here to do exactly that. Happy birthday weekend, Mum.' I didn't tell her that Peggy and I had been in touch earlier in the week, and that she was all set to bring over one of her famous lemon drizzle cakes – my mother's favourite – later in the day.

'Oh, thank you both,' she said, clapping her hands together and losing one envelope in the process. As Noah bent down to retrieve it, she added: 'I'm delighted you're here.'

After the usual tug of war with the bags, we bundled into the house through the back door, past my father's wellies and walking stick, which were right where he'd left them. When he died, I worried about my mother, too, but not for the same reasons as my uncle. My father's suits and shirts still took up half of the wardrobe. She still stayed up until half-past ten every night to watch the news, almost always falling asleep in her chair, because that's what he'd always wanted to do. I worried that, like the slugs that chewed at her salad leaves, the past would eat away at her future. For some time, though, she'd seemed to accommodate both quite comfortably.

In the kitchen, my nostrils began to tingle, and not in a good way. 'Is something burning, Mum?'

She scrunched up her forehead and for a few seconds nobody moved, nobody spoke. Eventually:

'Allow me,' offered Noah, slipping on the pair of oven gloves resting on the side and opening the top door of the Aga. 'Phew, stand back.' He took the smoking tray of blackened ginger biscuits – usually my mother's speciality – back out the door and into the garden.

'Blast.'

'Did you set the timer, Mum?'

She looked at me with raised eyebrows and said, in a tone that told me she thought I was criticising, 'Yes, I did.'

'Well, don't worry, they're only biscuits.'

She started rootling around in the cupboard, mumbling something about measurements.

'Mum?'

'Yes?'

'What are you doing?'

'Making another batch.'

'You don't have to do that, really.'

I considered telling her about Peggy and the cake, but before I'd opened my mouth again, she'd started sifting flour.

Like the rest of the house, my room was in the exact state I'd left it when I moved to London: there was a tall tower of old videos in one corner and a slightly shorter tower of CDs beside it; I'd tacked photos of friends and family directly onto the walls and by now half were hanging at wonky angles; lined up neatly on my desk were folders filled with colour-coded notes from my school exams; beside them, beaded bracelets and necklaces dangled from a handmade jewellery stand. More than once I'd offered to go through my belongings and do a clear-out, but my mother said they weren't any trouble and she would tell me if they ever were.

Because of the childhood tokens, Noah and I tended to sleep in the spare room whenever we came to stay. The first time we did, he said he was relieved, that it would make him uncomfortable getting sexy surrounded by snapshots of me as an adolescent. It was plain in the way that spare rooms often are, with lemon-yellow walls and a matching furniture set – wooden wardrobe, chest of drawers, bedside tables. One of my mother's hand-stitched patchwork quilts covered the bed, this one in various shades of blue, and on the windowsill were some shells we'd collected at the beach. The window overlooked Peggy's garden. There was no sign of her, but I could see her old blind terrier, Billy, nosing his way between potted plants. It was a peaceful room, a good room to be ill in.

'Here, I'll do this,' said Noah, slipping my bag off my shoulder. 'You go and spend time with your mum.'

'Are you sure?'

He planted a kiss on my lips. 'That's why we're here.'

I went in for another kiss.

Downstairs, the smell of burning had been replaced with the sweet scent of melted butter and golden syrup. As I walked up behind her and curled my arm around her waist, she was adding sugar and fresh ginger to the saucepan.

'Can I help?'

'Do you remember what comes next?' she asked, taking the pan off the heat.

For a moment I thought she was being serious, but when I laughed, so did she. She'd been making those ginger biscuits from a recipe inherited from her own mother ever since I was born. 'How could you doubt me?'

She waited, then she began to list the rest of the ingredients. 'So, flour . . .?'

'Flour, ground ginger, bicarbonate of soda.' I recited them as I would the lyrics of a song and grabbed a wooden spoon and a bowl. Next, I cracked an egg and stirred in the bright-orange yolk. 'OK, we're ready for you.'

After she'd poured in the cooled sugary mixture, I kneaded the lot to make a dough. Then, together, we scooped up small handfuls, each of which we rolled into balls and placed on the tray she'd pre-lined with baking paper.

'There, quick and easy,' she said, as she slid the tray into the top oven.

I was about to remind her to set the timer when I heard it ticking.

Later that afternoon, after a pot of tea and a plate of the biscuits, the three of us went for a walk on the beach. It was windy and I'd forgotten to bring a hair tie with me, which meant loose strands whipped at my cheeks. When I resorted to walking along holding them back from my face with both hands, Noah offered me his scarf. I'd told him he wouldn't need it, that it wasn't cold out, so he smiled smugly when I snatched it from him and eagerly wrapped it around my head, tying it in a knot beneath my chin.

'So, how does it feel, Janey,' he asked, 'the final day of your sixties?'

'Strange,' she said, brushing away from her forehead a strand of her own hair, shorter and salted. The rest was covered in a proper waterproof bonnet of sorts.

'Why strange, Mum?'

'Well, it doesn't feel all that long ago that I was your age and you'd only just been born.' As she spoke, the lines on her face moved, like they were listening to the rise and fall of her voice.

'You were my age when you had me?'

'I was; thirty-five.'

Noah's coat pocket started to ring, and she said she was surprised he managed to get any signal out here.

'Sorry, I should take this.'

As he answered and walked ahead, she linked her arm through mine. She didn't say anything and neither did I, but the air was thick with expectation. In an instant, I was fifteen again and she and I were walking towards the sea, as we often did, her waiting for me to pluck up the courage to put into words what was bothering me.

Even though the tide was low, and the waves small, we could hear the water rocking against the sand. We were wearing wellies. Noah had the same size feet as my father and had taken to borrowing his whenever we visited. The first time I'd suggested it, I'd bitten down on my lower lip as I'd waited for my mother to answer, not sure how she would respond. In fact, she was thrilled and said something about it being like dear old Dad was walking with us. After, she gave them a brush and returned them to their place by the door.

When I turned back towards the house to see how far we'd come, I could spy three sets of prints, which gradually faded away in the distance. 'Mum?'

'Yes?' She kept her gaze forward, as she always did when she could sense I was about to open up, not unlike the flowers in her garden at the start of spring.

'How did you know?'

'What's that?'

I paused, my train of thought swept up with the gulls overhead, who were having no trouble voicing their opinion.

She too looked up to the sky, tilting her head left and right in line with their arched wings.

'How did you know that you wanted children?'

If she was surprised by my question, she didn't show it.

I still remember the moment when I told her, early on in my relationship with Noah, that she shouldn't expect to become a grandmother. I remember my voice cracking with regret as I said it, regret that I was taking something elemental away from her, and the relief I felt when she said, her face unchanged, that she was more than happy to remain, simply, my mother. Looking back now, I suppose it must have been similar to the relief that Noah felt when I reassured him that I wasn't yearning for motherhood.

That day on the beach, though, she did squeeze my arm before she said, with a slight shrug of her shoulders, that she just knew. 'I think I always had done, ever since I was a little girl. Things were more straightforward then, or more predictable, whichever way you want to look at it. Your father and I got married, and it was the next step.'

I glanced at Noah, who was still talking on the phone, his free hand animated, and asked, in a hurry, 'But did you long for it?'

'Motherhood?'

'I suppose, yes.'

'I think so, after a while. But it took time. Most of my friends had their children in their twenties, and at that point I hadn't even met your father. We were quite old, by those days' standards, when we had you.'

'And you were happy you did?'

'Happy we had a child?'

'Yes.'

'Well, of course, darling; otherwise I wouldn't have you.'

When I looked at Noah again, he was returning his phone to his pocket and waiting for us to catch up. He smiled at me, and I smiled back.

'So, what's for dinner?' I asked my mother.

Before answering, she squeezed my arm again.

*

It turned out that, as well as dropping round the lemon drizzle cake while we were out walking, Peggy had delivered three dressed Norfolk crabs. Apparently, she'd called my mother that morning and asked if she could pick up any shopping for her while she was in town. I was pleasantly surprised. Usually, my mother made a point of cooking a roast when we came to stay because she knew that in London we tried to avoid eating too much meat. Protein, she would announce, as she piled flesh and bones onto our plates.

After showering I returned to the kitchen to find her sighing at her homemade chips, which hadn't crisped up to her liking.

'Do you want some help, Mum?'

'No, I'm all right,' she said, shuffling them about in the tray and returning them to the oven. 'Unless you want to trim that samphire?'

'Absolutely.' I unwrapped the vibrant green stalks and gave them a good rinse. As I reached for a knife, she told me it would be easier and quicker with scissors. I found a pair in the drawer and started snipping.

'Why don't you sit down?' she asked, flicking her wrist towards the table.

'I'm fine,' I said, tapping my toes, wondering if she was going to resume our conversation from the beach and why she suddenly seemed tetchy.

Five minutes later, her lips were pressed together, and I was standing still. She'd never been good at multitasking and right now the mayonnaise required her undivided attention.

'Janey, what can I do?'

Noah had appeared in the threshold, wearing a cotton jumper with a high neck that nudged up against his stubble, his winter beard hibernating in anticipation of the summer.

'How's work, darling?' She was whisking, and clearly talking to me. Occasionally Noah was darling man, but never darling.

I widened my eyes at him, and he shrugged his shoulders and nodded for me to go ahead. 'Work's great, thanks, Mum.' I started to talk about my progress with the seascape, then I paused. 'Can Noah help with anything?'

Her eyes flashed towards him. 'Oh, Noah, I didn't see you there.'

We exchanged another look.

'Not to worry, Janey,' he said. 'How about I lay the table?'

'That would be lovely. Plates are up here, in this cupboard, and cutlery is in that drawer.'

'Great. And in the meantime, you should ask Cathy about her whale.'

'What whale?' she asked, looking me in the eye for the first time since I'd come downstairs.

'In the painting.' I smiled, her peculiar mood forgotten as I launched into the latest news of Hendrick.

I was stuffed when we went to bed and as I crept downstairs the following morning to make my mother's card – a birthday tradition – I still felt full. I knelt on the carpet in front of the TV and opened the cupboard below, which was filled with old family photos. That Christmas I'd helped her organise them into three broad categories: family, friends, holidays. We'd laughed at past fashions and more than a handful of dodgy haircuts. She regretted that my father had always been the one behind the camera.

I pulled the family box out of the cupboard and onto my knee. I knew what I was letting myself in for, and yet, my stomach started to jitter when I saw the first photo. It showed my mother on the living-room floor with me, fresh from the womb, with sallow skin; it must have been just a few minutes later that the midwife phoned for an ambulance. My dark hair was wet and flat against my tiny skull, my legs like a frog's, and my fingers sticking out at crooked angles – not unlike my mother's now, old and arthritic. She looked exhausted, her own hair wet with sweat, shoulders slumped, face red. Exhausted, but ecstatic. A grin extended across her cheeks, which were streaked with tears of joy, relief.

The jitteriness soon turned to nausea, and I hadn't drunk enough wine the night before to call it a hangover.

'Everything all right in here?'

The photo slipped through my fingers and back into the box, which I returned to the cupboard. In its place I pulled out the holidays compilation.

'Cathy?'

I turned around and smiled at Noah, who smelled fresh after a shower and was already dressed. 'All good, just finding a photo for Mum's card.'

He came and sat in the nearest chair, and I handed him a small pile.

'How about this one?' he asked, a minute later, holding up a picture of her dressed as if for the runway with the green and pleasant Welsh hills rolling in the background.

I remember my father telling me that it was one of the first photos he'd taken of her, on his first camera – a bulky black thing that he wore around his neck on a thick leather strap. They were on their honeymoon. Her hair was blown out and a pair of big dark glasses concealed half her face. Again, she was grinning, but not with the same abandon. Still.

'It's perfect,' I said. 'Thank you.'

He touched his hand to my shoulder and told me he would put the kettle on. When I was done with my card, I joined him in the kitchen. Together we made pancakes – another birthday tradition – and when my mother appeared we sang to her. The three of us sat at the table and I told her to make a wish before blowing out the candles I'd poked into the stack between blueberries.

She grumbled.

'Don't worry, Janey, seventy is the new fifty,' said Noah.

'I'll remind you of that when you turn fifty, Noah. When is that?'

'Touché.'

'Do you have to rush off after breakfast?' she asked, popping a blueberry in her mouth. Then, while chewing: 'Is there somewhere you need to be?'

'No, Mum,' I said, glancing at Noah, who smiled and nodded. 'Nowhere other than here.'

He knew I always found it hard to say goodbye, especially now that she was living on her own.

In the end, we stayed an extra night and got up at five o'clock the next morning to drive back to London, the sky brightening above us, a wash of pink and lilac.

Back at work, I'd uncovered the tip of the whale's tail and now it was time to make a start on its head. Strictly speaking, only conservationists are supposed to enter the studios, but I'd had more than a few curious members of museum staff poke their heads in as they 'just happened to be passing'. I'd also had a visiting request from seven-year-old Allie, who had been sitting between me and Daniel at dinner earlier that week and caught her father's enthusiasm. So, you were right about that triangle being a fin? he'd asked, a forkful of green beans hovering mid-air. That's amazing, Cathy! Allie quickly swallowed her mouthful and echoed his sentiments: Amazing! Amazing!

As I chipped away at the overpaint, I began to think again about my body and the way it sheds hair, skin, blood. The way it's constantly changing and renewing, dead cells breaking away to make space for new cells to grow. To grow, or, as in the whale's case, to reappear. While the human body flushes those cells of its own accord, works of art need a helping hand. For a moment, I imagined a layer of overpaint on my skull, cloaking any unsolicited thoughts.

Frank could tell I was distracted, I'm sure. He was across the room carrying out a moisture treatment on a canvas and kept sneaking glances at me and – unlike my mother – probing.

He slipped on his Latex gloves, the artificial shade of mouthwash, and asked me if I was feeling all right. 'You know, the whale can wait if not.'

'I'm fine,' I said, pushing my optivisor up onto my head as I would a pair of sunglasses and leaning back to get a broader look at the work I'd done so far. As if to prove it, I turned to him and started talking about the first time I'd tried the kind of treatment he was doing. 'I was terrified,' I said, shaking my head as he pulled the cork out of a glass bottle of white spirit with a satisfying pop and tipped a small amount directly onto the surface. 'I mean, I knew it was harmless, but that didn't make me any less anxious about pouring solvent onto a centuries-old painting.'

'You and me both,' he said, temporarily accepting my diversion. He picked up a cloth and spread the clear liquid across the canvas, rubbing it in a circular motion until he was satisfied it had soaked in. I watched as he picked at the corners of the protective tissue covering the surface and, like human skin after it's been badly burned, peeled it off in mostly large pieces.

'So?'

I glanced up from his fingertips to his face, which was steady, giving nothing away. 'So, what?'

'Are you going to tell me what's on your mind?'

I laughed.

'You know I'm not one to give up.'

'I'm not sure if you want to hear it this time, Frank.' We'd never spoken about anything to do with reproduction – perhaps because we had a mutual understanding.

'Try me.'

I looked at the whale, then back at him. 'Children.'

He repeated the word back to me, nodding thoughtfully. 'You're considering it – or, rather, them?'

'Not exactly.'

Again, he nodded.

'Did you?' I asked. 'Consider it.'

'Ah, well,' he said, smiling, 'I thought we were talking about you.'

'We are.'

Again, he accepted the slight digression. 'We considered it.'

We. He and Douglas. Together.

'Too seriously, you might say.'

'What do you mean?'

'Parenting isn't something that could just sort of *happen* for us, for obvious reasons,' he said. 'It would require extra steps, and the logistics and money involved in those steps meant we had to be sure – beyond sure, really.' He laughed as he added, 'If we were heterosexual, we might have just said, Fuck it.'

I felt myself stiffen on my stool, and Frank must have noticed.

'No, of course, it's better this way – to carefully consider it rather than just do what everyone else does.' He waved a hand towards the door, as if indicating the general public.

'Do you think they know something we don't?'

'They might. Or they might just feel a pull that, for one reason or another, hasn't exerted itself on us quite so forcefully.'

My thoughts wavered to the sea, pushing and pulling against the beach.

'So, your turn,' he said. 'What does "not exactly" mean?'

'God, where to start.' I told him about my almost-missed period, Anna's pregnancy, and the way both had made me feel. The way that, lately, thoughts of responsibility and care were slipping in and out of my consciousness with greater frequency. 'Maybe it's an age thing.'

'Maybe.'

'A phase, even.'

'Could be.'

I gave him a small smile. A phase. Like flares and skinny jeans.

'I take it Noah isn't experiencing the same awakening – if we can call it that?'

'No, he isn't.'

'Well, take your time, think about it – you owe it to your-self, and to him.'

It was that afternoon that I began what I'd envisioned would be a brief foray into Dutch marine biology, culture, theology. I discovered that, as well as bringing wealth and wonder, these beached sea monsters were bad omens, warning signs of an impending disaster or God's wrath. I peered at an etching on my laptop of a whale stranded on a beach and, above, the calamities that ensued: plague, an earthquake, solar and lunar eclipses. When I tried to predict what kind of misfortune was lying in wait for me, I pictured Noah sleeping first in the spare room, then in a separate flat. Making dinner for one. Showering alone. End credits. A closed curtain. When the visions threatened to pull me under, I cast around for an alternative, and at last one came to me, a bitter blow I told myself I could cope with: I'd been so stumped by the way I was feeling, or not feeling, lately that I hadn't stopped to consider the fact that me having a baby might not be possible. A calamity, yes, but also a life raft for my marriage.

I had no idea what state my ovaries were in. How could I? But there was that inconclusive smear test a couple of years back – a letter typed out in small black font had informed me that my results were 'abnormal', and I would have to book a biopsy. After, the young male doctor said I was fine; everything looked healthy. I think he might have even compared my ovaries to a type of fruit. But still, it was something. Then there was the cyst I'd had removed in my late teens. And simply the fact that my childlike body – straight, hipless – didn't *feel* capable of growing and giving birth to a baby. I'd certainly started my periods later than most of the girls in my year at school. I looked again at the foreboding etching and wondered, maybe procreation isn't possible for me. Maybe Noah and I can move on, forget the whole thing. That accident early on was a one-off, our only shot. The prospect brought with it both pain and relief, like when you tweeze a splinter out from under your skin.

I touched my fingertips to my keyboard and felt a current run through them. Not really, but all of a sudden I experienced a sense of urgency, my heart rate quickening. Whether he'd picked up on my inner frenzy and was actively trying to counterbalance it, or whether he was simply absorbed in his task, Frank was slowly and carefully placing a new tissue facing over his canvas. I watched as he started in the middle and moved outwards, taking care to avoid creating any creases. As he worked, the painting – a tender self-portrait of the artist, Italian, eighteenth-century – started to re-emerge, first vague shapes and colours, then finer details.

When he was done, he checked the new facing was even and removed his gloves. He asked, 'Are you staying late?'

Thoughts of my fertility, or lack thereof, were churning in my head, and it wasn't until he cleared his throat that I registered the question and gave him an answer. 'I'm just going to finish some reading, I think.' I tilted the screen of my laptop towards me, even though I hadn't yet started the search I had planned.

He smiled a knowing smile as he shrugged on his coat and rummaged around in his pockets for his tobacco. I recalled what he'd said earlier – it's better this way, to think it through – and wondered what he would say now if he knew I was trying to convince myself that I wanted my body to fail.

'Frank?'

'Yes?'

'Thank you for today.'

He nodded. 'I'll be back in the morning to iron through the beeswax.' He walked away, and, as he did, I considered how this kind of moisture barrier would make the canvas less susceptible to changes in the environment, how the hope was to preserve the lining for as long as possible. I also considered what it meant, the fact that I was seeing fertility in *everything*.

Left alone, I moved my laptop screen back to its usual position and opened a new tab. I think the words I typed were 'fertility test'. I stared at the text cursor, blinking, waiting for me to either continue typing or press enter. I picked up my phone and scrolled aimlessly through social media until I felt my eyes glide back to it, still blinking, still waiting.

I started googling.

There were a few clinics to choose from, but the first in the list looked and sounded as good as any. On the home-page was a wholesome-looking mother and a toddler on a beach, both smiling candidly, wearing chunky knitwear, their skin kissed by the sun. I ignored the sceptical voice in my head telling me she was just a model and let myself wonder whether she was a single parent, or if there was a father or maybe a second mother in the background, just out of shot. My resolve began to waver as a very different set of visions flashed before me: the two of *us* on a beach – no, wait, not just us two, but us three. For a moment, I allowed myself to get swept up in them, even though something wasn't quite right – the visions were too polished, too saturated. I switched to WhatsApp, selected my conversation with Noah, and started typing: *How would you feel if . . .* I heard him exhale, loudly, felt his shoulders slump with disappointment, telling me I knew how he would feel. I felt a sharp stab of guilt. I deleted it.

Back on the website, my eyes skimmed the drop-down offerings running along the top and settled on Investigating Infertility, which lead me straight to something called a Fertility MOT. Really? My body a vehicle, my ovaries fiddly parts that had to be checked to ensure they met the required standards. I pictured an overalled man with oily hands standing between my legs, whistling.

Before I had a chance to change my mind, I scrolled down to the get-in-touch box and tapped in my details: name, date of birth, email address, telephone number, service (I decided to skip the offering of an initial consultation and go straight for the MOT). The final line was for the name, date of birth, email address and telephone number of my partner (if applicable). Again, I felt Noah's disappointment – this time because I'd lied to him. But if all was as I hoped – it *was* what I hoped, I told myself, loudly, firmly – this would make everything better again. My thumb hovered over Submit. I closed my eyes and clicked the trackpad.

As I collected my things and walked towards the door, glancing back just briefly at the solemn face of the dead whale beginning to emerge on the wood panel, I wondered if the leviathan would be my one and only warning sign, or if there would be others.

I heard back from the clinic the following afternoon. A sprightly email landed in my inbox, thanking me very much for my 'recent enquiry' and informing me of the price (four-hundred pounds!) and what was included: a blood test and a transvaginal ultrasound examination, plus a follow-up consultation about a week later. I was asked to send some suggested dates, which I did. Within the hour, a second email informed me that my appointments had been secured and requested that I call the clinic to provide payment details.

The singsong tone of the woman on the phone matched that of the email. 'Lovely,' she said, with a high-low lilt. 'Perfect, that's all gone through. Have a wonderful weekend!'

As I was leaving work, my fingers started to itch. Noah and I were going to see a new and apparently brilliant period drama at the cinema that night, but not for a couple of hours. He was having a drink with colleagues first, so I decided to do the same, except with a friend. Anna. In an instant, I pictured her face as I told her what I'd done and what I hoped would come of it: tilted up and a little to the left, eyes narrowed, lips pursed. The face she pulled whenever she didn't understand something and was trying to visualise it.

Walking towards Covent Garden, surrounded by strangers, I called her. I breathed in and out and rehearsed in my head what I was going to say: I need to know that I can't have a baby, because if I can't, my marriage is safe. That, and: Will you come with me?

I was about to hang up when, at last, she answered. 'Hi.' Her voice sounded small and far away.

I pressed the phone hard against my cheek and poked a finger in my other ear, muting the flurry of passers-by and churning rush-hour traffic. 'Anna, is that you? Can you hear me?'

'Yes.'

Still so quiet. 'Hang on, I'm having trouble hearing you.' I felt for my volume control and turned it up as far as it would go. 'Is that better?' I asked, ducking down a narrow side street, the ground a dirty grey and pocked with dried chewing gum and cigarette butts. I realised I was standing outside a shuttered entrance to a club; there were flyers outside, tacked to the brick wall. 'Are you free for a drink?'

She started sobbing.

'Oh, Anna. What's wrong?' My eyes skipped left and right, trying to work out what it could be. She'd only cried a handful of times since we'd met as eleven-year-olds, and I could probably pinpoint each occasion. When she didn't reply, only sobbed more, I asked again: 'Are you OK? Please talk to me.'

She was quiet for a few seconds, then she said it: 'I've lost the baby.'

Darkness. My eyes had closed. I felt suddenly empty. I remembered I hadn't eaten lunch, but it was more than that – the kind of empty that comes from scrolling mindlessly through the daily disasters in the news. Oh, but Anna, she should be feeling full, she should be . . . how many months now – three, four? 'I'm on my way.'

When I hung up, the stab of guilt had returned, but for a very different reason. It was my insides I'd been willing to be barren, not hers.

I rang the bell and Caleb answered. Before he did, I heard him coming – or rather, I heard Theo, who was in his arms, wriggling and wailing. Though it was still the shade of runny honey, the hallway seemed darker than usual. Duller.

'I'm so sorry, Caleb.'

Unlike Theo's face, his was eerily still. The whites of his eyes, normally bright against brown, were streaked with crimson, and his mouth was a fixed straight line.

I leant in to give him a hug and Theo wailed even louder.

'Don't take it personally,' said Caleb, pressing his palm briefly to his forehead before blinking, once, hard, and rubbing his little boy's back. 'He knows something's up.'

'Of course, don't worry about me. What can I do?'

He half smiled as he tipped his stubbled chin towards the stairs. 'You're already doing it.'

She was lying in bed, under the covers, one set of curtains open, the other closed. A pool of early evening light had let itself into the room and was twinkling with dust motes. I expected she might be sleeping but her eyes were open and staring up at the ceiling. Like her voice on the phone, her features were quiet, expressionless. When I tapped my knuckles against the doorframe, she craned her neck to look at me and in her small voice thanked me for coming.

'Anna, I'm so sorry.' I walked towards her, and she lifted the nearest side of the duvet. I took off my shoes and, careful not to catch her with a limb, climbed in. I lay on my side, my head propped up on the other pillow, facing her, while she stayed on her back. 'What happened?'

She slid her hands back beneath the covers and down towards her stomach. She rested them there, unmoving, and for a moment neither of us spoke. 'I had cramps,' she said, at last, her cheek twitching. When her eyes started to glisten, she widened them a little and forced a smile. 'We thought it was wind.'

I reached out and started to stroke her hair, something she'd always liked. When we lived together, in the flat south of the river, she would plonk herself in front of me while I was sitting on the sofa watching TV, and ask, Can I have a hair tickle, please?

'Then I started spotting.'

'Oh, Anna.'

She took a deep breath, shook her head. 'They don't know why, at least not yet. There was no obvious problem.'

I kept stroking, she kept talking.

'I must have done something wrong.' She brought her hands back up and covered her face, her fingers trembling. Her nails, normally perfectly painted, were chipped and uneven. 'My body must have done something wrong.'

I squeezed her shoulder tight with one hand and pressed the other down on the crown of her head. 'You didn't do anything wrong, OK? And neither did your body.' As I said it, I heard my own voice break.

'Then why couldn't I keep him safe? Why did he die?' She said it through the gaps between her fingers, through sobs.

Another boy. Theo's little brother. 'I don't know,' I said, my own cheeks wet. 'But I do know it wasn't your fault.'

One by one, she unfurled her fingers from her face.

I quickly brushed at my tears with the back of my sleeve, then attended more carefully to hers.

'I'm sorry,' she said, again forcing a smile. 'I'm a mess.'

'Don't be sorry,' I told her, firmer now. 'You have no reason to be.'

She nodded, slowly. Then the smile slipped away, and again she looked up at the ceiling. 'It's so strange,' she said, blinking back more tears. 'I feel like I've been thumped in the stomach, and the ache won't go away.'

*

My fertility tests were the following week. I'd spoken to Anna on the phone most days since I'd been to see her, but I hadn't mentioned my appointment. I couldn't, not without explaining why I was doing it, what I wanted the outcome to be. And then what? It felt outrageously selfish of me.

During my lunch break, I caught the Tube from Charing Cross to London Bridge. En route, I reread the medical history questionnaire I'd filled out that morning. The clinic should have received an electronic copy, but I'd decided to print out a physical version just in case. All thirty-two pages.

The clinic wasn't far from the station. I passed people taking bites out of pulled-pork sandwiches, aromatic curries in cardboard containers, and other street food from Borough Market. It was warm, the sun blushing in the sky. A man handing out leaflets for a new restaurant down the street was singing a song I wasn't familiar with.

It was a brick building, with lots of windows letting in the strengthening spring light. I walked up the steps and through a glass door into the waiting room, which smelled like it had been freshly hoovered that morning. A receptionist with pearly teeth that probably once wore braces was sitting behind a curved white desk that resembled the prow of a ship. When I leant forward to tell her my name, she too smelled squeaky clean.

'Excuse me?' she asked.

I glanced around the room, which was empty except for a fretty woman chewing a biro and a couple who looked more or less composed. She had her palm resting on his shoulder and he was pointing out something on his phone, speaking in dulcet tones. 'Cathy,' I repeated, a little louder, wondering what Noah would say if he were here with me, how he would be. I imagined him with his ex-wife, holding her hand during the sonograms, sitting behind her in the antenatal classes, helping her practise her breathing.

I'd seen photos, of course, back when I searched for her online. She had pale skin and dark features, like mine but stronger, as if they'd been carved in marble. She was tall, as tall as him maybe, and though she was slender she wasn't at all fragile-looking, which was something a man once said about me. Noah described her as more handsome than beautiful, which isn't necessarily a negative.

'How can I help you, Cathy?'

'I have an appointment.'

'Ah yes,' she said, peering at her screen, clicking her mouse. 'Welcome.'

I took in her floral blouse and the little gold bees dangling from her earlobes and wondered if this was the same woman who I'd emailed and spoken to on the phone.

'Lovely. Perfect.'

It seemed so.

'Take a seat and the doctor will be right with you.'

I grimaced.

'No need to be nervous,' she added, with a sympathetic head tilt, bees swinging.

'Oh, I'm not—'

The phone on her desk started to ring and a raised index finger told me to wait just a minute. A few minutes later, she was talking in what sounded like her most reassuring voice, punctuating her usual sunny vocabulary with words such as 'cycle' and 'bleed'.

I wanted to explain that I wasn't nervous, at least not for the reasons she assumed. Instead, I squeezed onto the unforgiving banquette beside the fretty woman, the biro still

113

lodged between her teeth, her face a blotchy red. I flicked through the questionnaire again. Some of the questions were easy: age, height, weight. Have you ever had a sexually transmitted disease? No. Are you allergic to any foods or medicines? No. Others less so. I tried to work out how much I drank a week on average, then rounded it down, something my mother had once told me doctors expect of all patients. Have you ever been pregnant? Yes. Total number of pregnancies? One. Number of elective terminations? One. I stuffed the printed pages back into my bag.

I spotted a water cooler in the corner of the room and went to pour myself a cup. I was busy focusing on the feeling of the fridge-cold liquid filling up against my clammy palm when—

'Cathy?'

'Yes?'

Standing to the right of the receptionist was a man wearing a white coat. 'You can come through now.'

I took a sip of water. 'OK.'

The red-cheeked woman beside me gave me a lopsided grin, biro slung between her lips.

His name was Doctor Day, and he was a consultant gynaecologist and sub-specialist in reproductive medicine. I don't know why, but I'd assumed I would be seen by a woman. Still, once I got over my initial surprise, I realised that, for me, it didn't make much of a difference. He had icy blue eyes beneath eyebrows as thick and dark as Noah's. His face and hands, though, were more creased. Together with his receding hairline, they told me he was closer to his sixties. As he talked, he smoothed down his silky tie, which was already lying flat against his shirt, white with lilac stripes. Noah would have hated it, and I wasn't a fan either.

'So,' he said, after introductions had been made, 'you're in for a Fertility MOT.'

I curled my lip.

'Don't worry, you're not the only one to take umbrage at the name.'

I was about to ask whether his patients' displeasure at being made to feel like vehicles was a good enough reason for him to suggest the clinic considered changing it, when – without further chitchat – he started talking about the transvaginal ultrasound.

'The scan will give us a clear image of your uterus and ovaries, as well as your antral follicle count.'

Unlike the receptionist, his signature scent was body odour. I switched from breathing through my nose to breathing through my mouth.

'Don't worry, it's not overly invasive,' he added.

Interesting: my respiratory tack had come across as trepidation.

He asked me to remove the bottom half of my clothing and lie on the bed beneath the flimsy paper sheet provided. 'I'll give you some privacy.'

As he slipped outside, and I slipped off my skirt and knickers, I tried to imagine that I was in for a bikini wax. I'd pictured stirrups, but the bed – on the spongy side – was designed to separate and support your legs. Even so, when I was in position, my modesty loosely preserved, I had to try to keep my knees from instinctively clamping together.

A couple of minutes later, Doctor Day knocked on the door and asked if I was ready.

I squeaked an affirmative.

With him was a young, unsmiling woman, whom he introduced as his assistant.

This time, I stuck to nasal breathing – even his body odour was a welcome distraction from the slim probe scanning my womb and ovaries. As he slid it inside me, cold and wet with gel, he commented on the warm weather we'd been having. Then he started moving it around, his eyes on the screen, counting. Before pulling out the probe and peeling off his Latex gloves, he said my uterus was in good shape. His tone was congratulatory.

The scan only took about ten minutes, and after a short hiatus back in the waiting room, it was time for my blood test with the nurse. Though I'd somehow managed to shrug off the thought like an unwanted layer, I've never been good with needles. The few times I'd managed to get myself through the door of the donor centre to give blood over the years, I'd almost needed pinning down and felt faint for the rest of the day. It didn't help that, more than once, the person doing it had poked and prodded and been unable to find a vein.

'With the blood test, we'll measure the levels of AMH and that will give us a good indication of your ovarian reserve,' Doctor Day had told me, stroking his tie as he'd explained that AMH – anti-müllerian hormone – is given off by growing follicles. 'Measuring the levels of it in your blood will suggest how many eggs you have left and help us to predict how your ovaries might react to stimulation.'

'Stimulation?' I'd asked.

'If you decide to go down the egg-freezing route.'

'The egg-freezing route.'

'Exactly.'

As the nurse readied the needle, I thought back to what Anna had said about her single friend, and looked down at my fingers, tightly interlaced in my lap.

The glint of my wedding ring.

Noah.

'Ready?'

When I looked back up, she was brandishing a needle.

'I think I need a minute.'

Noah and I knew from the moment he proposed that we wanted a small wedding. Neither of us come from big families and he'd always had a tight-knit group of friends. Although my own friendships are slightly more scattered, I was aware that, if we ended up going over a certain number, I would invite people because I felt I had to rather than because I wanted them there. A distant second cousin. A friend of a friend who'd invited me to her own wedding. So, we made a decision: we'd have a total of forty guests.

We got married at Hackney Town Hall. It was a cold but clear afternoon in October, the autumn leaves a mix of copper and saffron, curled and crisp on the trees. There was a small fete on that day, something to do with raising funds for the local fire station, and the pavements were filled with people and face-painted children, and makeshift stalls selling helium balloons, homemade jams, and cakes.

I wore my mother's going-away outfit from the eighties, a belted oversized blazer and a knee-length skirt, both a warm ivory that looked soft to the touch. I did my own make-up and Anna helped with my hair, twirling a few strands around her fingers and loosely pinning them back behind my ears.

My mother had picked a handful of creamy white anemones and greenery from the garden in Norfolk that morning, and she and my father brought the lot to London in glass jars of water carefully cradled in the boot of the car. While I finished getting ready, she tied a silk ribbon around my bouquet and sweetly helped Noah, who didn't really need help but went along with it as if he did, with his buttonhole.

Moments before the service, my heart started thumping hard against my chest. Noah must have sensed a change inside me. He dipped his head towards mine, kissed me and asked, with a smile, Need me to rub your feet warm? In an instant, my heartbeat steadied. I had zero doubts and I said so as I interlinked my fingers with his: No cold feet here. After some wrangling back and forth, I'd agreed to us writing our own vows on the proviso that we keep them short, and when I turned to face him and he told me, simply, that he loved me and always would, I felt the happiest I'd ever been.

A week after my initial tests I was booked in for my follow-up consultation. By the time I got home it was growing dark outside and Noah was cooking something spicy. As soon as I opened the door my nostrils began to tingle. Tom was splayed across the entrance to the kitchen, and when he saw me, he started purring, the sound coming from deep within his soft white belly.

'How was work?' asked Noah, leaning over to kiss me mid-stir. He tasted of chilli.

I didn't tell him I'd left early to find out if having a baby was an option for us, for me. That this was my second visit to the clinic in the space of ten days. That I wanted to be told it wasn't possible. That I wanted my confusion stamped out. That even so, there was something unsettling about seeing my womb vacant on a screen, black and white, no noise. A snowstorm at the start of summer. I'd only ever seen pictures of wombs with babies in them – in comparison, mine looked faulty, like it was missing something.

'Cathy?'

'It was good, thanks. And you?' I gave Tom a stroke, then unbuttoned my coat and folded it over the back of a chair. On the table in a glass vase was a bunch of daffodils he must have bought, their petals open wide and buttery yellow. Beside it, a bottle of our favourite red. I'd discovered it at our local wine shop not long after we'd moved in; I'd admitted to Noah that I'd chosen it because I liked the label, which was cream coloured with a classical-looking sketch of three women bathing in a fountain, and it turned out it was more than drinkable. I turned to him and asked, 'Are we celebrating?'

He looked at me and smiled. 'A publisher wants to buy my book.'

'Oh, Noah, that's wonderful!' I walked towards him and hugged him from behind. 'When did you hear?'

'My agent rang when I was walking back from the Tube.'

'I'm so happy for you.'

He thanked me and told me he was happy, too. 'I wouldn't have done it without you.'

'Well, I don't know about that.'

'Truly, Cathy.'

I was about to run upstairs and grab some champagne when I realised I hadn't bought another bottle. Instead, I found the corkscrew and started opening the red. 'Tell me about it?'

As he talked me through the ins and outs of the deal, including the editor's suggestion of structuring the book in three parts, all I could think was: normal. I had a normal uterus for a woman of thirty-five. Normal ovaries. An AMH level slightly on the lower side of normal. You might not want to wait much longer before trying to have a baby, said Doctor Day. As he shuffled some papers into a file – my file – he added, If you're not ready, you could consider egg freezing.

'What do you think?' asked Noah.

It was the question I'd been asking myself. What did I think, now that I knew having a baby *was* an option? What did I think, now that I knew, deep inside me, that I wanted to cling onto it? To hold it tight and keep it safe. To make up for tossing it aside so easily before. The scientific part of my brain knows there's no such thing as karma, but in that moment, it was muted.

'Cathy?'

I buried my face between his shoulder blades. 'Brilliant.'

He kissed my hands.

'Right, this is about ready. Could you just grab some cutlery and napkins?'

'Course.'

We ate and we drank, and that night I barely slept, consumed by pattering thoughts of my body's betrayal of both my mind and my marriage.

June

During those months of not knowing – not knowing what to say or do or how to move forward – work was a solace. By June, the whale was truly beginning to take shape: I'd uncovered its head and was moving along to the widest part of its body, in line with the fin, which I could now see was inaccurate and in the wrong place. In Hendrick's time, whales presented artists with a challenge; little was known about these strange and beautiful giants, which were both closely observed and fancifully imagined. Frank was on holiday for half of the month, visiting Douglas's family near Edinburgh, which meant it was just the two of us. I felt its black eye, still and sombre, watching me as I worked.

Some days, I came and went without speaking to anyone. After my morning run and breakfast at home with Noah, I would arrive at the studios, slip on my noise-cancelling headphones and in an instant be both startlingly present and entirely absent. I don't always listen to music – at times, I need to be laser-focused. When I do, it's always the same mellow playlist. I let it run from start to end, the songs shuffled, a background beat that doesn't require me to think about what to listen to next or whether I don't like something and want to skip forward. As I chipped away at the thick layer of paint on top of the whale's blubbery belly, the tempo was rising. I remember daubing a spot of lead white with solvent as one song came to an end, a full stop.

During my lunch breaks, I read books and articles on historical whale strandings. My research might have started out as a diversion, but before long it became an obsession. In the Netherlands, throughout the sixteenth and seventeenth centuries, these tragic incidents happened roughly every two years, with at least forty strandings recorded. The cause: the North Sea. After migrating north in the summer, male sperm whales returning south to their families during the autumn would become disorientated by the shallow, silty waters. Nature played a cruel and irreversible trick on them. I tried not to linger on the thought that it might also be playing a trick on me, pointlessly poking holes in the loving status quo that Noah and I had built. I certainly felt disorientated.

One Tuesday lunchtime I was reading in the *Guardian* about a more recent stranding, a little like the one my mother and I had experienced all those years ago in Norfolk. When I reached the end, I clicked on the homepage and saw, just below the photo of the whale, an image of a baby's dummy frozen in a block of ice accompanying another article. Doctor Day's deep voice sounded in my ear: If you're not ready . . . I glanced around the brightly lit café interior. Everyone was either absorbed in conversation or thumbing their phone. I sat up straight, clicked on the image and began to read about egg freezing.

It was an opinion piece written by a thirty-something woman who'd been through it herself. I skipped over the part where she described slowly pushing a blunt needle through her subcutaneous fatty tissue and instead focused on the statistics. That year, in 2018, twenty per cent of the women who froze their eggs weren't sure if they actually wanted children. I felt myself relax back into my chair, for the first time not feeling utterly alone and stranded in my indecision. I kept reading. About eighty-five per cent of frozen eggs went unthawed. My first thought: what a waste. Then: mine might be among them. My mind strayed to the food packed into our freezer and how, once a year, we mustered up the energy to do a clear-out. We almost always found Tupperware containers of hand-blended soups and sauces that we'd been too full to finish at the time but had conscientiously decanted and kept just in case we fancied them later. Often we didn't, but sometimes we did.

That evening, I took the long route home, which entailed catching a couple of buses rather than the Tube and the over-ground. I needed more time, more signal. After tapping in, I shuffled down the aisle and squeezed into a free seat. When the small child behind me started kicking at my chair, and her father said nothing, his nose in his newspaper, I turned towards the window. It was still light out, the sun winking through the buildings. The kicking became more persistent, and I shot the child a look. I wouldn't usually mind. On this occasion, it made me queasy.

There were more articles to choose from than there had been fertility clinics, which reminded me – there was some information on freezing on the website of the clinic I'd visited at London Bridge. This time, when I came face to face with the wholesome-looking mother and her cherubic son on the homepage, I decided that, yes, there was a father. Like my own dad, he was always the one behind the camera. He was there and he was happy. They all were.

I found the page I was looking for and skim-read, my eyes snagging on the three reasons why egg freezing might be used to preserve a woman's fertility:

- Ahead of medical treatments such as chemotherapy
- Ahead of gender reassignment surgery
- To alleviate apprehension about age-related fertility decline (otherwise known as 'social' egg freezing)

First *Fertility MOT*. Now *social egg freezing*. This industry really knew how to put off potential customers. As the bus pulled over and the child and her father stood up to leave, I shifted uncomfortably in my seat. This would be about more than offsetting my concerns. It would be about taking the time to consider things properly. It would be about keeping the option open in case one or both of us changed our minds and suddenly felt the pull more forcefully. Again, I turned towards the window, but my view was blocked by another bus, this one advertising a summer rom-com. And if only one of us felt it? I bookmarked that thought and scrolled on.

There was information about the process and a few fairly vague indications of the success rate. At the bottom, a big blue box invited me to book my place at one of the clinic's free monthly open evenings. I clicked on the link and saw there was one scheduled for the following week. A few minutes later, the bus dinged and lurched back towards the curb, and I looked up just in time to see that we were at my stop. Time to change. I took a screenshot and slipped my phone into my pocket.

I got back to the flat around half-past seven. Noah was on the phone with his brother. I could always tell who he was talking to from the tone of his voice. With Daniel, it was warm and good-humoured.

'Right, I better—' Noah clamped his lips together. Evidently, Daniel wasn't done talking. Noah mouthed a 'sorry' in my direction and I blew a kiss in return. 'Cathy sends her love,' he said, smiling. 'Yes, she's just walked in, so . . .' No luck. He raised one hand in the air in mock desperation while nodding and emitting the odd 'yes' or 'uh-huh'.

I kicked off my shoes and headed upstairs. After washing my hands, I splashed my face with cold water. I looked at myself in the mirror and wondered whether any of the little lines ticking up at the outer corners of my eyes were new. I tested the effect of a little lift above my upper lids, then I pressed my hips up against the sink and leant forward to inspect my hair for greys. After sweeping the strands left and right, I let out an audible sigh of relief. My skin might have started to wrinkle, but I had only dark hairs on my head.

They were still on the phone when I came back downstairs. I found a half-drunk bottle of white in the fridge from the night before and poured myself a glass.

'Right, will do,' said Noah, nodding enthusiastically when I raised a second glass in question. 'I'm sure that works, but I'll check and if we have any plans that I'm unaware of – ha, exactly – I'll let you know.'

I furrowed my eyebrows and before I passed him his wine, he lovingly clapped a hand to his heart.

'Yes, yes, speak to you then. OK, love to Griz and the kids. Bye bye, bye.' He exhaled and deposited his phone on the side.

'How's Daniel?' I asked, sinking into the sofa.

'Chatty.' He came over and kissed me hello.

'I gathered.'

'No, he's good,' he said, sitting down at the opposite end, putting his glass on the coffee table, and drawing my feet up onto his knee. 'They've invited us for lunch on Saturday.'

'Hm, I have a feeling . . .' I checked the calendar on my phone. 'Yes, sorry, can't – I said I would spend the day with Anna.'

'Oh well, don't worry. I'll go solo.' He began to massage my feet, one at a time, starting with the right, kneading the sole in the way he knew I liked. 'How's she doing?'

'She's OK, I think.' I paused, staring at the yellow liquid in my glass until my eyes lost focus. 'Sad, but OK.'

'Of course.'

My phone was nestled in the palm of my hand. I pictured the baby's dummy frozen in the block of ice and felt myself shiver.

'You're not cold, are you?'

'I'm fine.' I breathed in and out and, in as breezy a voice as I could manage, said: 'Actually, I was reading an interesting article on fertility today.'

He reached for his wine, took a sip, then continued to apply pressure to my foot, unfazed by the segue. 'You were? What was it about?'

'Egg freezing, mostly.' I recited the facts and figures that had somehow lodged themselves in my brain in the same way that paint gets trapped beneath my fingernails after retouching an artwork. 'Interesting, isn't it?'

'Interesting,' he agreed. He moved on to my left foot, starting with the heel.

I took a sip of wine myself, swallowed, and asked, 'What do you think?'

At this point, the massage was put on pause. He looked me in the eye – the first time we'd spent an evening alone together, it was his unwavering eye contact that got me. The corner of his mouth twitched. 'What do I think about egg freezing from a medical or ethical point of view?' he asked, calmly, still holding my gaze. 'Or what do I think about you saying you're considering it?' When I didn't answer, he added, softly, fairly, 'You said you were only having doubts because of Anna.'

'I think it might be more than that?' I didn't mean for it to come out as a question, but when it did, I decided to wait for him to answer. When no answer came, I said it again, with more certainty: 'I'm sorry, I know it's more than that.'

He closed his eyes, his fingers curling gently around my toes.

I hesitated, then told him about the Fertility MOT.

He too flinched at the name.

'I wanted them to tell me it wasn't possible,' I said, laughing just a little – a little hysterical, maybe. 'Because if it wasn't possible, we could forget the whole thing.'

Slowly, as if they might be breakable, he lifted my feet up and off his knee and lowered them back down to the floor.

I tested a crack between two floorboards with my toes. 'But it is, Noah. It is possible.'

He picked up his glass and walked into the kitchen. I followed and watched as he retrieved a packet of vine tomatoes, a bunch of parsley, some parmesan, and a tub of mascarpone from the fridge. 'Is anchovy pasta all right?'

'Anchovy pasta's fine, but . . .' My thoughts started to race, to tumble, out of control. I gripped the edge of the counter. 'There are so many ways we could do this.'

He hesitated, tomatoes in one hand, knife in the other, and for a moment I half expected him to turn it into a joke, to hold them up in the air and ask, This? But he didn't. It was too late for jokes, and he knew it. We both did. 'Such as?' One by one, he pulled the tomatoes from the stalk and started chopping.

'Well, for one, egg freezing.'

'To what end, Cathy?'

I wanted to suggest that he put down the knife while we were having this conversation in case he cut himself.

'You know I'm not going to change my mind.'

'But how can you be sure? How can any of us?' When he didn't answer, a word formed on the tip of my tongue: selfish. I swallowed it, wondering whether it was meant for him or for me.

Because he'd tried, hadn't he? To change his mind, to confront the trauma of losing a baby. Talking it through with a therapist, once a week, for several months, not all that long after he and his ex-wife separated. He'd known then that it would be a problem, a roadblock to future relationships, and he'd attempted to solve it. As it turned out, talking it through had only cemented what he'd already felt in his mind to be true.

He stopped chopping.

'Noah,' I said, gently, 'you know how unlikely it is that it would happen again.'

'It's more than that,' he said, shaking his head.

'You're allowed to move on.' Like she has, I considered saying but didn't.

128

'I have moved on, Cathy, with you. I'm happy.'

'You're sure?' I asked. 'You're sure you're not afraid?' I paused, trying to gauge his reaction. 'After all, you wanted one before.'

'That was different.'

'Why?'

'Because I was young, Cathy. I hadn't had time to weigh up what I wanted, how I wanted my life to be.'

In a smaller voice, I asked, 'And what about our baby? You said we would have made it work if I'd wanted to keep it.'

'Because you were already pregnant.'

'So accidentally having a child is OK, but intentionally having one isn't?'

'You know that's not what I mean.'

Of course I did. I bit my lip in an effort to stop myself from saying anything else that would leave me with a lingering pool of guilt in my stomach later in the evening.

'We would have made it work, but it wasn't what I wanted. It wasn't then and it isn't now. I'm sorry. It won't ever be.'

Selfish. I tried to swallow it again, but before I could, my lips started moving, rapidly. 'And what about me? Just because you're not going to change your mind, it doesn't mean I won't. Put yourself in my position. Can you imagine what it feels like for even a small part of me to question whether I might want to be a mother one day, and to have the pressure of knowing that, if I don't do something now, that might not be possible?'

He put down the knife and turned around to face me, except this time, he didn't look at me. Instead, he directed his gaze towards the ceiling, the way he does whenever he's unconvinced. 'I don't know what you want me to say. Great,

let's do it! Is that it? Always good to have a back-up plan!'
His eyes lowered to meet mine. 'Because that's what this
is – you know that, right? You stick with me for as long as
you can bear it, then when you can't wait any longer, you
leave me for a man who *is* willing to be a dad, happy in the
knowledge that it's still, as you call it, a "possibility".'

I felt dizzy, the kind you experience as a child after spin-
ning in circles with your arms outstretched. 'That's not it,'
I said, coiling my fingers more tightly around the edge of
the counter. 'Please don't say that.'

'Isn't it? I've been here before, Cathy. I know how it ends.'

Anna wasn't the only woman to call things off with Noah
when he told her he imagined his life without children. But
she was the only one to do so without hesitation. Others tried
to stick it out. They thought they would be the one to change
him, that he'd come around to what they saw as the default
conclusion. When he didn't, there were difficult conversations,
disagreements. Eventually, the relationships turned sour, and
he was left feeling like he was falling short, somehow deficient.

My face felt flushed. Maybe it was the wine. Water. I
needed water. I moved towards the sink, turned on the tap
and took a clean glass out of the dishwasher, the bottom
shelf of which had already been unloaded. I let the water run
until it was properly cold, then I filled the glass to the rim
and brought it to my lips. I tried to focus on the feeling of
the cool liquid slipping down my throat, but heated thoughts
of other women who had chosen the prospect of children
over the promise of him pricked at my skin. I kept drinking,
intent on drowning them out. When I was done, I turned
back around to Noah, who was still waiting. I could see the
disappointment in his drawn-in lips and heavy eyes.

My own eyes started to sting. 'I don't know if I'll want to have a baby one day, need to have a baby one day – I hope I won't. But can't you see that it's precisely because I don't know that I have to consider this? It might be my last chance. A second chance.' I felt the tears start to fall. I walked towards him, hesitantly, and without hesitation he wrapped his arms around me. Again, I told him I was sorry.

'I'm sorry too.'

We stayed like that for too many minutes to count. When we let go, he went back to preparing the pasta sauce, and I flicked the switch of the kettle. We carried on like nothing had happened, like everything was resolved.

On Saturday, Anna and I met at a spa just off Shoreditch High Street. I wanted to do something nice for her, to take her mind off the miscarriage. I'd originally booked us both in for massages, but at the last minute I wondered how she might feel about someone touching her body so soon and switched to facials. The woman on the phone was a bit huffy about the late change but agreed begrudgingly when I hinted at the circumstances.

We'd planned to go and get coffee beforehand, but when I was on the overground, I received a message from Anna saying she was running late. At the other end, there was a small café around the corner, so I picked up two lattes and one sachet of sugar to go instead.

The sky that day was the kind of blue a child would paint it, one single strip running across the top of an otherwise blank page. The few trees and flowerbeds were in bloom. Summer was upon us, and I was happy for even the slightest visual reminder. Standing outside the entrance to the spa, sipping my coffee, my thoughts turned to my mother and how she must have been enjoying her walks on the beach lately, barefoot instead of swaddled in thick socks and wellies. I hadn't spoken to her that week, and I made a mental note to call her later.

'Great minds,' said Anna, raising one eyebrow and two takeaway cups as she walked towards me along the pavement. Before I had time to tell her that the extra one I'd bought had probably gone cold, she was offering both of hers to an older couple heading in the opposite direction.

The man, who was shorter than the woman, shook his head and apologised without meeting Anna's gaze, as if she'd just asked if he could spare some change.

'Untouched, I promise,' she added.

I was about to suggest we try someone else when the woman waded in, reaching out her arthritic fingers, which were gnarled and knobby like ginger and would have made my mother's look positively straight. 'Well, thanks very much,' she said, smiling with her teeth clamped together. Turning to the man, she added, 'You'll only go and want one later.'

I did a double take.

Inside, Anna wrapped an arm around my waist and told me she was happy to see me. She was bundled up even though it was warm out, in a pair of jeans and a chunky rollneck that skimmed her chin, slightly pointed. She'd brought with her a handbag that probably cost close to my monthly earnings and was large enough to contain everything she needed.

I studied her face and noticed that the pouches beneath her eyes were a shade darker than usual. 'Are you sleeping OK?'

'Oh, see! I told Caleb it was noticeable,' she said, lightly touching her fingers to one eye. 'It's been fucking twitching for the past week.'

'I hadn't noticed,' I said, truthfully, leaning forward to get a better look, 'but I do hate it when that happens.'

'I'm scared it's going to stay like this forever,' she said, half laughing as she stretched out her lids with her fingers.

In the changing room, to a soundtrack of running showers and gusting hairdryers, we slipped off our clothes and squeezed into our swimming costumes, having agreed that we'd meet at the pool afterwards for a swim. I stripped down to my underwear, then awkwardly stepped out of my knickers and into my suit, slipping off my bra just before I pulled the straps up and over my shoulders. Beside me, Anna had casually joined the group of naked bodies around us, which the clinical space had rendered unidealised and anonymous. All I saw were child-bearing hips and malleable bellies with just the right amount of give. Breasts big enough to produce an adequate amount of milk. I curled my toes against the anti-slip tiled floor and avoided the mirror and my own body, too small, too straight.

A minute later, ready to go, Anna gave me a prod. 'Ready?'

'Ready.' I'd been looking at my phone to avoid seeing other people's flesh, never mind the woman walking around with a loop of string hanging out. I slipped it into the locker and punched in a four-digit code.

I felt better as we wandered into the lounge, which was also white but with splashes of colour that made it feel less sterile. We were both swaddled in the kind of fluffy dressing gown you would expect to find in a fancy hotel, and as we sat down on a comfy sofa, Anna made a sound that told me she was already feeling more relaxed. That's why we're here, I reminded myself.

133

Her name was called first and five minutes later, Mandy, the woman I was told would be taking care of me today, came to collect me.

'Sorry for the short delay,' she said, shaking her head with frustration. 'I've been on the phone with my ex.'

'Don't worry, I'm not in a rush,' I said, quietly surprised by her overshare.

She must have taken my indifference as an indication of me being a good listener, which didn't really bother me – after all, I assumed she would stop talking when the treatment started. Ten minutes later, my face was wet with lotions and creams, and she was moaning about the fact that he was never on time when he came to pick up the kids, which he did every other weekend.

I pressed my lips together and resisted saying running late must run in the family.

'You're married,' she said, a statement rather than a question. She must have spotted my ring.

'I am,' I replied, pointing and flexing my toes within the pair of slippers that matched my gown, and wondering why I hadn't taken them off before lying down. I held my breath, waiting for what would surely be the follow-up question.

'Kids?'

'Two.' It slipped out before I had a chance to stop it. And then, unprompted: 'A boy and a girl.'

'How old?'

No hesitation: 'Seven and four.'

'How's your husband with them?'

'Oh, he's great.' I was unstoppable. 'Loves them to pieces.' I was even talking differently. I never said 'to pieces'. A final flourish: 'I got lucky.'

I have no idea what came over me, but it did the trick. Mandy was quiet after that. From then on, the only words that left her mouth were related to pressure points and ointments.

At the end of the treatment, my face feeling fresh and new, I stood up and thanked her, and said I hoped she managed to sort things out with her ex. I think I might have even tacked on a 'life's too short'. She thanked me in return and said she hoped my own marriage would last longer than hers.

Anna was floating in the middle of the pool, at the point where it gently sloped between the shallow and deep ends, her plasticky pink skin stark against the azure tiles. As I lowered myself down the creaky metal steps into the water, which was warmer than I'd anticipated, I couldn't take my eyes off her stomach. She was stretched out, on her back. Instead of a dome, as it should have been, it was flat to the point of dipping in, her ribs flaring like butterfly wings.

'How was that?' she asked, swivelling onto her front and slowly coming to standing as I waded towards her. We were the only ones in the pool, which was dimly lit in the basement of the building, and her voice echoed off the walls and ceiling.

'Good,' I replied, deciding not to mention Mandy and her moaning. 'And yours?'

'Heaven. Just what I needed.'

We stood facing one another. I was submerged almost up to my chest, while the water, clear as glass, barely skimmed her belly button. A silence opened up between us, soft and inviting, and all of a sudden, I longed to talk to her about the fertility clinic. Instead, I stretched out my hands and tapped my palms on the water's surface. 'How are you feeling?' I asked. 'Generally, I mean.'

'Generally, OK,' she replied, nodding as she added: 'Occasionally, not.'

'And Caleb?'

She breathed in and out and said: 'He wants to try again.'

'And you?'

'I want to try again, too.' She smiled, though her eyes didn't squint as much as usual, the sadness of her loss coexisting with the excitement surrounding the prospect of something new.

Still, I felt a tug of jealousy, wishing things were so straightforward with me and Noah. Followed by a wash of guilt. How could I even think that, after what she and Caleb had been through? The past few months had been hell for them, the opposite of straightforward. I stopped tapping and instead started swiping at the surface of the water, a human windscreen wiper.

'Even if it works, though, and I get pregnant, then what?'

I was searching for the answer, but she already knew it.

'I would have to prepare myself, to plan for both outcomes. A baby, or not.' She took a breath. 'It would be like living at a fork for nine months.'

I swiped quicker, back and forth.

'Of course, it's worth it.'

I stopped.

This time, when she smiled, her eyes squinted a little more. 'There's a chance, isn't there? A possibility.'

For a moment I thought I could hear the distant sound of rain, then I realised the hammering was coming from my chest.

'The doctor says we can try again as soon as we're ready, that there's no need to wait. In fact, she said the longer we wait, the more daunting getting pregnant again might feel.'

When my chest began to burn, I sank lower into the water. It wasn't cold enough to cool me down, but still I stayed there, the water lapping softly against my lips.

'Cathy?'

I straightened up, too quickly, creating a small wave. 'I think that's exactly right,' I said, swallowing the surge of panic rising in my throat, clinging onto the sides of my thighs in an effort to keep still. 'There's no use waiting.'

All through lunch my thoughts kept straying to the clinic. When the waiter asked what kind of water we wanted, still or sparkling, I heard the gentle gurgle of the machine in the corner of the waiting room, the pop of a paper cone being let loose. When Anna started to talk about how easy everything had been with Theo, I felt the sponginess of the sonogram bed beneath my back, the pressure of the grooves spreading my legs. Usually swimming made me hungry, but after a few mouthfuls of my bread roll, which I'd generously spread with the restaurant's fancy salted butter, I felt full. We were sitting side by side on a banquette, our elbows touching, and yet, I felt alone.

As we emerged onto the pavement, Anna received a phone call from her mum, and as they talked, I considered calling my mother too. Something about their easy back and forth stopped me. Anna had mentioned that they'd spoken about the prospect of her and Caleb trying again, how happy her mum had been to hear the nearly good news.

Instead, I stared up at the sky, a little cloudy now, marked here and there with a single moving black speck, sometimes more. As I watched them swoop and soar, I reflected on what Anna had said, or at least insinuated, in the pool. That the grief in the event of another miscarriage would be more bearable than the uncertainty she'd have to live with if she never tried. That she could accept not having another baby, but not the idea of never giving it a chance.

'OK,' she said, slipping her phone into her pocket and looping an arm through mine. 'Ready?'

She would rather roll the dice.

As soon as I was back in the flat, I sat down on the sofa with my laptop and signed up for the open evening. I texted Noah to ask where he was before remembering that he was over at Daniel and Griz's. Things had been tense between us since the other night – our conversations shorter, our kisses more brisk – and, however much I loved them, the idea of him alleviating that tension by talking things through with his brother and sister-in-law made my skin itch. It also made me feel even more isolated than I already did. I got up and filled the kettle, then, cup of tea in hand, I phoned my mother.

She picked up after just a couple of rings.

'Hi Mum, it's me.'

'Darling, what a nice surprise.'

Her standard reply sounded a little passive-aggressive, but when I heard the news on in the background, I put it down to distraction.

'How's your weekend going?' I asked, wrapping my fingers around my mug, feeling its warmth. 'Have you been gardening?'

'Yes.' She said it with a huff, like I was checking she'd done her homework. As if to prove it, a detail: 'I'm pleased with the heleniums.'

'Oh, I don't know what those are.'

'Yes, you do.'

I was glad we weren't speaking over a video call so she couldn't see me frowning.

'Like bigger, brighter daisies.'

She was right – I did know that.

When I heard her lips part, I waited for her to continue. A few seconds later, the quiet stretching out between us, I asked, 'Mum, is everything OK?'

'Of course, why wouldn't it be?' She, too, must have picked up on the irritable tone in her voice this time, because she sighed. 'I'm sorry, it's just been one of those weeks.'

'That's OK, I know the feeling. Anything I can help with?'

'No, don't you worry – it's nothing a good night's sleep can't fix. Anyway, tell me, how's your whale coming along?'

My whale. I smiled. 'Slowly but surely. I'm just trying to keep up with the excitement building around it.'

'You'll do brilliantly.'

Noah still wasn't home when we said our goodbyes. I looked at the clock, tipped the dregs of my tea into the sink and changed into my running things. I could feel nervous energy billowing inside me, and if I didn't do something about it, I knew I wouldn't sleep.

The open evening was at half-past five the following Tuesday. I left work early, which I'd realised, a little guiltily, was easy to do when you worked alone. I caught the Tube to London Bridge and this time, when I walked into the waiting room, I was met with about thirty women. The smell of freshly hoovered carpet had been doused with perfume.

I made a beeline for the makeshift bar – a small table topped with a white paper sheet that looked a lot like the one that had attempted to preserve my modesty during my scan. I helped myself to a glass of white wine, which, like the bottles set aside for unofficial events at the museum, was lukewarm and a little fizzy. It was raining outside, and most people, myself included, had small umbrellas dangling from their wrists; although they were tightly bound, they were leaking onto the floor, which by now was marked with what looked like shiny snail tracks.

I stood with my back to the welcome desk and looked around the room. If I ignored the odd sighting of a white coat, I could just about convince myself that I was here for a talk that had nothing to do with fertility. A discussion of gender equality in the arts, perhaps. A study of the benefits of art education in schools. A call to action to get more works by—

The sputter of a speaker snapped me out of my cultural reverie. Doctor Day was straightening his tie and inviting us to make our way into the next-door events space. Like an obliging flock of ewes, we trotted along after the ram.

I'd been half disappointed by the lack of a baby wall before, and here it was in all its glory. A Warholian spread of white, black and brown babies beaming unanimously at the camera had been blown up on glossy card and tacked directly onto the back wall. My first thought was how they'd managed to get eight to ten babies to smile on cue. The second: if there's such an even spread of white, black and brown babies, where were all the black and brown women in the room? I searched each face for a self-conscious wince in the form of a stretched mouth or a squint. I detected

140

only one; a woman with mousey hair was apologetically nibbling her lower lip.

I looked back at the babies and, not for the first time, wondered what someone who was half me, half Noah would look like – whether they would inherit his full eyebrows, my amber eyes, whether their ears would be big like his or teaspoon-small like mine. I wondered about their character. Whether they would be fond of books or art or both. I tried to imagine if they would sneeze in twos or threes. How it would feel to have someone call me Mum. How their arrival might affect my relationship with my own mother. Would it bring us closer again, I wondered, to how we were before my father died, or at least make me miss her less when I wasn't with her? A mother for a mother.

When I imagined how it might affect my relationship with Noah, I felt my body grow tense, as if I was bracing myself, on behalf of us both, for a physical assault. I thought of our life together and how happy we were, how everything would irrevocably change whether we liked it or not. No more late nights out or long lie-ins, no more last-minute holidays or uninterrupted afternoons spent reading and sketching. No more just the two of us. The thought knocked the wind out of me, and I was questioning what I was doing there when, once again, Doctor Day's voice addressed the room.

'OK, ladies and gentlemen, please can you take your seats.'

I widened my eyes, then scanned the crowd and realised that, yes, there were a couple of men present. Both were holding their partners' hands, as if they were worried about getting separated from them and swept away in this choppy sea of women. I was also surprised to find that lots of the women looked younger than me. Contrary to medical advice,

I'd read that the average age of women freezing their eggs was between thirty-seven and thirty-eight. But at least a handful here had the kind of youthful skin and figures that made me suspect they were in their twenties.

I picked up a plastic folder off one of the blue chairs in the back row and sat down beside the woman with the mousey hair, who I guessed was closer to my own age. I began to leaf through the bumf, then apologised when she shifted her leg away from my soggy umbrella, which was rubbing up against her like a wet dog.

'Oh, no worries,' she said, smiling as she introduced herself. 'I'm Robyn.' It came out in a whisper, either because she was conscious that the talk was about to begin or because she wasn't all that comfortable being here either.

'Cathy,' I whispered back.

Both of us were already juggling our handouts and wine, so in lieu of a shake we politely dipped our heads in greeting. As she did so, the tips of her fringe kissed her eyebrows, which were fairer than her hair and pin thin. I decided that yes, she was my age, having grown up at a time when having almost non-existent eyebrows was a thing.

'Are you still considering it, or have you made up your mind?' she asked, nudging some hair away from her face with the back of one hand. She was still talking in a hushed voice.

'Oh, I'm still considering it,' I replied, nodding. 'And you?'

'My mind is pretty much made up,' she said, adding as if by way of explanation: 'I'm thirty-six and single.'

I nodded some more.

'I mean, I am still hoping that I'll meet someone sooner rather than later and it'll happen naturally. But if not, at least this will buy me some time.' She started nibbling her lip again, then pressed the pad of one finger to it, apparently conscious of the habit. 'What's your situation?'

I looked towards the screen at the front of the room, hoping to see Doctor Day standing open-mouthed in front of the microphone, ready to go, but he and his team were fiddling with various wires, clearly having technical issues. When I returned my gaze to Robyn, she was smiling and patiently waiting. Her eyes were the kind of luminous blue that reminded me of the precious pigment mostly preserved for the Virgin's robes in Renaissance paintings. 'Well, actually, I'm married.'

'You are?'

'I am.'

She paused and scrunched up her nose, the way you might if you were trying to solve a difficult sum, then asked, 'So why are you considering freezing?'

I laughed and she did too, though I'm sure both sounded artificial.

'Are you going your separate ways?'

I felt my body temperature rise a few notches and quickly shrugged off my jacket. It was the first time someone had said it out loud.

'Sorry, that's none of my business,' she said, her own cheeks flushed. 'I've never been good with small talk.'

'No, it's all right,' I said, bundling up my jacket even though it was linen and crumpled like newspaper, and stowing it underneath the chair in front. My eyes flashed towards the screen again, then back to hers, which were fringed with bare lashes so fair they were almost invisible. 'He doesn't want children. My husband doesn't want children.'

'And you?'

I tried to smile as I said, 'I'm not sure. I didn't think so.'
I paused, breathed. 'But now, maybe, one day.' Again, I
glanced around at the women who, like me, were fortunate
enough to be able to take out an insurance policy on their
fertility. 'It probably sounds terrible,' I said, shifting in my
seat, 'that I'm wondering whether or not to do something
that the majority of people could only dream of doing, just
to put my mind at ease.'

'Not *terrible*, no.' When I held my breath, she gave a gentle
shrug and continued, in a lowered voice. 'Look, I'm not
really comfortable with any of it – the courting, the access,
the cost . . . which I can only just about afford. The idea
of it being this quasi-feminist solution to having it all.' She
rolled her eyes. 'And yet, here I am. Does that make me a
hypocrite? I think so. But I also can't bear to take the risk.'
She shuddered, as if imagining she were to gamble and end
up with a future that was quieter and emptier than the one
she hoped for.

I opened my mouth to reply, but Doctor Day got there first:
'OK, everybody, apologies for the hold-up.'

Conversation petered out; chairs squeaked. There was at
least one cough.

'Let's get going.'

As he introduced himself then handed us over to one of
the clinic's medical directors, Robyn took a deep breath, and
so did I.

The talk concluded, and there was a clumsy applause, none
of us quite sure whether we should be clapping. People were
chatting again when I reached forward and snatched up my
jacket, which, as predicted, was crinkled with lines.

As I went to stand, Robyn said, 'Hang on, pass me your phone.'

I handed it over and she handed it back for me to unlock. I watched as she dialled her number and added it to my address book.

'If you ever want to talk to someone who gets it, even vaguely.' She smiled, a little embarrassed maybe, as she added, 'I don't know anyone else who's going through it either.'

'Thanks,' I said, smiling back, oddly moved by the small but generous gesture. 'And what you said before, about being a hypocrite?'

She nibbled at her lip.

'I don't think you are.'

'Thanks, Cathy.'

As I slipped on my jacket, she wished me good luck.

On the bus home, the slideshow replayed on a loop in my head. In between carefully curated images of proud parents and burbling babies, it had been filled with statistics – some comforting, others less so. We'd learned that women are born with around a million eggs, ninety per cent of which have been lost even before we're thirty years old; by our mid-thirties, the quality of those remaining eggs begins to dip, and quick. At this point, I'd heard Robyn gulp beside me. More positive murmurings had ricocheted around the room when we were told that if a woman freezes at thirty-five, she has a seventy-five per cent success rate. As the bus stopped at a red light, I pulled the plastic folder of extra information out of my bag and, although reading on the move makes me queasy, started to pick through the pages.

By the time I was back at the flat, I realised that I didn't want to put it off any longer. Noah was watching a game at the pub, so I had the place to myself. I made a tea with fresh ginger and honey and sat on the sofa waiting for it to cool down, not watching or reading anything, just thinking. After, I had a hot shower. I stayed in for longer than normal, enjoying the feeling of the water raining down on me.

I was in bed with the lights off when at last I heard the latch go on the door. I glanced at my phone and saw that it was almost eleven. Noah must have stayed on after for drinks. The sign of a good game, usually. Still, my chest felt bruised and sore at the idea that he could have been avoiding coming home.

He went straight to the bathroom and brushed his teeth. I listened to the whir of his electric toothbrush and then, after a few minutes, heard him swish and spit. He didn't turn on the light when he came into our bedroom, probably because he didn't want to wake me. But I wanted to see him. We had to talk. I rolled over and flicked the switch on my bedside lamp, my eyes blinking.

'Oh, hello you,' he said, his voice thick from beer. 'I thought you were asleep.'

'How was the game?' I asked, turning to face him, and propping myself up on one elbow.

If he was surprised by my sudden interest, he didn't show it. 'The game was great – we won two–nil.'

'That *is* great.' I waited until he'd taken off his clothes and climbed in to join me, his skin cool against mine, even though he was normally the one to warm me up, before I said I had something to tell him.

His mouth moved, almost imperceptibly.

I continued: 'I went to a talk about egg freezing at the clinic this evening.'

When he didn't respond, I carried on speaking, surprised at how confident – how certain – I sounded.

'I'm going to go through with it.'

'Cathy, please—'

'I'm not saying I need a baby, Noah, I just need the option. I know it sounds stupid – crazy, even – but I feel like I owe it to myself, to us, especially after . . .' I didn't finish the sentence.

He closed his eyes. A few seconds that felt like a few minutes passed and then he asked, with open palms: 'Is it even safe? Can we even afford it?'

He cared. Of course he did. 'It's safe,' I said, a superficial warmth spreading through me like central heating. 'You have nothing to worry about, I promise. And I have the money from Dad.' Life from death.

He rolled onto his back and craned his neck, looking up to the ceiling. I watched his neck ripple as he swallowed. His hands, which were previously down by his sides, rested lightly on top of his chest. 'OK.'

'OK?'

He angled his head back towards me, and in a voice that still sounded caring, he said, 'It's your body, I can't stop you.'

I reached out a hand to hold his, but he pulled away, gently. He wasn't finished talking.

'I love you and I'll support you, Cathy, always. You know that.'

I nodded. I did. 'I feel the same way.'

'But I don't want to be a part of it. OK?' He paused, then added: 'And I'm telling you again, I won't change my mind about this.'

Relationships are about compromise, they say. Where you live, what you have for dinner, how much money you throw at a holiday, whose family you spend Christmas with. That last one was easy for us after Noah's parents died, and Daniel and Griz had her extended family and the kids; it was Noah who suggested we make spending Christmas with my parents and later my mother a tradition. But some things lack a middle. In my head, I heard Robyn's voice: Are you going your separate ways?

For a while, we both lay there on either side of the bed. Together but apart. Not touching. A stalemate.

Then, when I couldn't take it any longer, I told him I understood, and I thanked him for his support. I reached out again to hold his hand.

This time he didn't pull away.

I was able to say goodbye to my father before he died. When my mother found him face-down on the living-room carpet, she called the emergency services, and an ambulance on its way back from a false alarm happened to be nearby. After surgery, the doctors were able to stabilise him, but only briefly. As the surgeon had gently told my mother, and my mother had a little less gently told me, there had been complications.

Noah and I arrived late that night. The sky was the kind of dark that, when you look at it for long enough, becomes tinged with colour. The motorway had been quiet, and the whir of sirens and voices in front of the hospital entrance felt like the opening act of a tragedy. It was the same hospital my mother and I had been rushed to moments after I was born.

My father was lying in bed, with my mother in a chair by his side, oddly upright and wide-eyed considering it had just gone midnight. There were drips and tubes and a round red button to push in the event of an emergency. Machines beeping in harmony.

There wasn't enough of him; he should have taken up more room. He was a tall man, but tucked in beneath the stiff hospital sheets, with a spotted robe hanging loosely around his collarbones, he looked small, like he'd shrunk in on himself. Above his pale-blue eyes, his lids were heavy. Beneath his oxygen mask, his cheeks were sallow. Standing before him, I felt the urge to cover up his lower neck, which was rarely exposed.

'You must keep that on,' my mother said, when he went to remove the mask.

He was wheezy, and his breathing made me think of a toy I'd had as a child that had eventually lost its squeak.

'Hello Dad,' I said, reaching for his hand, which was colder than I'd anticipated. I held it between mine and blew warm air at it. I'd promised myself I wouldn't cry – at least not in front of him – and when I felt my eyes fill with tears, I shook my head.

Again, he went to remove his mask.

Again, my mother told him to keep it on.

This time he didn't do as she said.

He pulled it down and let it rest on his chest, then he moved his jaw, stretching out the muscles on his face. I was still holding his right hand, and with his left, he reached for my mother on the other side of the bed. We stayed that way, three links of a chain, until quietly his link came loose.

Before it did, he looked at her, a smile on his lips, and said, 'It's OK.' Looking at me, he added: 'It's OK because I have you.'

July

The night before my first run in July, Noah and I were due to meet one of his oldest friends for a quick drink down the road. He and his new girlfriend – very beautiful, apparently, very young – were having dinner in the area, and he wanted to introduce us beforehand. The day's warmth had leaked into the evening, and I was glad to be leaving the flat without my coat. We'd thrown open one of the first-floor windows overlooking the street, and Tom was sprawled in front of it like a damp item of clothing.

Noah was locking the door when my phone started vibrating and the number of the clinic flashed up on the screen.

'A bit late, isn't it?' he asked, when I told him who it was. 'Why don't you ring back in the morning when it's more convenient.'

'No, I should take it.'

'We haven't got long as it is,' he said, glancing at his watch. 'They have to be at the restaurant in forty-five minutes.'

'You go ahead,' I said, nodding in encouragement as I fished my own set of keys out of my pocket and fumbled with the lock. 'I'll be right behind you.'

'OK, but—'

'Hello, Doctor Day?'

I turned around to mouth an apology to Noah, but he was walking away.

Doctor Day said that, since my fertility was as expected for a woman of my age, I should be able to get away with just the one cycle of egg freezing. I stiffened at his choice of 'get away with', as though I'd lucked out in this certain situation. He told me I would need to drop by the clinic to pick up some more paperwork and the injection packs, and after some to-ing and fro-ing we settled on first thing the following Wednesday.

After I hung up, I sat on the stairs and added the appointment to my calendar, with a notification set for an hour before. Then I switched to Safari and started skipping through my open tabs, searching for something I'd read about whether you should try to avoid consuming alcohol beforehand. When I couldn't find it, I started googling, my heart rate quickening, and before I knew it, I was poring over an endless stream of posts in an unregulated fertility forum. There was advice on what to do, and what not to do. Herbal tea suggestions. Supplements. Intimate images. The telephone numbers of acupuncturists and masseuses.

I'm not sure how it happened – it felt like no time at all had passed – but the next thing I heard was a key turning in the lock.

'Cathy?'

Noah's voice reached me before he did.

'I'm so sorry,' I said, shutting off my phone and coming to stand.

'What happened?'

'I wanted to check if it was OK for me to drink in the run-up – it turns out it is, which is good – but I ended up going down a bit of a rabbit hole before I found the answer.' I tried to make light of the situation, adding, with a smile, 'Now I know why people recommend avoiding these crazy online message boards.'

His own mouth was fixed in a straight line. 'Is this how it's going to be from now on?'

I felt my smile slip and made a concerted effort to keep hold of it. 'What do you mean?'

'You do your thing, I do mine?'

'That's not fair.'

He dragged a palm wearily across his face.

'I said I was sorry, Noah.'

'I know you did.'

'So, what else is there to say?'

He took a moment, and then he asked, 'Is this you checking out?'

'Of course not.' I reached for his hand, and he let me.

'We want different things, Cathy.'

'No, we don't – that's not what's happening.' I wanted to be firm, but my voice was wavering.

'Isn't it?'

'We've talked about this. We're going to be OK.'

He shook his head and smiled, a sad smile. 'How can we be, when we're aware that, whichever way this goes, one of us will have to take something away from the other?'

I didn't answer – I couldn't – and I forgot we were still holding hands until he gave mine a squeeze and let go. He walked past me and up the stairs. I stayed where I was, my ears ringing in the silence.

After a few minutes, there was a rustle of papers. I, too, went upstairs and found him at his desk doing some marking. I propped up my pillows, sat on the bed and caught up on my emails. Because what else?

There was one from my mother, sharing the latest news about the offshore windfarm – to her dismay, it had all gone quiet since the proposal – and mentioning the hotel that Noah and I had bought her the voucher for. She suggested some dates for our mother-daughter night away.

I looked on the website and saw that it was already fully booked over the summer. There was, however, a double room available at the weekend, and a last-minute deal. I hadn't seen her since her birthday, and I wasn't sure how I would feel when I started injecting. I looked up at Noah, sitting very upright, red pen poised.

'Would you be OK with me and Mum doing the hotel thing this Saturday?'

I could sense him closing his eyes, taking a breath. With his shoulders raised, he said, 'I think that's a good idea.'

The following morning, on the towpath, my legs were moving more quickly than usual. It was light out, the sky tinted yellow and blue. The overhead lights in the offices of start-ups and tech companies that should know better had been left on overnight. As lamps on bedside tables began to flicker on in flats, I caught glimpses of human silhouettes lumbering from bedrooms to bathrooms – full bladders, furry breath. I ran my tongue over my teeth, which I would brush after showering.

I tried to focus on my feet: left, right, left, right. I curved around the bend and continued beneath the bridge, its dark and abrasive stone softened by brightly coloured bubble writing and other more graphic graffiti. When I emerged, one foot – I don't know which one – slipped. In a moment I was a child again, falling over in the school playground. Stinging palms as my hands went splat on the rough concrete, a bloody patch on each knee. Another runner passed by without offering to help, glancing at his watch, evidently intent on keeping up the pace. I came to standing, shakily, and tried to keep going. That's when my ankle started throbbing. Sluggishly, I hobbled home. When I eventually arrived, I noticed that Noah's keys were missing from the small brass hook by the door. He'd either skipped breakfast or eaten without me.

The throbbing had morphed into a slight ache by the time I got off the train at Bury St Edmunds. It was bright out, and I brought my hand to my forehead as I scanned the car park. I quickly spotted my parents' old Volvo, straddling one-and-a-bit spaces. As I walked towards it, I tried to smooth down the back of my dress, which had stuck to my bare legs in the stuffy and surprisingly crowded carriage.

Before I'd even reached the door, I could hear the dulcet tones of Radio 4. I didn't want to make my mother jump, so rather than opening it or even tapping on the window, I walked around the bonnet and waved at her through the windscreen. To no avail. Her eyes were closed, her mouth hanging open like it had got caught on the end of a fishing line. She used to arrive at least half an hour early to collect me whenever I took the train home from university, and on the rare occasions that I'd been abroad with friends, she would get to the airport even earlier, repeating her refrain about how you could never trust the traffic. I smiled. She clearly hadn't kicked the habit.

When the sun started to beat down on my forehead, I resorted to letting myself in. Unlike me, my mother is a heavy sleeper, and it wasn't until I nudged her shoulder that she slowly blinked her eyes open.

'Darling, you're here.'

'I am, and so are you.'

We hugged – somewhat awkwardly, since she was safely buckled in.

'Did you have an OK drive?' I asked.

'I did, thank you. Was everything all right with the train?'

'Yes,' I told her, passing my weekend bag between us and onto the back seat, 'everything was fine.'

The radio was still on, and I asked if she would mind if I turned it down a bit.

'Oh, now you're here we can switch it off.' She pressed the power button as I slipped on my own seatbelt. 'So,' she said, 'do you know where we're going?'

'I do,' I replied, bringing up the directions on my phone. 'It's just a fifteen-minute drive from here.'

'Lovely,' she said, turning on the engine and moving her hands to the correct position on the wheel. She looked at me expectantly.

'So, Mum, first we need to leave the car park.'

She rolled her eyes with such gusto that I couldn't help but laugh, and as she took the handbrake off, she started laughing too.

I'd warned my mother that we would be sharing a bed beforehand, but still she seemed surprised when we walked into our room and were faced with a double.

155

'At least it's a big double,' I said, cheerily, 'a king, I'm sure.' I dropped my bag on the floor and hopped on, demonstrating to her how little space I would take up, and adding that we could even build a display-cushion wall if that was what she wanted.

'Oh, don't be so dramatic,' she said, as I got to work on construction.

She walked towards the tray of teas and coffees and lifted the lid of a small silver tin, gasping with delight at the freshly baked chocolate-chip cookies inside. Offering one to me and then, when I declined, shrugging her shoulders and taking a bite out of it herself, she settled into one of two low-slung armchairs and put her feet up on a leather pouffe. 'Aren't we lucky?' she asked, nibbling.

The room was light and airy, with a pitched ceiling and exposed wooden beams. The headboard of the bed was upholstered in green velvet, and the wall behind was covered with wallpaper in a botanical print. The other walls were white and hung with abstract art. On each bedside table was an olive-green Anglepoise, hunched over like it had been tapping at a laptop too long. I slipped off the bed and inspected the bathroom, which centred on a free-standing tub and had a little basket of mini shampoos, conditioners and body lotions that we would squirrel away into our washbags before leaving. Above the sink was a big mirror in a gold frame.

We were also lucky with the weather. The sun was still shining, but now its rays were being filtered through a light breeze. After unpacking the few bits we'd brought with us, we decided to get out and explore the grounds. Our room overlooked the back garden, which sloped down towards an oblong pond that the receptionist told us was home to two swans and their cygnets. Beyond that, a public footpath stretched across a grass field and into a wood. Even with the breeze it was hot, and we didn't have any water with us, so as soon as we reached the treeline we doubled back and headed to the walled garden instead.

It was neat and orderly, with gravel paths wending in between raised beds of vegetables, herbs, edible flowers. My mother marvelled at the globe artichokes and announced that she, too, would introduce a signage system in her patch at home – by which she meant she would buy some little white labels to stick beside different types of produce. While we were there, a young male chef arrived, ready to pick greenery for the evening's menu. He was wearing a white apron and carrying a shallow wicker basket that made me think of period dramas, with their ribbons and bonnets. Noticing that my mother was tailing him, he asked if she would be interested in hearing about what was in season. She nodded eagerly. As the pair of them moved from bed to bed, I sat down on a wooden bench painted pebble grey. I closed my eyes and soaked up the earthy floral scent of the lavender sprouting beside me in a large terracotta pot. The sound of my mother's voice reminded me of a time when I used to fall asleep feeling the weight of her sitting beside me on the mattress and listening to her telling me a bedtime story fresh from her head.

One thing our London flat was missing was a bath, so whenever I stayed somewhere that did have a tub, I would make the most of it by soaking for up to an hour, sometimes more than once. That night, after tipping in a generous glug of bubble bath, I lowered myself in and stayed there until my skin began to wrinkle like the overripe pears that dropped from the branches of the tree outside the back door in Norfolk. I looked down at my body, its edges blurred and softened by the water, and wondered if it was a glimpse of what was to come.

I decided in the bath that I would talk to my mother about the egg freezing over dinner. She woke from her nap feeling fully rested and hummed as she picked out her outfit for the evening, a pair of straight black trousers and a long silvery top that was strangely sparkly for her. She nodded approvingly at my own choice of a simple cream dress and cherry-red pumps, and happily hooked her arm through mine as we made our way downstairs to the restaurant.

When she ordered the green beans, anchovy, mustard and quail egg starter, I decided to hold fire on my news until the main course. The dining room was filled with a mix of overnight guests and locals, and I soon realised that you could spot one from the other by the presence or absence of a room key on a heavy metal fob. To our left was another mother and daughter who could have been us about a decade ago. They, too, looked strikingly similar, with fine high foreheads and bow-shaped lips. I overheard them discussing wedding plans, and the prospect of having it here. I wondered how old the girl was, and how much time would pass after the nuptials before she would begin to contemplate motherhood. Then I shook my head in a hopeless attempt to loosen the links my mind kept insisting on making.

'How was everything for you, ladies?'

I hadn't noticed the waiter standing by my side.

'Lovely, thank you,' said my mother, parroting something the chef had said about the first of the green beans. 'Do tell him I send my compliments.'

He smiled and cleared our plates, the china clinking.

I drank some wine.

Right on cue, a second waiter came to refill both our glasses from the bottle of white chilling in a silver bucket at the table's edge.

'Thank you,' I said, before turning to my mother, who was buttering the second half of her bread roll, which to her delight was stuffed with salty black olives. Before I could change my mind, I opened my mouth and pushed out the words: 'Mum, I have something to tell you.'

She stopped buttering and turned to me, too, a smile playing on her lips. 'You're not . . .?' She didn't finish the sentence, but she didn't have to.

'No, I'm not,' I said, smiling, warily, 'although it is related.'

She tore off a piece of bread and popped it in her mouth, chewing as she waited.

'Mum, I've decided to freeze my eggs.'

I paused, gauging her reaction.

She continued chewing.

'You know what that means, don't you?'

She rolled her eyes, just like she'd done in the car, and swallowed. 'Yes, Cathy, I know what it means to freeze your eggs.'

'So, what do you think?'

'What does Noah think?'

Noah. I swallowed down the knot twisting in my throat and said, confidently, 'He thinks it's my body and I can do what I want.'

She waited, and so did I.

Then, a little less confident: 'He says he won't change his mind about having children, and that he doesn't want to be

159

involved.'

Her face softened. She held out her hand.

I took it, and instantly regretted it. I knew what she was going to say before she said it – maybe because, ever since Robyn had asked the question, a small, sequestered part of me had considered it myself. Still, I wasn't anywhere near ready to hear it spoken aloud.

'You're going to have to leave him.'

My stomach dropped, the way it does when you drive too fast over a hill. I laughed, instinctively. It was either that or cry. I could feel tears prickling in my eyes and I squeezed out a smile as I repeated what she'd said to me earlier that morning, in relation to the barricade of display cushions: 'Mum, don't be so dramatic.'

'But what's the point in doing this then, darling, if he won't change his mind?'

I took a breath and recited to her the same thing I'd said to Noah: 'It's not that I necessarily see a baby in my future, it's just that the picture of my future is hazier than before.' I waited for her to say something, and when she didn't, I kept talking. 'I want to have the option,' I said, my voice a little shaky now, 'in case I do decide that I want to have a baby later. I want it to still be possible.'

At some point during my monologue our mains arrived. As the waiter placed two pieces of salmon in front of us, all pink flesh and crispy skin, along with an assortment of sides, I wetted my mouth, suddenly dry, with wine. As he walked away, I went to continue, but my mother got there first, saying again what she'd said before:

'Cathy, you're going to have to leave him.'

'But Mum—' the shaking was becoming audible '—you're

not listening to me.'

'I'm listening.' She said it gently, but firmly. 'You don't know if you want to have a baby, but you want to have the option. And with Noah, there is no option.'

I hadn't realised, but my hand was still in hers.

'Cathy.'

'Please.' At this point my voice broke, and I paused. 'Please, I can't.'

'But—'

'I can't.' Slowly, I slipped my hand away, and I picked up my knife and fork.

The next morning, I woke to the sound of birdsong, and my mother snoring. She'd done so throughout the night, stopping every now and then, abruptly, prompting me to lean over and check she was still breathing. I reached for my phone on the bedside table to see if I had any messages from Noah, and when there were none felt an emptiness inside me, as though I'd gone without dinner. I climbed out of bed, pulled on yesterday's clothes, and left a note on the hotel's branded notepad:

Gone for breakfast. See you downstairs. C x

I was on my second round of the complimentary breakfast buffet – a blueberry muffin and a couple of mini pastries followed a bowl of creamy yoghurt, homemade granola and fresh fruit – when she arrived. She strolled over and sat down and smiled, then she said, 'Oh, this looks nice!'

I smiled back, or at least I tried to. My lips felt faulty. After our conversation the night before, we'd tiptoed around the subject, talking about the food on our plates and whether we might want to watch some TV before going to bed. In the end, we went straight to sleep, or at least my mother did – I lay there, trying to make out pieces of furniture in the dark, and the feelings clattering around in my mind. I must have drifted off eventually, and I woke up ready to talk.

Again, though, I felt a knot in my throat. I tried to dislodge it with a swig of iced water, which had been laced with fussily peeled ribbons of cucumber.

A chirpy waitress appeared and asked my mother what she would like to drink, then invited her to help herself to the buffet and let her know if she wanted anything hot from the kitchen.

My mother pushed herself up and out of her chair and shuffled towards the display of freshly baked goods. She walked from one end of the long, thin table to the other, slowly, considering her options, then retraced her steps.

My water glass was empty when she sat back down beside me and began tucking into the first of three plates. Still, the knot remained. When I couldn't ignore it any longer, I said, in as steady a voice as I could muster, 'Mum, I think we need to talk.'

She looked up from her mini-Danish and I noticed that she hadn't yet applied her make-up. 'What is it?' Her eyelashes, usually thick and dark, looked delicate and oddly pale. Her cheeks were a shade lighter than usual too, and her lips were dry and a little cracked in the middle.

I felt my own lip tremble. 'We need to talk about last night, the conversation we had over dinner.'

'OK,' she said, taking a bite, bits of pastry falling on and around her plate.

'Would you mind putting that down for a moment?' I

asked, the pitch of my voice rising involuntarily.

Her eyes narrowed in confusion, then widened as they clocked mine flashing towards the Danish. 'Yes, of course,' she said, swallowing and wiping at the corners of her mouth with her napkin. 'What is it?'

'I'm not going to leave Noah.' Suddenly, I felt sick. Even saying the words out loud.

She laughed.

I felt my entire body stiffen, even as my lip continued to tremble. 'Why is that funny?'

Still laughing and now looking around as if she expected others to be doing the same, she said, 'Because of course you're not! Why would you?'

It's hard to explain how I felt at that moment: hurt, frustrated, embarrassed even. Three feelings I rarely, if ever, associated with my mother. I went to reply, but I was so close to the edge now that the only word I could manage was 'Mum'.

Her laughter slowed and quietened, then stopped altogether.

A few seconds went by, then I managed to push out a full sentence: 'I know you might not agree with the way I'm handling things, but it's the only way I can think to handle them right now.'

'But I don't—'

'Please, Mum.' I paused. 'I've made up my mind, and I'm going through with it.'

She was shaking her head. 'I don't understand.'

'I know you don't.' My eyes were filling with tears, and I widened them to make room. 'But please don't tell me to leave him.'

'Darling!' She held out her hands, which were trembling too. 'I would never tell you to leave Noah. I don't remember

163

saying it. If I did, I . . . I must have had too much to drink.'

My stomach lurched, but in my desperation not to break down at the table, I ignored it. 'Right,' I said, finishing my coffee and slowly pushing my chair back and away.

'Where are you going?'

I don't know whether it was because I was standing by this point, but through my blurry vision she looked small and vulnerable.

Another lurch, this one harder to ignore. 'To pack,' I said, taking a second, then adding softly: 'We have to check out by eleven.'

When she looked down at her open hands and started to move her mouth, as if she was replaying our conversation, a single tear spilled over my lower lid, and I quickly wiped it away.

'Mum?'

She looked up at me, her own eyes watery with worry.

'There's no rush, take your time.'

I've always hated confrontation, especially with my mother. I packed as she finished her breakfast, and when she came back upstairs and bundled her own things into her bag, I went to check out. On the return journey to Bury St Edmunds, I turned on the radio in the hope of reinstating normality. But the only conversation that took place between us came in the form of my directions.

She pulled into the car park, put on the handbrake, and turned off the engine. I leant over and kissed her goodbye. I was quiet, but my insides were whirring. Mostly with the same blend of sadness and frustration I'd felt earlier, but also with worry. Worry that I might have made a horrible mistake. Worry that she truly had drunk too much and didn't remember. Worry that she *hadn't* drunk too much and didn't remember. Worry about what that meant.

'Thank you, darling, for such a lovely weekend away.' Her voice was quieter than usual and a little wobbly.

'You're welcome,' I said, reminding her with a small smile that it was a gift from Noah, too.

'Of course,' she said, momentarily lifting her expression before letting it fall again, like it was too great an effort. 'I am sorry if I said something to upset you.'

My internal whirring rose in volume at the 'if', then faded again as a flicker of confusion crept across her face.

She said it again – 'I'm sorry, I don't know what's wrong with me' – and turned away, hastily pushing some stray grey hairs from her forehead.

The whirring was muted, and in its place rose a wave of guilt. I felt my cheeks burn with shame. This weekend away was supposed to have been about her; it was her birthday present. 'I'm sorry too, Mum.'

She turned back to me then.

'Please drive safely, and message me when you get home, OK?'

She nodded and said she would. She did.

I remember when I introduced Noah to my parents. They were coming to London to see a play at the National Theatre, something they did only once or twice a year, and when I told them we'd be next door that night, watching a film at the BFI, they suggested we get together afterwards for a quick dinner.

Throughout the film I felt fidgety, and I recognised it was

the kind of fidgetiness that crept up on me before exams and interviews. I crossed and recrossed my legs, and at one point Noah put a hand on my knee and exerted a small amount of pressure to stop it from jiggling. He paused, chin lifted, the brightness of the screen reflected on his cheek, and said, No, we're good. I must have looked at him questioningly because he explained that he thought he'd felt the rumblings of London's first serious earthquake. Haha, I said, very funny.

It was almost ten o'clock when we emerged from the low-lit cinema, and my parents usually ate dinner at seven. Not wanting to delay them any further, I'd booked us a table at a small-chain Italian around the corner. We arrived first and ordered a bottle of red and some antipasti, and when they walked in ten minutes later, I had a plump green olive stuffed with a blanched almond in my mouth.

When Noah stood up to greet them, he towered over my mother, as he did me, and he even made my father, a tall but skinny man, look a few inches smaller than he was. He navigated the potentially awkward first-encounter greeting with grace, reaching out to shake my father's hand and taking hold of my mother's shoulders as he planted a kiss on each of her cheeks. I hadn't told my parents much about him, other than where he'd grown up and what he did for a living. I definitely hadn't mentioned the fact that he'd been married before or why that marriage had ended. When my mother had asked how old he was, I'd said something vague like a few years older than me.

I needn't have worried. That night, there was barely a pause in conversation. Noah politely enquired about life in Norfolk and my parents were eager to hear all about his job. I kept sneaking glances at Noah, expecting his brow to be damp, or his wine glass low, but he was as relaxed as he had been when the two of us first went out for dinner together. Even when my mother began to talk about a documentary that she and my father had watched recently on the community of Orthodox Jews living in north London, and he told her that sounded interesting but actually his family wasn't Orthodox, the tone of his voice was even, and he was smiling. When the food had been eaten, and a second bottle of red had been drunk, we said our goodbyes, already planning a second get-together.

It was the hottest July on record, and as I walked from the Tube station to the clinic, I wondered how the probability of my frozen eggs surviving compared with that of the ice caps. I was wearing a loose sundress the colour of peach flesh; it had a V-neck and short sleeves and fell to just below the knee. I hoped the cotton wouldn't soak up the bead of sweat that I could feel sliding down my spine. On my feet was a pair of leather sandals that announced my arrival from a distance. Whenever I wore them, I would notice people glance up from their phones, intrigued or perhaps even excited by the smart clip on the pavement. When I was level with them, they would be staring at their screens again. I tried not to take it personally.

In the waiting room, I got talking to a fresh-faced woman with striking blue eyes made even more striking by heavy lids. She told me her mother had given her a round of egg freezing as a thirtieth birthday present.

'Ah, ill-advised mothers,' I cringed.

She pursed her lips. 'I asked for it.'

I tried to conceal my surprise, then excused myself and went to phone my own ill-advised mother. Just before voice-mail kicked in, she answered, her voice chipper. Like me, though, she seemed distracted, trailing off halfway through sentences. I asked what she'd been up to in the couple of days that had passed since the weekend, eager to move on from our disagreement, searching for some reassurance about her state of mind maybe. I hadn't told Noah about what had gone on at the hotel because I didn't want him to get the wrong idea. When she happily filled me in on her weekly Monday evening game of Bridge, and tea with Peggy, I felt my shoulders drop with relief.

'Cathy?'

I looked up to find Doctor Day standing in front of me, hands clasped together behind his back.

'Mum, I have to go, I'll call you later.'

'OK, have fun, darling.'

I hadn't told her where I was or what I was doing. If I had, I suspect she would have used a different sign-off.

The temperature dropped as I followed Doctor Day into his office, and I heard the fly-like whir of the air-conditioning unit before I caught sight of the clunky white contraption on the ceiling. My attention moved towards his desk, where I noticed for the first time a couple of framed family photos. He had a wife, who was quite beautiful, with a dark bob and winged eyebrows, and two small girls who looked close in age and were wearing matching marigold-yellow dungarees. My mind strayed first to thoughts of his marriage and whether it was a happy one, then to the girls and the possibility that they'd been ice babies.

'Right,' he said, sitting down and straightening his tie, 'let's get this paperwork out of the way.'

Along with my treatment plan there was a breakdown of the fixed-price package, which was less fixed than the name would suggest, thanks to additional costs for everything from sedation to storage. I tried to keep a neutral look on my face as I totted up the numbers and worked out that, if I were to store my eggs for a year alone, I'd be looking at paying around six thousand pounds.

'And these are the consent forms for you to sign,' said Doctor Day, pushing the numbers to one side.

I took my time reading the part about me giving approval for the procedure, then skimmed the section about what would happen to my eggs if I died or became somehow incapacitated, scribbling my signature on the dotted lines.

'Any questions?' he asked, shuffling the paperwork into a neat pile.

'I don't think so,' I said, feeling like I was in an interview and should have prepared at least one insightful enquiry for the end.

'Well, if any arise, just give me a call.' He slid the papers into my file, then slid that file into the top drawer of a metal filing cabinet with squeaky hinges. 'OK, that's that, and these are for you.' He handed me my own breakdown of the costs, as well as a brochure on counselling. 'We offer a free session with all our treatments – optional, of course, though we would recommend it.'

My roaming gaze landed on the words 'individuals or couples'.

'I have another appointment, so I'm going to ask one of my colleagues to talk you through what will happen next.'

I nodded, still scanning the leaflet, which was now lying open on my lap. Seeing a counsellor can help you to 'understand your partner's responses to treatment'.

Doctor Day cleared his throat and picked up his phone.

He asked for someone called Amina, and a few seconds later there was a sharp knock at the door. He made some introductions: 'Cathy, this is Amina, one of our senior nurses. Amina, this is Cathy, who's going to be freezing her eggs with us.'

'Nice to meet you,' I mumbled, aware that this was all becoming very real.

'So,' said Doctor Day, with a smile that contained an air of finality, 'I'll see you in a few days.'

Amina was already walking away, and he gestured for me to follow.

She was about my age, I would guess, with a freckly face and scarlet hair so bright it had to be dyed. I followed her down the corridor and into another consultation room, which may or may not have been her office. I glanced at the desk but saw no family photos. Just some neon-rainbow Post-it Notes and a half-eaten Snickers bar.

In her hands she had a bin liner-like bag filled with colour-coded drugs, which she announced quite brusquely was my injection pack. She fished out a sheet of paper. 'See this flow chart?' she asked.

I nodded; I saw it.

'This is a breakdown of everything you need to do over the next fortnight,' she said. 'So, you'll see that you need to inject every night for two weeks and come into the clinic every three days for a scan.' She jabbed at various points in the chart with a long acrylic nail.

'How?'

'How what?'

I wondered if it was a stupid question to ask and was thankful not to have thought of it when I was with Doctor

Day. 'How do I inject?'

When she didn't sigh or raise her neatly shaped eyebrows, I relaxed in the knowledge that perhaps it was a question she'd been expecting.

She reached back into the bag and retrieved two smaller bags, one filled with a dozen thick needles with pink plastic tops, the other a dozen slightly thinner needles with yellow lids. 'You take a pink needle, suck up some saline solution from one vial and inject it into another vial containing the powder.' She paused to look at me, and when I didn't respond she must have taken my silence as tacit compliance, because she continued: 'Next, you remove the pink needle and shake the vial containing the mixture.' Another pause. 'Then you inject the yellow needle into the vial, suck up the mixture, about a teaspoon's worth, tap the syringe to make sure there are no air bubbles, and inject.'

'Inject?'

'Inject.'

'Into?'

'Your stomach or your upper thighs, whichever you prefer.'

I nodded, again, mute, wondering if this was a preference of which I should have already been aware.

'You got it?'

'I've got it.' But did I? I was about to ask if she could repeat the instructions, more slowly this time, so I could write them down, when she told me there was a leaflet in the bag, plus a sharps bin to dispose of the used needles.

She was already bundling the bits back in and reiterating Doctor Day's parting line about calling if I had any questions. Satisfied, she passed it to me and told me, not exactly insincerely, to have a good day.

'You too,' I said, folding the bag up into as small a parcel as possible and clutching it to my chest.

I held it there as I walked back towards the Tube. The sun was higher in the sky now, beating down on my forehead, and like cling film, my dress clung to my skin, which was damp with sweat. When I saw a police officer, my heart pounded hard and fast. He turned to look at me. I kept walking. I pictured his palm rising – Hang on a moment, Miss – and his free hand gesturing for me to hand over the bag. Me: It's for my ovaries, I swear! Instead, his gaze slid down my bare legs to my sandals, then back to his iced coffee.

It turned out Noah had no choice about being involved. On day one of my hormone injections, I was sitting cross-legged on the bathroom floor in nothing but my pants and bra, the grouting of the tiles imprinting itself on the backs of my thighs. I held one pink needle and one yellow needle in my palm and took a deep breath. When I started to feel faint, I closed my eyes, and kept breathing – in *one, two, three*, out *one, two, three*. When I reopened my eyes, the dizziness had mostly subsided.

I followed Amina's instructions, mixing the powder and saline solution, filling the syringe, and getting rid of the air bubble – then wondering what would happen if I forgot that part, my mind skipping to the terrifying story an older girl at school had told my own year group about the dangers of having sex in a swimming pool. Taking another deep breath, I tried to pinch a bit of fat and pierce my stomach. With the tip of the needle pressing up against my skin, I tested its sharpness, then I squeezed my eyes shut and pushed. Nothing happened. I pushed again, or at least I thought I did. It was only when Noah walked in and slipped the syringe out of my hand that I realised I was barely holding onto it.

'Here?' he asked, indicating towards my stomach with his eyes.

I nodded and re-pinched the skin.

'Look the other way,' he said, gently, rubbing my upper back – the way he'd done once or twice in the past when I'd been crouching beside the loo for another, altogether messier reason. 'OK, I'm going to do it,' he said, unfazed, his fingers now moving back and forth across my stomach, which was rippling with nerves. 'Just breathe, honey.'

I did as he said, I breathed.

A pop, then a slight sting. The dizziness returned as he slipped the needle out from inside me.

'Well, that's one down,' he said, disposing of the needle in the small, yellow sharps bin.

I thanked him, and together we sat on the cold tiles, my head on his shoulder, his hand on my leg. We stayed that way for a while, as though one of us had hit pause, then he stood up and brushed his teeth and I did the same.

Back at work, I imagined the hormones swirling around inside me, stimulating my ovaries. The whale was almost completely revealed, and it had become clear that the man balancing on its back was measuring its length with a rope. I just had to remove the final bits of overpaint from the tail, which was half submerged beneath the waves. As I daubed the surface with the solvent solution, I was acutely aware that I too was being primped and preened. But while the whale in front of me was coming to life before my eyes, even in death, I felt myself disappearing. It was like I'd slipped into a fugue state while the rest of the world continued, on mute, around me.

After my first botched attempt, Noah helped me with my injections. We didn't talk about it; it was more of a silent agreement. Every evening at eight o'clock my phone alarm sounded. I walked over to the fridge and retrieved the saline solution, which, after much deliberating, I'd decided should live in the bottom shelf of the door in between the orange juice and the milk, as if being among natural foodstuffs would make it less artificial. Then I climbed the stairs and resumed my seated position in the bathroom. By the time I'd done the mixing and got rid of any air bubbles, the syringe was ready, and he was with me. Sometimes the needle wouldn't go in for him either. I would bite my lip as unsolicited tears sprung up in my eyes and he would tell me to hold on, that in a minute it would be over.

On the third evening, Anna called. I stared at my screen, which whenever she phones me shows an old photo of the two of us that she found and sent to me during a particularly nostalgic period. We're in our south London flat, sitting side by side on the sofa, a plain grey; if you look closely, you can see the stark white of tiny feathers poking out in places. She's leaning back with one leg crossed over the other, a grin stretched across her face. I'm grinning too, while hugging my knees to my chest, my fingers interlinked. We both have bare feet, and her toenails are painted denim blue. We'd moved in that day, and beside us, half in shot, is a personalised cushion she'd ordered off the internet – a joke, but one that remained in our living room/dining room/ kitchen for the two years we lived together. Stitched onto its front are the words: HOME IS WHERE ANNA AND CATHY ARE. When she sent me the photo, the subject line read: *Where oh where is our beloved cushion?!?!*

That evening, I kept staring at the screen until the photo vanished and, in its place, a little message appeared saying I'd missed her call. I told myself that if she called back, I'd pick up this time. I wanted to talk to her, to tell her what was going on, and more than once that week I'd found myself clutching my phone, my thumb hovering over her name. Every time, something had stopped me. I'd experienced a needling pain in my chest, which I couldn't explain; I'd tried to physically rub the pain away and work out what I was feeling. Embarrassment perhaps.

I watched and waited and chewed at my cheek, which I'd accidentally bitten during dinner the night before and was providing a sort of solace. I unlocked my phone and checked when she was last on WhatsApp: a few minutes ago. A few minutes more of sitting and staring and I turned the screen over to face the table, wondering whether my side effects were kicking in.

The next morning, the day of my first scan, I felt them – jitteriness, hot and cold flashes, lethargy. I'd managed to avoid any more online forums since my argument with Noah at the start of the month, but now I found myself beholden to them, urgently scrolling in search of solidarity and some acknowledgement that yes, it was normal to experience heart palpitations, and yes, they would go away again.

'How are you feeling?'

When Doctor Day first asked the question, tugging at his tie, I found myself replying with a stock 'Fine, thanks'. But as I lay back and he swivelled his chair into position between my legs, I changed my answer: 'Actually, I feel a little queasy.'

'Well, you'll be pleased to hear that any side effects should settle down in a few days once the initial shock of the hormones has subsided.' Perhaps as a distraction from the wet probe he was slowly slipping inside me, he directed my attention towards the screen, which showed my ovaries – there, left and right.

'Is it working?' I asked, noticing the slightly frantic note in my voice, and lowering it as I added: 'Can you tell?'

'So far, so good,' he said. 'We'll have a better idea the closer we get to your final injection though.' He jotted some things down and when he was done, he pulled out the probe and passed me a piece of tissue to wipe myself with.

I was walking back through the waiting room when I saw her, sitting with one knee crossed over the other, holding a book in one splayed hand. She'd parted her fringe in the middle and it framed her forehead in two curves, like drawn curtains. She hadn't seen me, and I considered continuing towards the door. Then I felt my feet turn towards her. 'Robyn?'

She glanced up from her reading and gave me a toothy smile that told me she recognised me.

Still, I reintroduced myself, just in case: 'It's Cathy – from the open evening.'

'Of course, Cathy, good to see you!' She closed her book without marking the page and came to standing. 'Does this mean you went ahead with the egg freezing?' As she said the word 'this', she held out her hands, palms facing the ceiling, which I took to mean my being here at the clinic.

'That's right,' I said, trying to match her smile. 'I just had my first scan.'

'Oh, you're a few days behind me then. I'm here for my second. And how are you feeling?' She tilted her head to one side, as if she could already tell.

Before I had time to answer, Doctor Day appeared and called her name.

'Hey, do you want to hang around and grab some lunch?' she asked, giving him a wave, and slinging her bag over her shoulder. She half laughed as she added, 'We can compare notes.'

I wasn't sure whether that prospect made me feel anxious or less alone, but either way I heard myself saying, 'Absolutely.'

'Great, I'll be as quick as I can.'

By the time she was done my stomach was growling and I was conscious of the time – I really should have been getting back to work.

'There's a Vietnamese around the corner, if you fancy it?' she asked, as we walked out of the clinic. 'Or we can get a sandwich or something?'

Then again, it wasn't like anyone would notice my absence. 'Vietnamese sounds good.'

We set off at a brisk walk. As she talked, I felt a tingle of nerves on my skin. I couldn't remember the last time I'd made a new friend, and for a moment my thoughts returned to Anna and those other mums. I wondered what she would think of Robyn.

It was a tiny café, with a handful of clothless tables. Robyn nabbed the last free one, which was wedged into a corner by the window. Half the glass was covered with printed menus and handwritten specials intended to entice passers-by. I looked down at my own menu, which a harried man had placed in front of me before we'd even had a chance to sit down. It was laminated and featured numbered photos that corresponded to the dishes listed on the left-hand side.

'Any recommendations?' I asked her.

'Let me see – the fried rice noodles with prawns and vegetables are a must. And maybe we should share some pork spring rolls?'

'Works for me.'

She caught the same waiter's eye, and we placed our order.

'So, how are you?' I asked, as he took our menus away and disappeared through a beaded curtain.

'Busy, but good,' she said, smiling and nodding. 'I work for a homeless charity, and there are more people sleeping rough in London than ever, so . . . it's a lot.'

'Because there isn't enough social housing?'

'That, but also, before that, because there's no chance of these people being able to afford rising rents.'

I exhaled, and a look passed between us – the same look we'd given to one another at the open evening when talk had turned to price packages. Before we found ourselves down another tunnel of hard truths about the commodification of fertility, she shook her head and said, 'What about you?'

I told her about my work at the museum, and about the painting waiting for me back in the conservation studios. I realised halfway through the story of Hendrick and the whale that I was doing what I often did – talking about my work as if it were my life, my love. 'It hardly compares on the scale of doing good,' I added, a little sheepishly.

As she sucked some Diet Coke through a straw, her blue eyes blinking at me from behind her fringe, she said that wasn't true and that art and culture were important. 'Plus, it sounds fascinating.'

'It makes me happy,' I conceded, moving my hands off my plastic placemat as the waiter hurriedly set down our noodles before taking the order of the next-door table.

As we ate, we moved on from small talk, which I belatedly remembered she'd said she was no good at, to the subject that had brought us together.

'How are you feeling about everything?' she asked, raising her skinny eyebrows. As she waited for me to reply, she dipped a spring roll into some sweet chilli sauce that was unnaturally saturated.

'I'm feeling . . . OK.'

'It's kind of lonely, isn't it?'

All at once I felt happy to be seen, and sad to acknowledge that, yes, lonely was exactly how I was feeling. Sad, and also guilty. Robyn was *literally* going through this alone, while I was married. Happily married.

As if she could read the thoughts roiling in my mind, she asked, 'You don't feel able to include your husband?'

'It's more that he doesn't want to be included.' Conscious of not wanting to paint an unflattering portrait of Noah, I quickly added, 'He is supportive.'

'Do you think you would want children if you weren't with him?'

I half laughed, half exhaled.

'You don't have to answer.'

'It's not that,' I said. 'I just can't imagine it – not being with him.'

She studied me for a moment, then she asked, 'Have you taken them up on that free counselling session?' I must have given her a blank look because she clarified: 'The one they offer to all patients. They should have given you a leaflet.'

'Oh, that.' I'd forgotten. 'No, have you?'

She nodded while her mouth was full, then after swallowing said it was well worth it. 'I know what I want, and I still found it helpful.' In descending order, she listed on three fingers three hopes: 'To meet someone now and conceive naturally, to meet someone later and use my frozen eggs, or, if I have to, to get them fertilised with donor sperm.'

If I have to. I wished I was as sure of myself.

'Anyway, I'd recommend it.'

'Well, maybe I will take them up on it then.' I pincered some noodles between my chopsticks and struggled to keep hold of them. 'And you?' I asked. 'How are you feeling about it?'

She poked at a prawn, still half in its shell. 'To be honest, I'm scared it's not going to work.'

The noodles slipped out of my grip and back into the bowl. 'But you don't have any reason to think that, do you?' I asked, taken aback by the chink in her resolve.

She picked up the prawn with her fingers and peeled the shell away from the flesh. 'Not really, other than a gut feeling. It's silly, really.'

A gut feeling. In my mind, I could see my mother earnestly nodding. I opened my mouth to tell her I was sure it would be fine, but how could I be? Instead, I tried again to pincer some noodles as I said, 'In my experience, gut feelings can be misleading.'

Doctor Day was right – the side effects did subside, but not before the late arrival of the tender breasts. The combination of the July heat and the drugs was pushing me over the edge, physically, emotionally. Soon I was so bloated that when I turned side-on in front of the floor-length mirror in our bedroom, I could fool myself into thinking I was pregnant.

Every three days during my lunch break I dragged myself from the museum to the clinic for a scan, during which Doctor Day would comment on my oestrogen levels and follicle growth. I didn't bump into Robyn again, but we messaged – as she said, comparing notes. Some symptoms we shared, others one of us experienced and the other didn't. Take bruising. She could barely see where she'd been injecting, whereas my stomach was pockmarked with dots of grey, which I would rub with Arnica cream before bed. I was reminded of my father, who always said I bruised like a banana. Each time I would sigh and say, I think you mean a peach.

One night, as I lowered myself onto the mattress beside Noah and opened the small tub of cream, he offered to do it for me. His hands worked around my stomach, up over my breasts, which were still sore, then lower. In an instant, my discomfort was dispelled. I felt drunk with desire, my mind a blur. He kissed my neck and chest and pressed himself against me, then I climbed on top of him.

After, we lay on our backs, staring up at the ceiling. Slowly, in the same way that grief creeps up on you when you first wake in the morning after a misleadingly good night's sleep, the aches and pains returned. In a panic, I reached for my phone and found myself googling if it was a good idea to have sex during treatment. I think the words I used were, 'Is it allowed?'. When I read on more than one site that it was fine, I tried to relax again.

Noah was quiet beside me. He didn't ask what I was doing – perhaps he knew – and when I leant over to plug in my phone, he reached to turn off his bedside light.

I put my hand on his chest and asked, 'How are you feeling?'

He let out a sigh.

'Noah?'

'I feel like you're leaving me behind.'

I rolled over to face him. 'I'm not.' When he didn't respond, I held on tight around his waist and said, 'I'm not going anywhere.'

He smiled, a sad smile heavy with doubt.

Aside from Noah, the folk at the clinic, and the odd person I bumped into at work, I didn't see anyone during those two weeks. I'm sure even Tom could sense that something was up, so my solitude was probably a good thing. During the final few days, I would sit on the sofa clutching a hot-water bottle to my pulsing womb, and he would come and sit as close as possible without sitting on top of me, licking the back of my hand with his sandpaper tongue. When at last I would get up and walk away, he would follow, his snowy paws kissing my heels. When he asked for extra food, I gave it to him without question.

And so, I was surprised when Noah decided to invite Daniel and Griz over for dinner on Saturday, the night of my penultimate injection. He sprung it on me when I was getting out of the shower the day before.

'You don't mind, do you?' he asked, waiting as I wrapped my body in a towel and passing me an extra, smaller towel for my sopping hair.

I padded into the bedroom with wet feet, my body feeling its most vehicle-like, carrying around precious cargo. I'd started to think that 'MOT' might have been the right term for the fertility test after all.

'I just thought, we haven't seen them for a while,' he said, standing in the threshold, casting a tall shadow on the wall. 'And the past couple of times we've been to theirs, so we owe them.'

I opened my mouth, then I closed it again.

He was still talking, telling me that they were going away the following week.

He'd been so good to me. I could do this for him. Finally, as I started drying myself, I said, 'Of course not, sounds fun.'

A couple of hours before they were due to arrive, I received an email from my uncle, Duncan, telling me that my mother had missed their weekly Saturday morning Skype call for the second time in a row. He'd tried phoning her landline and no answer. Had I heard from her? I felt jittery. She loved those calls and looked forward to them all week. Duncan had moved to the States in his twenties, got married and had two children – my cousins, who I'd only met in person twice. He rarely came home, but every year my mother sent emails and cards and looked forward to her annual two-week sojourn with them.

I left his email unanswered and dialled my mother's number.

She picked up after just a couple of rings. 'Hello?'

'Hi Mum, it's me.'

'Who?'

'Me. It's me, Mum, Cathy.'

'Oh darling, hello. Sorry, the front door is open, and someone's got a lawnmower going, I can't hear a thing. One minute.'

I heard the shuffle of her house slippers on the floor and

the click of the latch.

'Is that better?' I asked, when I could tell from the sound of her breathing that the receiver was pressed back against her cheek.

'Much,' she said. I pictured her sinking down into her chair and thought I might have even heard its springs heave. 'How are things?'

'Oh, I'm fine, thanks, almost done with the injections.' As soon as I said it, I regretted it, and I steeled myself for another comment like the one that had spoiled our weekend away.

'The injections?'

I must have pulled a face, because Noah walked past me at that moment and asked if everything was OK. I waved my hand and nodded. 'You, know, for the egg freezing.'

For more than a few seconds, she didn't say anything. Then: 'Of course.'

I waited for her to elaborate, and when she didn't, I decided that was that. 'So, Mum, Duncan emailed me and mentioned you missed today's Skype call?'

'No,' she said, defensively, as though my question was an accusation. 'I didn't.'

'You spoke to him and Sal this morning?' Sal, my uncle's American wife, who worked in luxury real estate.

She went quiet again, and then she asked, 'Is it Saturday?'

'It is, Mum.' My jitteriness must have subsided before because, at this point, I felt it return. Or not jitteriness so much as low-level tingles creeping across my chest. The kind of feeling that spreads from your fingers across your knuckles and towards your wrist when you touch an electric fence with a single blade of grass. 'Have you got your diary in front of you?' I asked.

Quietly, she said, 'I lost it.'

'You lost your diary?' I failed to conceal my surprise. 'But you always keep it by the phone.'

'I know I do,' she said, audibly irritated by my stating the obvious.

I balked and wondered what had put her in such a bad mood. I was about to ask if she was feeling OK, when:

'I think Peggy took it.'

'Mum!' I couldn't help but laugh. 'Why would Peggy take your diary?'

'Well, I don't know, do I? But she did, I'm sure of it.'

I stopped laughing. The tingles were spreading along the length of my arms and down my back. 'OK, Mum, I'm sure this is just a misunderstanding. Perhaps Peggy moved your diary when she was dusting?' I tried to sound convincing, even though I knew Peggy would never do that – she was aware of how much my mother relied on that thing. 'How about I give her a call, get this straightened out? And maybe you can talk to Duncan tomorrow instead?'

'No, tomorrow I'm busy.'

'Doing what?'

She paused, and then said in a brittle voice that cut straight through me: 'I don't know, it's in my diary.'

'OK,' I tried again, taking a deep breath. 'Listen, Mum, you wait there. I'm going to call Peggy.'

'OK.'

'OK,' I repeated. I hesitated. I could hear the moisture in her lips as she opened and closed them without saying anything. 'We'll figure it out, Mum, don't worry.'

I put down the phone, took another breath, and found

Peggy's name in my recent contacts. It started ringing.

'What's going on?' asked Noah, from the kitchen.

I was about to reply when Peggy answered.

She was as baffled as I was, and of course she hadn't touched it. But she promised to nip next door and help my mother look for it. I expected her to call back right away and say she'd found it on the floor, that it had simply slipped off the side table and was hidden behind one of its legs. Instead, it was almost an hour until my phone rang. When I answered, she paused, and then she told me she'd found it in the freezer.

'What?'

My body was a mess, and now so was my head. I thought back to the weekend away with my mother and asked Peggy if she'd noticed any other unusual behaviour.

'Not unusual, no, though I haven't been around all that much.'

'You haven't?'

'Your mum didn't tell you? I've been helping Nicole with the boys – you know she's on her own now.'

Before she began criticising her daughter's soon-to-be ex-husband: 'She's forgetting things, Peggy.'

'Well, who doesn't forget things?'

'I think it might be more than that.' In my head, I heard the faint whisper of the word I associated with my grandmother. My mother's mother. One or two of my mother's older, frailer friends. 'She's seventy.'

'And I'm seventy-three!'

I bit down on my bottom lip. 'I know, I'm sorry. I just wonder if it's worth me taking her for a check-up, if only to rule it out.' I didn't have to say what I meant by 'it'.

When Peggy didn't respond, I told her I had a bad feeling.

A gut feeling?

'Look, there's nothing you can do tonight,' she said, when I started to hypothesise.

She was right, and when she promised to keep a close eye on her, I tried to temporarily push my worries – and that word, rising in volume – to the back of my mind.

I was running late and only just changing when Daniel and Griz arrived. As I attempted to conceal what felt like a mixing bowl beneath my most loose-fitting shirt, I heard Noah thanking Daniel for the wine, and Daniel offering to put it in the fridge. I held my breath as I heard the fridge door swing open, then sighed aloud as it closed again, and Daniel started talking about something sports-related. The saline solution had gone unnoticed. I was busy letting an alternate scenario play out in my head when Griz said my name and Noah called up to tell me they were here.

'Cathy, how are you?'

I still had one foot on the stairs when Griz kissed my cheek.

'I'm fine, thanks,' I said, holding onto her bare shoulders for balance, my eyes taking in her colourful crochet vest. 'And you?'

'Oh, you know, just trying to make it through the summer holidays without the children killing each other.'

I pushed out a 'ha' and followed her back into the kitchen.

'Cathy, looking lovely as always.'

Well, now I knew that was nothing more than politeness. 'Thanks, Daniel, good to see you.'

More kissing. Griz bent down to greet Tom, who was mewing at our ankles.

'Yes, sorry it's taken so long for us to get you guys over,' added Noah, pouring wine from a bottle that was already chilled. When he got to the fourth glass, he paused, and then continued.

I hadn't drunk since that weekend with my mother, just in case, and we hadn't talked about how this evening was going to pan out. He was extending a glass towards me before I said, 'Actually, I have a bit of a headache, so I think I'll stick to water for now.'

I could have sworn Griz's eyebrows rose infinitesimally, but I also could have imagined it.

'Oh, before I forget,' she said, reaching for her handbag and pulling out two or three neatly folded pieces of A4 paper. 'From Allie.'

Whenever Noah and I saw Daniel and Griz without the children, Allie sent along some drawings for me. I smiled at the underwater images of stripy fish, mottled crabs, stringy seaweed. On the third sheet, a whale on a beach, with people standing around and pointing. Speech bubbles were filled with 'wow!'s and 'amazing!'s. I held it close to my chest. 'Please thank her from me.'

Dinner that night was one of Noah's staples, courtesy of a cookbook I'd given to him a couple of Christmases back: tomato and coconut cassoulet, with butter beans and basil and torn-up pieces of sourdough. We milled around in the kitchen chatting while he cooked, and when we sat down to eat, candles flickering on the table, we were still sharing pleasantries about the unusually long stretch of time that had passed since we'd last seen each other.

'How's work going, Cathy?' asked Daniel, helping himself to some extra bread from the cast-iron dish between us. 'I still can't believe there's been a hidden whale in the painting all this time.' He shook his head. 'Incredible.'

I smiled, and so did Noah. 'Thanks, Daniel, it is exciting. And it's going well – I've uncovered most of it now.'

'It must be fairly big news in the art world, a discovery like that?'

I was telling him how the press office was already making plans for a media announcement that would go out towards the end of the autumn when I heard Griz ask Noah how his research into the origins of the US-Vietnam War was going. I put down my fork, dumbstruck. I hadn't asked him the question myself. Before Daniel had finished whatever he was saying, I looked at Noah and told him I was sorry.

Worry leaked across his face and his upper body became eerily still. Instead of putting down his own fork, he gripped it tight, his knuckles turning bone white. 'Sorry for what?'

'I haven't asked you about the book in weeks.'

He physically relaxed, his shoulders falling from his ears, and scooped up another mouthful. 'That's OK,' he said, kindly, 'you've had a lot on your mind.'

'Has work been very full-on, Cathy?' asked Griz, turning to look at me.

'Well, yes,' I said, letting my gaze fall to my plate, contemplating, if only for a second, 'and then there have been the injections.'

For a moment, nobody said anything. I kept my eyes on my plate, and the burnt basil leaf pressed like a flower on its outer edge.

'Cathy.'

I looked up at Noah, who was sitting opposite me. He was tired, I realised, the bags under his eyes unusually pronounced, as if they were ferrying something.

'What do you mean, "the injections"?' asked Griz.

'Oh, Cathy,' said Daniel, solemn, his lips curling upwards as he continued, 'I had a feeling those DAA meetings might have been in *vein* . . .'

He laughed at his own joke. Griz smiled. Noah didn't.

I craned my neck, and then I said it, out loud, for the first time, to people who weren't my husband or my mother or my doctor: 'Actually, I'm freezing my eggs.'

I heard the scrape of a chair leg, wood on wood. Noah had stuck small felt patches to the four feet of each chair to prevent them from scratching the floorboards, but I wasn't wholly convinced that they worked. The scrape had come from Daniel, who was sitting further back from the table now. He was wiping the corners of his mouth with his linen napkin, which he proceeded to fold up and put on his plate, even though there was sauce there and we still had the salad to come. I felt my fingers itch and held them securely together on my lap.

It was Griz who broke the silence, asking, tentatively, 'But only recently you were saying you didn't want children?' As if to double-check that she was correct in her understanding of the situation, she added: 'Both of you.'

I looked again at Noah, whose expression was blank. He caught my eye and gave a slight nod of the head that said, Over to you.

'Well, we,' I began, stumbling over the pronoun, 'I decided it would be sensible to have an option. You know, just in case we . . .' There it was again. This time I held firm. 'Just in case we change our minds.'

'Oh right, that makes sense,' said Griz, too quickly, sensing, I suspected, that this was a sticky subject, and thoughtfully trying to move the conversation along. But it was too sticky. More than sticky. Thorny, with the potential to draw blood. She was nodding at Daniel, who looked less certain.

'But you don't want kids now?' he asked.

Noah reached for the salad bowl and gave the leaves a toss, making sure they were all coated with the oily dressing, before tumbling some onto his plate. He passed the bowl to Griz, who thanked him, smiling, still overcompensating.

I gave her a small smile in return.

'Noah?' asked Daniel, looking at his brother. When he didn't reply, and Griz shook her head at him, he said that he was sorry, he just didn't understand.

'You and me both,' said Noah, stabbing some leaves with his fork and funnelling them into his mouth without cutting them first.

I felt my belly flop, and shook my head at the salad bowl, which Griz then passed straight to Daniel.

We carried on eating for a few minutes, then Noah stood up and started to clear our plates. Before he took mine, I picked up the burnt basil leaf and put it on my tongue. I kept it there for a few seconds, thankful for something else to focus on, before chewing it into nothing.

When he returned to the table with a couple of those fancy chocolate bars and some mixed berries in a white bowl with a scalloped edge, conversation gradually started up again. Not between me and Noah, though. That night, the only time he looked at me was after Daniel and Griz had left, when I asked if he still felt comfortable piercing my stomach. He didn't answer, but he did do it.

'Thank you,' I said, as, without a word, he stood up from the bathroom floor and started walking away. 'Noah, I'm sorry.'

He paused in the threshold, one hand on the doorway, and finally, without turning around, he spoke. 'I'm not sure where we go from here.'

The words swept the air out of my lungs.

He stayed where he was. 'It's impossible.'

That word, even more than the others . . . I gripped at the tiles with my fingertips. 'What is?'

'This. The situation. Our situation.'

'No,' I said, growing increasingly breathless. 'Please don't say that.'

'Why not?' He pressed his palms to the sides of his head, as if it was starting to ache. 'It's the truth, isn't it?'

Air. I needed air.

'This can only end one way, Cathy.' Still clutching his head, he asked, his voice cracking, 'Are you planning on leaving me?'

'No, Noah!'

He turned around and dropped his arms to his sides when he saw my face.

'No!'

He walked towards me, crouched down in front, and held onto my shoulders. 'Hang on, just breathe, Cathy.'

I did as he said.

'Slowly.'

I closed my eyes, and gradually, I started to feel better. When I opened them, I repeated myself: 'Please don't say that.'

August

There's a surrealist painting by the British-born Mexican artist Leonora Carrington that shows a giantess cradling an egg. Her feet are bare, her pale face moon-like and fringed with a golden mane. Geese flock around her while a hunting party of tiny men, women, children and dogs scurry past her toes. On and in the water are white-sailed ships and ghostly sea creatures. In the distance, mountains rise and rain lashes down from an overcast sky. The egg, a symbol of new life, is safe in her dainty hands. At least for now.

That was the image projected onto the inside of my shuttered eyelids as I sat on the bathroom tiles waiting for Noah to administer my trigger injection. I'd picked up the final pre-filled syringe from the clinic that afternoon and caught the Tube home with it clutched to my chest like a loaded gun. I tried to remember how I'd felt before the hormones, and I tried *not* to think about what it would be like to live with them for nine months. I considered that my eggs would soon be released, and that one of those eggs could one day become a baby. At least in theory.

'OK, are you ready?'

In my semi-delusional state, I decided to test that theory. I exchanged the image of the giantess cradling the egg for an image of me holding my baby. Me, alone, a single mum. Me, with Noah, a part of a team. I thought of my parents, and the fact that even though I'd always been closer with my mother, we were three.

'Cathy?'

'Sorry, yes, I'm ready.'

He pushed the needle into my side and pressed down on the plunger. When all the liquid was gone, he slipped it out.

In its place, I saw a single spot of blood.

'Here,' he said, handing me a piece of loo roll.

I thanked him and dabbed at my skin. It was the only time I'd bled.

Thirty-six hours later, I took the day off for the procedure, which meant being put to sleep while a needle perforated the wall of my vagina. The eggs would be harvested by draining the fluid in each follicle, which, during my last scan, Doctor Day had told me were looking 'mostly good and even'. That would happen in one ovary, then the other; the needle was attached to a scan probe that would enable him to see if he needed to move it up, down, left, right. If Noah had been there when Doctor Day was telling me this, he would have laughed and said something about it sounding a lot like a computer game. He wasn't.

He did message me, though, saying he was thinking of me. The night before, as I was removing my nail polish, Robyn had done the same and I'd remembered with a jolt of guilt that I hadn't wished her luck for her own procedure or checked in since. I thanked her and apologised and said

I would call her after. She told me not to worry and wished me luck in the form of a four-leaf clover emoji.

Doctor Day said the actual process would take no longer than fifteen minutes, but that I shouldn't expect to be back in my room for about an hour. Waiting to be wheeled down, I lay flat on my back, arms by my sides, rigid. I tried to ignore my rumbling stomach, which beneath my backless gown felt both empty – cheated out of that morning's breakfast – and the most bloated it had ever been. I poked at it, gently, with one fingernail, and imagined it flattening like a helium balloon, pricked with a needle. I shook my head and tried something different, cradling it in my palms, waiting to feel . . . something. I imagined it swelling, slowly at first, then quickly. Up above me, one of three strobe lights was flickering, on the blink. I bit my lip and told myself there were no such things as bad omens. An image of the whale spilled out of the surf at Scheveningen flashed before me.

Ten minutes later I was in theatre, and the anaesthetist who'd taken my blood pressure when I'd first arrived was talking me through what was about to happen. In my field of vision were white lights and scraps of blue fabric. The radio was sounding, a song I vaguely recognised. A cannula was eased into the back of my hand. I was instructed to count down from ten. There was a metallic taste on my tongue, and that's the last thing I remember.

When I woke, my jumble of emotions – anxiety, fear, longing – had been replaced with a dull ache. In the recovery room were three other women, with whom I exchanged a half-smile. I thought of Robyn and how it would have been nice to have seen a familiar face. Still, there was a sense that, although we were strangers, we were in this together. One woman looked significantly younger than the rest of us, her skin soft and dewy even in the garish hospital light, and I couldn't help but wonder if she was here because she was unwell. When a nurse came to wheel her away, she turned to us and made a joke about heading for the *eggsit*. I laughed, thinking it was the kind of thing Noah would say.

Half an hour later, I was back in my own room. Beneath the hospital bedsheet, I inched up my gown and peered down at my flesh. To my surprise, I still felt bloated. Again, I tested the skin with my fingers, then I reached over to the bedside table for my phone and typed into the search bar: *Is it possible to miss eggs during egg-retrieval?* I scrolled through the first of many forums, frowning at some comments and feeling my heart speed up at others. I told myself I would close the tab as I neared the end of each page and message Noah instead. I didn't.

Doctor Day interrupted my self-induced spiral to tell me how the procedure had gone and to give me my initial results. 'We've retrieved fourteen eggs.' I must have been grinning like an idiot because he promptly reminded me that they wouldn't all be mature. 'Still,' he said, the corners of his own lips curling upwards, 'you should be pleased.'

After eating a slightly soggy cheese-and-pickle sandwich and proving to the nurse that I was able to go to the loo, I was allowed to head home. Noah had said he would collect me, but when I called him, it turned out there was a last-minute lecture he couldn't miss.

'You can't sneak out early?' I asked, pressing my phone to one cheek and the palm of my free hand to the other in an effort to prevent my voice from wobbling.

'I'm sorry, Cathy, I'm the one giving the lecture.'

If he was giving it, had he also arranged it? I felt a curdling in my stomach, a sour mix of disappointment and resentment.

'I'm sorry,' he said, again.

I accepted that he really did sound it, and when he swore under his breath, I knew that he too was frustrated. 'Maybe Anna can help?' he offered.

The thought made my throat pinch. 'Don't worry,' I said again, doing my best impression of a smile. 'I'll think of something.'

When I said being collected wasn't even mandatory, that some people head home by themselves on the bus or the Tube, he made me promise to find someone, anyone.

'OK,' I said, smiling for real now.

'And message me when you're home? I'll be back as soon as I can.'

'I will. Bye.'

Before he hung up, I heard a sigh that made me think of the sea.

I considered my options, then I called Anna. I had to tell her at some point, and this was the nudge I needed.

She answered after the first ring, which caught me off guard. I thought I would have longer to recite in my head the information I intended to share with her. She was saying something about the fact that she'd been messaging me. 'Where are you?' she asked, a tad sulkily. 'Why haven't you been getting back to me?'

I waited until I couldn't wait any longer, the hiatus stretched tracing-paper thin, then I mentioned the clinic.

She remained quiet. I heard her lips part before pressing together again. Eventually she asked why.

'I'm freezing my eggs.'

'You're what?'

'I'll explain. Please, Anna, can you come?'

She was pissed off that I'd kept something from her, I could tell from the sound of her voice, which was even more brisk than usual, and only forming short words and sentences. I couldn't blame her – I would have been pissed off too. We were each other's confidantes; we had been since school. She'd told me when she'd overheard her dad yelling at her mum about another man, how her mum had cried and begged as her dad had walked out the door; he hadn't come back that night, but the following morning he'd been there at the kitchen table, the pair of them eating breakfast like nothing had gone on. She'd told me when she'd said to her first boyfriend that she didn't want to touch him, and he'd taken hold of her hand and shoved it down below his waistband – neither of us knew at the age of thirteen what we know now. Even after she'd suggested that Noah and I get together, and he'd asked me on a date, I wouldn't give him an answer until I'd spoken to her again, recounting what he'd said, word for word, making doubly sure she was all right with it.

Forty minutes later, she was walking towards me, with a squashy handbag slung over her shoulder and a firm expression on her face. She put the handbag down on the small table at the foot of my bed. Unhooked her sunglasses from the V of her shirt and slid them into the bag's side pocket. Eventually, she lifted her gaze to meet mine. I don't know what she saw, but there was no more frostiness.

'Oh Cathy.' She walked towards me and went to give me a hug. 'Wait, is this OK?'

I smiled a small smile and opened my arms wide.

Her shirt was the kind of silky that probably had to be handwashed. Her hair smelled of shampoo, citrusy and fresh. When she let go, I saw that she was wearing a sticky paper name badge printed with a red balloon that announced she was 'Anna – Theo's mum'.

She must have noticed me staring at it because she promptly picked it off and screwed it up into a ball. She tossed her head back as she explained she'd been at some god-awful children's party – her words, not mine.

'Anna, I'm sorry,' I said, my eyes unexpectedly filling with tears.

'Oh, don't be,' she replied, waving away my apology and looking taken aback. 'You saved me. And Theo's still there – my friend Maddie, whose daughter's there too, said she'd take him – so that's a few hours of free childcare.'

I gave a half-hearted laugh and scraped my hair back from my face. 'I'm sorry about everything, Anna, not just today.' I paused. 'I wanted to tell you.'

'But?' She was still looking at me kindly, but her eyebrows had become knitted. As she waited for me to answer, one tooth started testing her bottom lip.

I closed my eyes, hoping that when I reopened them, the tears I could feel brimming would be less threatening. I was wrong, and as I told her that I was embarrassed, that I didn't know how to explain it because it didn't really make sense, even to me, they started to fall.

She took my hands in hers and looked at me. 'You have nothing to be embarrassed about,' she said. 'I'm proud of you, for taking control, for following it through.'

A nurse joined us then. Clocking my damp cheeks, she told me not to worry. Turning to Anna, she added, with a sympathetic head tilt, 'Her hormones will be all over the place for the next few days.'

Anna smiled, self-assured, and asked if she could take me home.

'I should think so,' replied the nurse, checking the clipboard at the end of my bed, then her watch. 'Yes, it's been long enough, and I see you've eaten your lunch,' she said, her eyes skipping towards the plate on the bedside table, clean except for a few crumbs. 'You're good to go.'

Anna went to make a phone call while I pulled on that morning's clothes. I was tying my laces, which I still did in the childlike way my mother had first taught me, when she came in and told me a taxi would be here in three minutes.

I felt something like comfort as I buckled myself in and rested my head against the leather seat. As we rolled over London Bridge, the Thames was glinting in the sun, its surface pixelated.

When we reached the other side, Anna turned to me and cautiously asked what all this meant for me and Noah. She knew as well as I did that he still had no desire to be a father. 'Cathy, are you leaving him?'

My thoughts turned to my mother and whether she really had forgotten saying the same thing, except hers was framed as a piece of advice rather than a question. Peggy had been sending me regular updates since she'd found the diary in the freezer, and as far as she was concerned my mother really had just been having a bad day. In my head, I'd heard that same word, the one I hadn't yet dared to say aloud. I'd told her I wasn't so sure it was an isolated incident, that there were other things my mother had said and done, other slip-ups. She'd promised to continue to keep a close eye on her.

'Cathy?'

My heart flickered inside my chest. When I tried to imagine my life without Noah, I felt hot and faint, as if I hadn't eaten. I kept looking out of the window and, again, I tried not to cry and failed, just like I tried to ignore the cramps and the pad stuck to the crotch of my pants.

Anna made me a cup of tea and sat with me until Noah got home. Gradually, the sedative wore off and my stomach, though still tender, began to feel closer to its usual self. After being bloated for so long, the change should have been welcome. Instead, I felt like my insides had been harvested. Lying on the sofa that afternoon, I couldn't shake the sense that I'd been stripped bare.

'I know you don't want to talk about it,' said Anna, blowing at her tea, 'but how has Noah taken it?'

I started stroking Tom, who was curled up beside me and promptly began to purr. When I'd told Noah that animals could sense when humans needed comforting, he'd said that he could say the same thing about me – that I always seemed to know when something was bothering him. It was, he'd said, one of his favourite things about me.

'Cathy?'

I kept stroking as I started talking. 'He didn't want me to do it, not really, but he also didn't want to stop me. He helped with the injections, even though he said he wasn't going to be involved. He was supposed to pick me up today, but . . .' I was avoiding eye contact, keeping my gaze fixed on the way Tom's black fur bled into white fur on his belly and feet. I took a gentle hold of one of his tiny paws, which, underneath, were marbled with black and pink.

'But what does this mean for you two as a couple?' she asked.

As Tom stretched out all four legs and I started to scratch his back, the purring got louder. 'I don't know,' I said, raising my voice over the hum. 'I suppose we wait.'

'Until you decide you can't wait any longer?'

'That might never happen.'

'And if it does?'

The sound of my phone vibrating on the table saved me from having to answer.

The results and Noah arrived at exactly the same time.

'Hi, how are you—'

I turned around and Noah saw that I was on the phone. He mouthed an apology, then went to hug Anna hello.

'Ten eggs fit for freezing,' said Doctor Day, with a lilt that told me there was hope.

I wasn't sure how to respond, other than to thank him. I half listened as he talked me through the next steps, while also half listening to Noah and Anna's hushed voices – because I was on the phone or because they didn't want me to hear? I turned my back on them and dug my nails into the palm of my hand, telling myself to get a grip.

'All good?' asked Doctor Day.

'All good,' I repeated. 'Thank you again.'

As I hung up, their hushed voices broke off. I returned my phone to the table, and Anna reached for her bag.

'You don't have to go,' I said, refilling the kettle as if to tempt her with more tea. 'Stay.'

'I would, but I can't,' she said, reaching around inside her bag for her own phone and checking her messages. 'Maddie will be leaving soon, and I don't want to be judged by the other mums . . .'

Other mums. It was like the words sucked all the air out of the room in one quick sweep.

She clamped her lips together to prevent any other comments about the club called motherhood from spilling out.

The three of us stood there, not talking, then Noah walked towards her and gave her another hug. 'Thanks for coming to the rescue.'

Later, I would blame what I said next on the hormones: 'Yes, it's good to know I have someone I can depend on.'

'Cathy.' As he said it, his eyebrows bent into a frown.

I realised it wasn't Noah I was frustrated with, not really. 'I'm sorry,' I said, first to him and then to her. 'Thanks for being here, Anna.'

She smiled. 'Always.'

After she'd left, the flat felt smaller somehow. I walked towards the window and watched her look both ways before crossing the road and continuing around the corner to the overground. It was still light out, the sun filtering through faint clouds. Come evening, people would be strewn across London Fields, sitting on summer jackets and picnic rugs, sipping from cans.

'So,' said Noah, 'how did it go?'

'It went well,' I said, turning around and leaning back against the radiator, which always lost a lot of its heat to the window above during winter. 'The doctor thinks we have a good chance.'

Noah didn't react to my use of the word 'we', and I pretended I hadn't planted it there just to see if he would. Instead, he suggested we have a drink: 'Negroni?' His favourite.

The kettle, which I'd filled to the rim, had finally boiled.

'Yes, let's.'

He grabbed an orange from the fruit bowl while I opened the freezer in search of ice. As I pulled at each drawer, I couldn't help picturing my eggs, three to a straw, in a tank along with thousands of others. Frozen, glass-like, in a storage room with no natural light. I wondered if the tanks were locked up and clearly labelled. What if there was a mix-up? Goosebumps pricked up on my forearms, and Noah must have noticed. At last, he hugged me too, just once, but we stayed that way for some time, our bodies pressed together, moving without music.

I experienced a shift inside me after my abortion. Wherever I was, whatever I was doing, I felt the scratch of anxiety, a tiny coil enmeshed in my skin. I knew I'd done the right thing – I wasn't in any doubt – but at the same time I couldn't shake the sense that I'd knowingly destroyed a part of me. At night I would lie in bed, the sheets soaking up my cold sweats. When I passed a pregnant woman on the street, I would squeeze my eyes shut. Just occasionally I would catch myself believing that I, too, was still pregnant. My mind was clouded with melancholy like a glass of water swirled up with ink. At some point, I suppose, the clouds cleared.

It was the same after the egg collection, which I hadn't anticipated. The feeling of emptiness that I'd experienced once I'd left the recovery room stayed with me until I began to worry that, once again, I was missing something – a vital organ maybe. Things with Noah returned to normal, or at least as normal as could be expected. We slipped back into our old routine, pre-injections. And yet, there was a palpable distance between us. When we were eating dinner or watching TV, when we were lying side by side in bed, his elbow brushing against mine, even when we were showering – I felt it. I assume he did too, but I couldn't bring myself to ask in case it tipped our precariously maintained balance and one or both of us toppled over the edge. I watched us tread carefully, as if our marriage were built on foundations as fragile as eggshells.

Instead, belatedly, I phoned Robyn.

'Hey! How are you?' Just after she asked the question, a siren sounded at her end.

I waited until the screeching had died down before I replied. 'Phew, that was loud!'

'Just walking to the office,' she said. I could hear her footsteps on the pavement. 'So, how did it go?'

'It went . . . well,' I replied, wondering what the etiquette was when it came to sharing the number of eggs retrieved, and experiencing flashbacks to getting exam results at school. I decided to keep it vague: 'Doctor Day was pleased.'

She laughed. 'And you?'

I tried to laugh too, though it came out as more of a gurgle, the kind you make when your mouth is full of toothpaste. 'I'm still trying to figure that out.'

'Did the counselling session help?'

I exhaled.

'You forgot?'

'I did.'

'Well, it's not too late.' When I didn't respond, she added: 'Like I said, I would recommend it.'

'OK, I'll book an appointment later today.' As I said it, I thought of the wavering balance between me and Noah and felt nauseous. 'Anyway, what about you?' I asked, trying to sound positive. 'How did yours go?'

The few seconds it took her to answer gave me a clue. When she spoke again, her voice sounded softer. 'Mine didn't go so well actually.'

I felt my cheeks flush as I scrambled around for the right words. In the end I told her, unhelpfully, that I was sorry. 'Sorry to hear that, I mean.'

'That's OK,' she said, audibly pulling herself together.

'And for, well, you know . . .'

'What?'

I screwed up my face as I said, 'It should be the other way around.'

'Cathy, don't be crazy.'

'Am I? Being crazy?'

'Yes. You are.' I could no longer hear footsteps. She must have stopped walking. 'Being uncertain doesn't mean you deserve less of a chance.'

'I'm not so sure.'

I could almost hear the forced smile, see the fatalistic shrug, as she said, 'It's just one of those things.'

'What are you going to do now?'

'I'm going to try to save up and do another round if I can.'

Technically, if I'd wanted to make use of the free counselling session, I should have done so pre-egg retrieval – so the receptionist told me over the phone, matter of fact, when I followed Robyn's advice and said I wanted to cash it in. When my voice cracked with uncertainty, she didn't budge, but a few minutes later – to my embarrassment, yes, but also relief – my tears got me somewhere. She interrupted my list of reasons as to why I hadn't taken them up on it before to ask when I was available. Before I had time to respond, she said there was a gap the next day, mid-afternoon. I thanked her and said I would take it, jotting down the name and address of a practice in west London.

I caught a couple of buses from the flat to Notting Hill. On the second, I phoned Peggy.

Still, she said everything was fine and good. 'Actually, there is one thing – though I'm not sure whether it's worth mentioning.'

'Go on.'

'It happened earlier. There was a coffee morning at the village hall, and when your mum went to put some change in the charity pot, her purse was empty.'

'Completely?'

'No cash, no cards, nothing.'

'Did she say why?'

'Something about switching purses.'

'Right.'

For a moment, neither of us said anything.

Then: 'Peggy, I'm going to come home at the end of the month and take her for a check-up. In the meantime, please can you—'

'I will.'

'Thank you. And Peggy, one more thing.' I paused, conscious of what the question I was about to ask represented. 'Do you think she's fit to drive?'

'You want to try stopping her?'

I closed my eyes, and when I did, I saw my mother's frowning face, indignant.

After a ten-minute walk the other end, I arrived at a red-brick building with a small white sign that told me I was in the right place. I tried to get a glimpse through the sash windows, but slatted white blinds blocked my view.

The front door was pigeon grey with a brass number nailed to its middle. When pushing it didn't work, I tried pulling. Eventually, I gave up and rang the bell. There was a buzz and the door clicked open.

Inside, the air was faintly infused with the smell of flowers that needed to be tossed. Around to the right, a welcome desk. Jostling for space in a slender glass vase was a bunch of sunflowers, their downy stems slimy in murky water, their petals curling back on themselves like neglected cuticles. I glanced around at the rest of the waiting room, which was very white and very clean, and decided the flowers must have got a free pass because of their sunny disposition.

'Cathy?' inquired a bespectacled boy, angling his neck until his oval face emerged from behind a bulky desktop.

'Hello, yes.'

'Great, Jos will be with you in a couple of minutes. Would you like to take a seat?' As he asked the question, he nodded towards a single row of empty chairs, also white.

I was leafing through an interiors magazine, barely pausing on each page before flicking to the next, when Jos appeared in the threshold. She had bobbed hair, which she'd let go naturally grey, and bow lips that curved as she greeted me. My legs felt a little wobbly as I came to standing.

'Cathy, lovely to meet you.' She held out a hand with painted nails the shade of marmalade.

'You too,' I said, pointing them out to her as if she might not have noticed them herself. 'I like the colour.'

'Thank you,' she replied, smiling. 'I do, too.'

I followed her up a single flight of stairs, willing the wobbliness to cease, and into her office, which was small and tidy and smelled – more appealingly – of freshly brewed coffee.

'Fancy a cup?' she asked, pointing to a half-filled cafetière on a wooden side table and reaching for a second mug. Her own was on a felt coaster by her computer, steam rising from the dark liquid.

'Please,' I nodded, sitting down as she gestured towards a chair opposite hers.

Her own blinds were pulled to one side and the windows were thrown open, the room absorbing the bustle of the street below. She poured the coffee to a background beat of passing cars and muddled conversation. She was wearing a beaded necklace that swung away from her chest as she leant forward. The beads were small and brown like lentils.

'Milk? Sugar?'

'Milk, please.'

I reached into my bag for my cardigan, then decided, one arm hooked in one sleeve, that I wasn't cold after all, and bundled it back up again. I touched a finger to my lips, which were chapped, and reached back into my bag for some lip salve before realising I didn't have any with me. I breathed in and out.

As she handed me my coffee, she smiled kindly, lines ticking up at the outer corners of her eyes. 'It's OK to be nervous, Cathy.'

'Thanks,' I said, cupping the mug in both hands, grateful to be able to hold onto something solid. Robyn was right – Jos was nice.

'So,' she said, settling into position, 'I understand you've just frozen your eggs?' As she asked the question, she glanced at a small, cubed clock, the kind you might keep by a bed. The session had started.

'I have, just last week.'

'And how are you feeling?'

A ball formed from nothing in my throat. I took a sip of coffee, and when that failed to dislodge it, I took another. I smiled apologetically and tried clearing my throat. My voice broke as I uttered two syllables: 'OK.'

She rested her coffee back down beside her computer and clasped her hands together in her lap, her marmalade nails complementing her navy-blue trousers. 'You know, it's OK not to be.'

A tear had made it halfway down my cheek before I realised I was crying without sound. 'Sorry,' I said, instinctively, raising my eyebrows at myself as I wiped it away with my fingers. 'It's probably the hormones, or what's left of them.'

Again, she smiled. 'Probably.' She passed me a box of tissues, ready and waiting within arm's reach, then asked me to tell her a bit about myself. 'Life, work, family, friends – anything.' She paused. 'I notice you're fiddling with your wedding ring.'

I peered down at my fingers, interlinked around my mug. I told her the first thing I tell most people – that I work in conservation, that it's my job to preserve centuries-old paintings for future generations. As I said it, I wondered when my work had become such an important part of my identity, and if that was a good or a bad thing. I told her about Noah – I even shared our private joke about me slowing down his inevitable ageing process, which made her laugh – and the life we'd built together in London. I talked about my mother and Norfolk, how we were close but no longer saw each other as much as I would like. I mentioned the weekend away, the diary, the purse. Without saying the word, the one that was beginning to haunt me, I hinted at what I was afraid it all meant.

When I was done, she asked: 'And why did you decide to freeze your eggs?'

I took a breath and said the four words I'd been twirling around since I first set foot in her office: 'Noah doesn't want children.' I parted my lips to say 'at least not right now' then changed my mind and pressed them together.

'And you?'

'I used to think I didn't want them either – a part of me still thinks that. But another part – now I'm not so sure, maybe, one day?'

She either didn't notice the rising note at the end of my sentence, turning it into a question, a question I was hoping she might answer, or she chose to ignore it. Either way, she responded with a question of her own: 'And your mother?'

I felt my brow furrow. 'What about my mother?'

'Do you think the change in that dynamic has affected your feelings towards having children?'

I could feel a headache coming on and realised I was frowning. I blinked. 'I don't know, maybe?'

She kept quiet.

I should have realised by now that it wasn't her job to answer my questions. 'I miss her when I'm not with her,' I said, pushing out a small laugh as I added, 'I probably shouldn't at my age.'

'Why do you say that?'

'Oh, you know.'

After a pause, she asked, 'And do you think that might be making you crave motherhood yourself?'

I let out a long audible breath. 'You think that – is that what you're saying?'

'I'm not saying anything,' she said, her hands still comfortably clasped in her lap, 'I'm just asking the question.' When I didn't respond, she asked another. 'So, what now?'

'Now? Now I don't know what to do,' I said, the words spilling out all of a sudden, unchecked. 'I assumed that doing this would make me feel better, like I had an option,' I added, cringing at my frequent use of that word, and the privilege tangled up with it. 'Instead, I feel even more stuck.'

Again, she kept quiet, listening.

'Now I have all these frozen eggs, and I feel so lucky and grateful, I do.' I paused, blinking back more tears as I thought of Robyn and the second round she was prepared to go through, the emotional, physical and financial toll. 'But I also feel like they'll only ever be that – frozen.'

She waited for me to continue, and when I didn't, she started talking. Her voice was slow and steady, the kind that would be well suited to those podcasts that are supposed to help you sleep. 'What you've done here *is* give yourself an option, Cathy – that's exactly what it is.'

'Then why do I feel like this?'

This question she did answer: 'Well, what follows an option is generally a decision.'

'But when?' I asked, hungry for more advice, to be told what to do. 'How do I know which is the right choice?'

In the same slow and steady voice, she said, 'There's no right or wrong here. It's just deciding.'

In the days that followed, I found myself craving Noah. Things between us continued as normal, but I couldn't shake the sense that we were existing within a clear, fragile bubble. When we were in the flat, I felt myself following him, keeping physically close to wherever he stood or sat, my body shadowing his. When I was at work, my thoughts strayed to him. Whenever I tried to steer them away, they would turn to my mother, and in anticipation of my upcoming visit, my heart would begin to race.

By this time, the whale was fully realised, slumped on the beach, and I'd turned my attention to the overpaint shrouding the sand and the rest of the sea. I'd always been passionate about my work, but Frank said he'd never seen me so animated – a coping mechanism, maybe. As I unearthed the coloured pebbles in the foreground, they assumed a newfound clarity. A similar thing happened with the old wooden fence, which Hendrick had carefully incised. When I removed a thick layer of ochre from the shoreline, it seemed softer somehow and more receded. Like the whale, most elements were in good condition, but every now and then I uncovered small losses and abrasions. In restoring the work to its original condition, I discovered cracks – deeper issues that would have to be addressed before we were able to move forward.

It appeared that Hendrick had devoted more time and energy to the painting than we'd initially assumed. These Dutch maritime scenes tended to be made quickly and with very few changes, but he'd tweaked and trimmed the composition as he went along. Beneath patches of overpaint were pentimenti, visible traces of earlier figures and forms that he himself had added and then painted out. They resurfaced as I worked, and Frank confirmed their presence with infrared reflectography.

There had once been a carriage, or a cart, which explained the parallel tracks disappearing into nothing in the sand;

as well as bad omens, beached whales brought with them a bounty of oils, fats and meat that would be extracted and barrelled away, the blubber boiled down. More figures appeared among the crowd, gathered as if at a market or a fair. The whale itself had originally been depicted on its side, long and thin, its mouth ajar; in the final version, it was upright and firm, with that weirdly prominent fin. The shoreline around the whale had also been repainted. Hendrick no doubt had trouble getting right a subject he was unfamiliar with.

Ghosts of the past, these shadow-like stains taunted me as I worked. In them, I saw my own past, present and future, my mother, Noah, and our unborn child. Every day, I would return home happy with the progress I'd made, but at the same time shaken.

One evening, after an early dinner, Noah suggested we go for a walk along the canal. It was still warm, without even a hint of a breeze, the sun winking at us as it dipped down and then reappeared in the vertical gaps between buildings. He was wearing shorts – a sight that always made me imagine him as a young boy, tearing around a playground – and I'd purposefully put on a striped sundress he liked. That was another thing I appreciated about him from the start, the way he showed an interest in my appearance.

'When are you going to start running again?' he asked, as a woman dashed past us, tinny music leaching out from the small buds poked into her ears.

'I haven't really thought about it,' I replied, which, to my surprise, was true. When Doctor Day had first told me to avoid doing any aerobic exercise during the injections, I'd told him I wasn't sure I could. My morning routine was about more than keeping fit; it was a way for me to recharge, clear my head. Now that I did think about it, I wondered whether my lack of movement might have been at least partially responsible for my inner restlessness.

'Well, it might help,' said Noah, as if he were reading my mind.

'Remember the time I took you running with me?' I asked, a smile tugging at my lips.

'I do.' The tone of his voice told me he was trying not to smile, too.

'You were excellent,' I said, 'really.'

'Yes, all right.' He laughed and reached for my hand, which fitted snugly in his, like a perfectly sized shoe.

We continued walking like that for a while, hand in hand, looking left at the still water and the lined-up house-boats named after beloved wives, mothers, daughters. Our own quiet was pierced at various intervals by happy people drinking by the water's edge, their bare legs dangling over the side of the stone, and the squeals of children not yet back at school after the summer holidays.

'Cathy.'

The first time he said my name, I tried to ignore it. Something in his tone had shifted. I kept walking, kept squeezing his hand tight in mine.

'Cathy.'

When I couldn't ignore it any more, I stopped. The sun caught in my eyes as I turned and gazed up at him, and I looked away like I'd been blinded. He moved a little to the left, providing me with shade, and I gazed up at him again. That's when I saw it. All this time I'd been thinking of him, staying close to him, but I don't think I'd really *seen* him since he'd given me the trigger injection. Now, as I did, I noticed the red in his eyes, the strained look on his cheeks.

'I've accepted an exchange for next term.'

'What?' I heard him.

'I'm teaching the next term in New York.'

I took a breath and said, 'That's wonderful.' I think I meant it. 'The whole term?'

'We talked about it when I got the promotion, remember?'

I nodded. I'd forgotten, but now it came back to me.

'Well, I have book research to do there, too, some archival diplomatic texts, so it seems like a good opportunity.' He paused to brush a strand of hair away from my face. 'And some space might be good for us, give us both time to think.'

'You didn't tell me you had book research to do there.' That wasn't the problem and both of us knew it. He might have been holding back, but so had I.

'I'll be home in just a couple of months.'

Just.

'Cathy?'

'But I need you here now,' I said, feeling the sting of tears, a sensation that was becoming all too familiar. 'I'm still trying to figure things out, what I want, what I need.'

He smiled, but it was the kind of smile that didn't reach his eyes. 'For that, you don't need me here.'

He booked a flight for the end of the month, which coincided with the weekend I'd planned to visit my mother. Though I longed for us to make more time for each other in the days leading up to it, I said nothing, for fear of making his going away into a bigger deal than it already was. The night before, we went out for dinner, to one of the less fashionable pubs in the area that we'd always liked for precisely that reason. We hadn't thought to book, and it was busy; a waitress I didn't recognise asked if we would mind sitting at the bar. The menu had changed, which threw me more than it should have. Still, we smiled and clinked glasses.

We walked back to the flat in silence, and when we closed the door behind us the lack of sound became more noticeable. After a few minutes, Noah held my hands in his and said he was going upstairs to pack. I was clinging on, trying to find the words that might make him stay, while at the same time not wanting to hold him back, when my phone rang.

I saw Peggy's name flash up on my screen and felt a jab of guilt. The past week had been such a blur that I'd barely spoken to my mother, despite asking Peggy to keep me updated. We'd exchanged the odd email and a handful of texts, but that was it. The egg freezing had taken up all my head space. And now Noah. Now this.

'Go ahead, answer it,' he said. I screwed up my eyes and he reassured me he wasn't going anywhere just yet. As if to prove it, he pulled up a chair.

I did as he said. 'Peggy, hi, how are you?' I asked, trying to sound chipper, preparing for her to tell me it wasn't good enough, that I needed to put in more effort.

'Cathy, I'm sorry to call you out of the blue.'

'That's OK. You can call me anytime, you know that.' When she didn't respond, I asked, 'Is everything all right?'

'I'm afraid it's not good news.'

The jab morphed into something stronger – a gash, bone-deep.

'Don't panic, she's OK.'

Noah looked at me, tilting his head in question.

My mind was running away with me. I walked towards the window. I needed air. 'What then?'

'I think you're right, that it's time we take Janey to see a doctor.'

'What's happened?' I lodged the phone between my cheek and shoulder and tried to open the window. When I couldn't make it budge, Noah took over. 'Peggy?'

I could hear her breathing at the other end of the line.

I looked across at the flats opposite. One woman was reading. Two children were playing, peeping out from behind a blind. A man was standing at a sink doing the dishes. 'It's got worse?'

More breathing, and then: 'Yesterday she couldn't figure out how to turn on the television.'

I rested my elbows on the windowsill and, like a child, fished around for an explanation that would make everything OK, that would erase the word that had presented itself to me first as a whisper. Now, it was like someone was screaming it in my ear. Or was it me screaming it inside my head? Desperately, hopelessly, I tried to fight it.

'Maybe it was on the blink?'

Dementia.

'I know it sounds silly, but I've had trouble with that TV before.'

Dementia.

'Maybe—'

'Cathy, today she drove to the farm shop, and I got a call from the owner.'

I looked to the right and noticed the old lady who was never not lying in bed. A bed topped with a patchwork quilt, pushed up against the window to give her a nice view of the street.

'Cathy?'

'Why?'

'He was concerned.'

'*Why?*'

'Because for a moment she couldn't remember where she lived.'

September

My mother talked to me about rising sea levels long before news reporters began to write about them in earnest. Often the conversation would come up as she was tending to the garden, which in summer she would do from under the wide brim of a straw hat that cast half her face in crisp shadow. I would squint with concentration, and then, struggling to keep up, watch the way the shadow slipped up and over her nose, across the moving gap between her lips, down towards her rounded chin. She would say that nature gives and takes, and that it deserves respect like any other living being. As she said it, she would be pruning, trimming, deadheading.

Based on the same low-lying stretch of Norfolk where I grew up are several people I know who refuse to believe that their coastline is slowly being returned to the waves. They read articles about homes and roads and fields at risk of rising sea levels and soft eroding shores, shrug and think how lucky they are, every morning, when they open their curtains to a calm blue expanse.

My mother had never been one of those people. She loved our family home because it reminded her of her marriage, my father, me. But she knew all along that it was under threat. From nature and from human beings. It was her memories she cherished, not material things. And she accepted that, in time, they too could wear away.

The sky was a hazy blue, hovering somewhere between night and day, when I caught the overground from London Fields to Liverpool Street. From my seat, I glanced around at the early-morning commuters and noticed that there were more uniforms at this hour than when I usually took the Tube a little while later, around nine-thirty. There were a handful of construction men in hi-vis. A couple of suits, top buttons not yet done up beneath hastily wound ties. Opposite, a young woman in hospital scrubs, a wash of blue. Her eyes closed and her body still, except for her fingers, worrying at a scab on the back of one hand. Beneath her eyes, puffy bags; the crease of a pillow imprinted on one pale cheek.

The night before, after I'd hung up and relayed to Noah what Peggy had told me, he'd offered to stay. He said this changed things, that my mother's health was more important than any teaching post; he could call the university and explain that there had been a family emergency. I flinched: my mother's health was more important than any teaching post, but I wasn't? He walked towards me, and I tried not to stiffen as he held me. He was still holding me when I told him that I would be fine and, besides, it wasn't like him to leave his students in the lurch. Slowly, one finger at a time, I loosened my grip and told him to go; really, I said, there was no need for him to worry. When he didn't argue, something crunched inside my chest, like treading on broken glass.

The carriages charged into the station. Checking I had both my bags, I got off and made my way towards the national rail service. After buying my ticket I still had a few minutes to spare, so I picked up a milky coffee and a croissant, hoping some food would settle my flighty stomach. I didn't know what to expect when I arrived at the other end, but that hadn't stopped me from staying awake for most of the night, trying to guess. I felt the kind of tired that usually comes with being hungover; that, or being a new parent.

On the quiet outbound train, I let the weight of my head tip back against the seat. I thought about the past year, the times I'd seen and spoken to my mother, and the things she'd forgotten. The Noah comment. Anna's miscarriage, now I came to think about it. My birthday even. There were more things, little things – mishaps that, if only for a moment, had made me stop and think. Her repeating herself. Dressing differently. Burning her ginger biscuits. I sipped my coffee and again went over the things she'd said and done, and the times I should have reacted and sought help. The signals had been there. How had I not seen them? My thoughts turned to the beached whale, another warning sign, hidden in plain sight.

When my heart started to skip, and not in a good way, I turned to the window and watched the cityscape switch to countryside. Glass and metal were replaced with trees and fields. I realised I hadn't yet touched my croissant and told myself that must be it – I was always hyper-sensitive to caffeine on an empty stomach. I rolled down the paper bag and started nibbling, flakes of pastry falling like dead leaves onto my lap. Then I closed my eyes and waited for my heart to steady itself.

Peggy offered to pick me up from the station, but I told her I would take a taxi. She understood in an instant what I meant to say, or rather ask, and assured me that she would stay with my mother until I arrived. She also offered to make an appointment with the doctor, but I said I would do that myself; if possible, I wanted to talk it through with my mother first rather than spring it on her unannounced. I considered emailing my uncle Duncan, then decided against it; there was no use in worrying him until we knew exactly what we were dealing with. I said a similar thing to Noah when he suggested I call Anna and let her know what was going on – that, right now, there was no need.

'You from around here, love?'

I'd hoped that staring down at my phone would save me from having to make conversation with the driver, but he was having none of it. I looked up to find his oval eyes flitting between the wheel and the overhead mirror, his irises dark and round like raisins behind thick-rimmed glasses. He had an equally thick Norfolk accent.

'I'm visiting my mother,' I told him, returning my own eyes to my screen, and hoping that would be it for our interaction.

'Ah and where do you live then? The big smoke?'

'I do.'

Thankfully it was only a short drive and he spent most of it talking, his head, which was bald and as shiny as a freshly polished apple, bobbing up and down enthusiastically. All that was required of me was the occasional nod of agreement. When we arrived, though, and he carried my bags from the boot of the car to the front door, and refused to accept a tip, I felt my face redden with embarrassment.

'Thank you,' I said, trying to make up for the coldness, 'that's really kind.'

He gave me a sad smile, lips locked, and told me, 'You look after yourself now.'

Before opening the door, I fished a pocket mirror out of my handbag and held it up to my face. There, sprouting from my lower lids like weeds, were two or three faint streaks of mascara. I thought back to my journey and wondered when I'd cried, then I licked my finger pad and wiped away the greyish black from my cheeks.

She was watching TV when, eventually, I pushed open the door and called out a 'hello'. I heard the mumble of voices coming from the living room, where I found her sitting upright in her favourite armchair, eyes fixed on the screen.

'Hello, Mum,' I said, smiling uncertainly.

'Darling!' She sprang to her feet and came to give me a kiss. 'What are you doing here?'

'Oh, you know, I just thought I would come and visit, see how you are.' I paused, scanning her for some sign of erosion, a physical manifestation in the form of an inside-out top or mismatched shoes. Finding none, I extended my smile and asked, 'How are you?'

'Very well, thank you.'

We stood there for a moment, her hand resting on my arm, then she returned to her armchair and carried on watching. 'Here, come and sit down. Have you seen this one?'

I glanced at the gameshow and told her I hadn't. 'How about I make us some tea. Do you fancy a cup, Mum?'

'Yes, lovely.'

In the kitchen, Peggy was already boiling the kettle. As she'd reminded me on the phone, she was three years older than my mother, her hair a whiter shade of grey, her step less springy. She was taller too, with a slight hunch that I'd always suspected she picked up in her youth, when other girls hadn't yet experienced growth spurts and she wanted to take up less space. As the kettle clicked and steam spurted from its spout, she looked up and caught sight of me lingering by the door.

'I thought I heard you come in,' she said, smiling, pouring the boiling water from kettle to pot. 'How are you?'

Such a simple question, and yet, I struggled to formulate an answer with either thoughts or words.

She returned the kettle to its stand and enveloped me in her arms. 'Here, take a seat,' she said, gesturing towards the kitchen table. 'You've said hello then?'

'I have. She seems OK?' I hadn't intended for it to come out as a question. 'Apart from the daytime TV. Is that new?'

'Fairly, but she's had a good morning.' She raised a hand as if she was about to say more, then she lowered it again.

'Is there something else, Peggy?'

She lifted the lid of the teapot and peered in at its contents, then muttered something about giving it another minute. She looked up at me and told me that last night, my mother had suggested a game of Bridge. 'She wanted to deal, which she did very well.' Peggy smiled and shook her head with disbelief. 'You know how quick she is with cards?'

I nodded; I did. 'What happened?'

'Well, after she'd dealt us each a hand, she couldn't remember how to play.'

I was glad I was sitting. 'How did she react?'

'She was upset,' said Peggy, giving up on waiting any longer and pouring the weak tea into three mugs. 'You know how she laughs it off sometimes, or tries to come up with an excuse?'

With a wince, I thought of her blaming the fact that she'd forgotten what she'd said about Noah on having too much to drink. 'Yes?'

'Well, this time she didn't. I could tell, just from looking at her, that she was worried. After that, she wanted to go to bed. I didn't want to stop her, or press the issue, so . . .' She trailed off and added three splashes of milk.

'And this morning?'

'What?'

'Has she mentioned it?'

'It's like it never happened.' She picked up a teaspoon and started stirring, the watery liquid turning pale.

When Peggy went home, I suggested to my mother that we go for a walk on the beach. I'd always found it easier to talk to her in motion. That way, if the conversation became stilted, we could simply walk, free from eye contact, looking out at the sand and the sea.

That day, I found myself sneaking glances at her as we walked, searching for clues, something in her appearance that would tell me what she was thinking. There was a breeze, but the sun was shining, and we were plenty warm enough, bundled up in coats and wellies. The rubber of one pair – I think it was mine – was squeaking. We'd brought with us a flask of tea, and cheese and pickle sandwiches wrapped in tinfoil. My mother had a tartan blanket tucked under the crook of one arm.

226

'How's Noah?' she asked, after a while, scanning the dunes for a suitable lunch spot.

'He's good,' I said, touching my fingertips to my phone, nestled in my coat pocket. He would be up in the air by now, I thought, drinking the first of several Bloody Marys, his favourite thing about a long-haul flight. 'Actually, he's on his way to New York; he's teaching there this term.'

She kept walking but turned her face towards mine, her mouth open with expectation.

'It's OK,' I said, ignoring the empty pit in my stomach and parroting what he'd said about it only being a couple of months. 'And besides, it's a good opportunity for me to spend some more time with you.'

'Well, as long as you're happy, then lucky me,' she said, smiling.

I let go of my phone and smiled back.

'Here we go,' she said, gesturing to a sheltered patch overlooking the sea. 'You sit down.'

I smiled as she shook out the blanket and joined me, stretching it across both our legs, the way she used to do when I was little. She held out a couple of plastic cups, and I poured some tea, the liquid piping hot and letting loose swirls of steam.

'Sandwich,' I said, handing her a small, silvery parcel.

'Sandwich,' she repeated, nodding.

As we sat there, listening to the waves rocking softly against the shore, I tried to work out how to approach the subject of her forgetting, what it was I should say. I looked left and right; as far as I could tell, we were the only ones here. It struck me that I should have checked if confronting her was the best course of action, and again I fingered the phone

227

in my pocket, wondering if I could get away with a quick search. Very occasionally, back when we lived together, Anna used to sleepwalk, and I remember her telling me I mustn't wake her up if she did. But this was different, wasn't it?

By the time I'd plucked up the courage, the crinkle of her tinfoil told me she was done eating. The September sun was warm on our faces, and when she leant back and rested her head against a grassy dune and closed her eyes, I did the same. She sighed, a cheerful sigh. Relaxed, content. I scrunched my already shuttered eyes tight, taking a mental picture of the moment.

I remember the feeling of fatigue sweeping over me, limbs softening, thoughts becoming clouded, but I don't remember falling asleep or how many minutes had passed by the time I woke. I was starting to feel the cold – especially my fingers, without gloves, clutching at my tinfoil ball, the skin pallid. I turned to my mother to ask if she was cold too, to suggest we head home. That's when it happened.

'Mum?' I tossed away the blanket and scrabbled to my feet.

The patch of sand beside me was vacant, the only sign of her being there a few tufts of grass lying flat rather than poking up towards the sky.

I looked out towards the waves, which were rocking harder against the shore now, but not as hard as my heart was thumping in my chest.

'Mum?!' I called her name louder this time.

I scanned the dunes then ran out into the middle of the beach. Looked one way, and then the other. I saw nothing. No one.

A far-off ship, maybe, swelling clouds, empty air.

I called her name again. And again.

Back to where we'd been sitting. Up into the dunes and over the edge, facing out towards the marshes between the beach and the house. More nothing, until something. There. A man, walking this way.

'Excuse me!' I ran towards him, heart thumping harder still. 'Have you seen my mother?'

'Your mother?'

'She's about my height, wearing a navy-blue Barbour and green wellies.'

His eyebrows lifted. Surprise? Pity? Judgement?

News headlines of distracted parents flashed before my eyes. Parents losing track of their child. Getting caught out by the tide.

'Is that her?'

My eyes followed his pointing finger towards the house. Another figure, walking in the opposite direction.

'Mum!'

I was running again.

By the time I'd caught up with her, I was out of breath and tears were streaming from my face. 'Mum.' I hugged her. 'Are you OK?'

For a moment, she didn't say anything. Tears slowly welled in her eyes, which looked a lighter amber in the daylight, with less noticeable flashes of green. She pursed her lips together in the sort of tight smile that I knew from experience wasn't genuine.

'Mum, talk to me.'

It took another moment for her to say, 'What's happening?'

'Oh, Mum.' I held out my arms and she clung to me. I held on tight, then I stroked her back, remembering how soothing I used to find it when she did the same to me when I was just a child.

'I'm frightened,' she said, her voice uneven, the way it often sounded when we were talking on the phone and she was busy gardening or cooking. 'I don't know what's wrong with me.' She was growing breathless.

'It's OK, Mum, we're going to figure this out. Just breathe.' I tried desperately to keep a lid on my own emotions as I put my hands on her shoulders. Each time her chest rose and fell I counted to three.

In her bulky coat, she looked even smaller than usual, with a birdlike face and petite hands and feet. As she breathed in and out, she peered down at the tips of her wellies, the green rubber lightly coated with grains of sand.

'We need to call the doctor when we get home,' I said, still holding on. 'Are you happy for me to do that?'

She nodded, still staring.

'OK, that's good,' I said, puffing out my cheeks. 'Now, shall we go home?'

She looked towards the house and said, in barely more than a whisper, 'I think that's what I wanted to do.'

That night, sitting up in bed in my old room, with my laptop balanced on my knees, I read stories of dementia-driven wandering. There was a woman who would leave her house in the middle of every night, and a man who was often seen walking in the road. Some people wandered across borders; others simply wandered up and down corridors. One died, another mysteriously disappeared. They were either bored, or curious, or they thought they needed to do the shopping or pick up the kids. They were trying to get home – in some instances, even when they were at home, in their pyjamas, ready for bed. I pictured my mother heading in the opposite direction, away from our house, towards the waves, in nothing but her thin cotton nightdress.

When finally I fell asleep, I dreamed of my childhood. It was as if my mother's forgetting had sharpened my own remembering; that, or the quiet of the countryside made space for echoing memories drowned out by the thrum of the city. Sights, sounds and smells of days spent on the beach once again stirred my senses. A bumpy crab with a cracked shell. The slipperiness of seaweed. The sting of a jellyfish on the sole of my foot. My father's gravelly voice trying to coax me into the ice-cold winter sea. My mother lifting her dress up above her knees, so it wouldn't get wet, watching the way the water rippled against her legs. Her body imprinted in the sand. A Thermos of tomato soup and more sandwiches wrapped in tinfoil, sunlight on silver.

I woke up to an email from Noah. It was short, but it said all there was to say. He loved me. He was thinking of me, and of my mother. He was only a plane ride away if things got too much. I longed to talk to him, to be grounded by his voice, but I worried that in doing so I would realise just how much I needed him, and I had to be strong. Instead, I wrote back saying that I could manage, I hoped the start of term went well, and I loved him too.

Before I forgot, I messaged Robyn to thank her for recommending the counsellor, and to say that I hoped she was doing OK after her disappointing results. I also called Anna, who sounded somewhat distracted until I mentioned what had happened and where I was.

'Oh, Cathy, I'm sorry,' she said, focused now. 'Is there anything I can do?'

'I don't think so but thank you.'

'Are you OK? Probably a stupid question.'

'I am. I just feel . . .' I shook my head, forced a small laugh. 'Irresponsible.'

'Cathy.' She continued, warily: 'You know this doesn't mean anything?'

'I know.' There was no need for her to say what she meant by 'anything' – that losing my mother didn't mean I would be an irresponsible parent.

'Maybe I can come and visit one weekend? You know, depending on your movements.'

'That would be wonderful,' I said, my mind skipping forward over the days, weeks, months aching out in front of me, all of which were suddenly blurred.

My mother was dressed and sitting at the kitchen table with her handbag on her knee when I came down for breakfast. She'd made an effort, blow-drying her hair and lining her lower lids with kohl. Beneath her plum-coloured coat she was wearing a silky white shirt printed with blue feathers. Plain silver studs pierced her lobes.

'I like that shirt, Mum,' I said, glancing at the clock and wondering how long she'd been waiting. I'd managed to get an appointment for midday, and it had only just gone half past ten. 'I'm not sure I've seen it before.'

'Thank you, darling.'

'Have you had breakfast?' Before she had a chance to answer, I added, 'I could make us some eggs if you like?'

'I've eaten, thank you.'

'What about some tea or coffee? We're in good time – Peggy won't be here for another hour.'

'I know, Catherine.'

I couldn't work out if the use of my full name was yet another sign of her forgetfulness or simply a symptom of her frustration at my fussing. Either way, I opened the door to the fridge and took a moment, gathering my thoughts. Then I closed it again and opened the breadbin, fishing out a single slice to make myself some toast.

'Do make your mind up,' my mother mumbled.

I was taken aback, but I tried my hardest to smile.

Peggy drove, with my mother in the passenger seat and me in the back. The surgery was only fifteen minutes away, and for the entirety of the journey my mother faced the window, her nose close to the glass. I suggested we listen to Radio 4, her station of choice, but she said she needed some quiet time to think. I wanted to ask her what she was thinking about, to say that we could talk it through together, like we used to do, but I resisted.

She'd been going to the same doctor for the past thirty years, the same doctor my father had gone to. By this point we all referred to her by her first name, Edna. She was a slight woman, with sculptural features that were more malleable than they looked, softening as she spoke. Her hair, the colour of straw, was always scraped back from her face and her wide-set eyes were shaped like almonds. She greeted us personally and invited us to follow her into her office.

To begin with, Edna carried out some checks that, if the purpose of our visit had been different, might have passed for preamble. 'How have you been spending your time lately?' she asked my mother. 'Are you still managing to get out into the garden despite the cold and the wet? What have you been reading over the past couple of months?' That sort of thing.

My mother did a fairly good job of recounting her days, even if she couldn't remember the author of the book that was currently sitting on her bedside table, or the name of a particularly gripping TV drama she'd seen. 'I sowed some spring cabbage and spinach seeds last week,' she said, adding that she would soon need to cover them with fleece.

My eyes flickered between hers and Edna's, alert to anything that could pass as a reaction, positive or negative.

When she was done, Edna asked how she was feeling in herself. She asked how she'd been sleeping – 'sometimes good, sometimes bad' – and whether she would consider herself to be depressed.

My mother parted her lips to say something, then closed them again and pulled her shoulders back. When she reopened them: 'I would not.'

Then: 'Do you have any worries about your memory, Janey, or complaints?'

At this point, my mother's posture crumbled. She looked at me.

Edna nodded and followed her gaze. 'Go ahead, Cathy,' she said. 'Why don't you share your concerns?'

I felt my throat close up and quickly swallowed some air.

'Anything you've noticed over the past few months? Changes in mental abilities, behaviour, mood?'

I shifted in my seat, a little uncomfortable talking about my mother with her sitting right beside me, recalling how cross I used to get when, as a child, she spoke openly with other adults about me. At dinner parties and parent-teacher conferences. This time, she was the one being graded.

'When did these changes begin?'

'May I?' Sensing my discomfort, Peggy came to my rescue, and I told her, too quickly, to go ahead. 'It's been quite gradual, I think.' She looked at my mother, who dipped her head in agreement. 'To begin with, we didn't think much of it – the forgetting, I mean. After all, it happens to the best of us!'

I recalled her saying the same thing to me a couple of months ago.

'But recently it's been more than just little things.'

'Can you give me some examples?' asked Edna, jotting down a few notes in a lined notepad. When her biro appeared to dry up, and scribbling didn't help, she touched its tip to her tongue and the ink started flowing again.

'I didn't know where I was,' my mother interjected, wrinkling her nose as she tried to explain how it felt. 'It wasn't like forgetting the name of something, or not recognising someone. I really thought . . .' She trailed off like a loose piece of thread.

I reached for her hand. 'This was when you went to the farm shop, wasn't it, Mum?'

She nodded sadly, and said in a quiet voice, 'I don't know what happened.'

'And a similar thing happened on the beach just yesterday, didn't it?' I asked, squeezing her hand.

Silently, she nodded.

'Well, I think we should run some tests,' said Edna, giving a small smile of encouragement. 'I would like to take a blood sample and I'm also going to test your vision and hearing, Janey, if that's all right?' My mother must have looked nervous because she added that there was no need to be. 'We're just ruling things out.'

My mother uttered an almost inaudible 'OK'.

'Perhaps you could take a seat in the waiting room, Peggy?' Turning to me, she said, 'It might be nice for your mum to have you stay.'

'Of course,' I said, trying to keep check of my own nerves, which I could feel quivering beneath my skin.

I hadn't anticipated it – that being in a surgery would bring up the feelings I'd experienced at the fertility clinic. But it was no wonder, really, especially when Edna started to talk us through the next stages and share her initial findings, using words such as 'time' and 'deterioration'. Like triggers, those words turned my thoughts to my body and my frozen eggs and what would happen if, as I still hoped, I never needed to use them. Hurtling through my mind immediately after those thoughts was another about how self-centred I was to be thinking about anything but my mother at this moment.

Edna booked her in for a second appointment. She wanted to conduct one or two more mental ability tests, including a memory test with a pen and paper. She asked if I would be able to accompany my mother each time, and without hesitation I replied, 'Of course.' As we left her office and rejoined Peggy in the waiting room, I found myself contemplating the future again and how we would cope. Maybe it was a good thing that Noah was away; I didn't feel torn about where I needed to be. On the journey home, my mother said she would like to listen to Radio 4 now, and when Peggy turned it on there was a segment on the value of solitude. As we listened to a group of writers talk about finding inspiration in isolation, I imagined my mother's reaction to having a carer in the house.

The days and weeks that followed were out of control, bleeding into one another like the liquid shades of a watercolour. I spent half my time in London, the other half in Norfolk. When I was in London, Peggy all but moved into the house under the pretence that her boiler was on the blink; if my mother was suspicious, she didn't show it. Every evening, I would call when I got back from work, and the two of them would be watching some TV show together, eating their dinner on trays like an old married couple. Peggy's own husband, a grumpy but good-hearted man called Ted, had died just a few years before my father.

I got to know the view from the train by heart, a blurred backdrop imprinted on my brain: brick tunnels, tower blocks of flats, golden-brown hedges and trees, electricity pylons marching towards the horizon like malnourished giants. As we peeled away from London and its industrial outskirts, I would recognise, just briefly, the familiar feeling that used to settle over me whenever I headed home from the city. Body relaxing. Mind slowing. By the time we were cutting a smooth and uninterrupted path through the fields – the farmers hard at work ploughing, cultivating and drilling – my thoughts were racing, and I felt feverish.

I convinced HR to let me go down to four days at the museum, and every Friday morning I would drag myself to Liverpool Street, my limbs sluggish from lack of sleep. There was too much empty space in our bed without Noah beside me, too much quiet without his heavy breathing. I remember perfectly clearly the feeling I had lying alone on the mattress, wide awake in the middle of the night: it was as if I was adrift at sea, far from the shore, the water green and cloudy.

Of course, we would have been apart during the day anyway, but not having him there in the evening, and in that small pocket of time each morning between waking and work, left me alone with nothing but my unspooling thoughts, free from their usual buffers. I thought incessantly of my mother, my marriage, my eggs, all tumbled by waves, a mental wreckage. Even Tom had deserted me, off on one of his extended neighbourhood adventures. When he finally reappeared, his black-and-white coat was rough and stained and he was even more hungry than usual. I gave him a good brush and filled, and refilled, his bowl.

While we were apart, we emailed every day, Noah and I, at least once, sometimes twice. We didn't share much in terms of updates. Rather, each of us reminded the other that he or she was there, as had always been the case.

Thinking of you.

Sending love this morning.

Goodnight, my love.

Sweet dreams.

Every other day, we would try to talk over the phone while he ate lunch in Washington Square Park and I rode the bus home from work.

Noah must have told Daniel what was going on, because I received a kind message from him and, one evening, a visit from Griz and Allie.

'These are for me?' I asked when Allie presented me with a bunch of sunflowers. 'Thank you, sweetie, they're beautiful.'

'They're happy,' she said, with sweet sincerity. Then, wrinkling her nose, 'Where's Uncle Noah?'

'He's away at the moment,' I said, trying a bit too hard to smile, 'teaching.'

Her nose remained wrinkled. 'When will he be back?'

'Soon, I think.'

'Why isn't he teaching here?'

'Well—'

'Allie,' said Griz, 'why don't you go and find Tom?'

'Tom!'

'I bet he's asleep on the bed,' she said.

As Allie crept up the stairs, Griz turned to me and whispered, 'I'm sorry, she's been asking incessantly about Uncle Noah and Auntie Cathy, and why they no longer visit.'

I mumbled something about finding a vase and turned around before she could see my eyes fill with tears.

After a third appointment at the surgery, Edna referred us to a specialist an hour's drive away. There was an almost four-week wait. On the train back to London, I phoned her to ask first if it was necessary and second if we could afford to delay.

In response to my first question, she told me that in some cases, patients chose not to continue with further assessments. 'Very occasionally, they don't want to find out if they have dementia.'

'But surely it's better to know what we're dealing with?'

'Yes, of course, it's in everyone's best interests.'

'And so, in our case?'

'I would wholeheartedly recommend it.'

I bit my lip to stop myself from asking if that was in some way a reflection on our case's severity. 'And the wait?'

'I'm afraid there's no way around it,' she said. 'But I don't think we're going to see any sudden changes over the next few weeks. From what I can gather, the rate of your mother's deterioration so far has been fairly steady.'

She meant it as a positive. Rather than swallowing her whole, whatever was eating away at my mother was doing so in small bites. I'd often wondered what was harder – losing a loved one suddenly, without warning, or gradually, like a bleached photograph left in the sun, the contours and colours slowly fading. When my father's heart stopped beating while he was searching for something to watch on TV, and he died in hospital later that night, I thought there was nothing worse. I wasn't ready, I didn't have time to prepare. The sense of loss was too blunt. But then, I hadn't yet experienced the alternative – awaiting death as you await swelling seas.

It's an interesting if ever so slightly morose exercise to rank a life's worst moments. Up there with mine, for reasons unrelated to my recent nuptials, was my honeymoon.

Noah and I had been in the south of France for three and a half days when Daniel called to say their parents had been in a car accident. Everything from that one terrible moment in time is suspended in my memory like a film still, high-definition.

The warmth of the autumn rays on my limbs, slippery from sun cream. The reflections of the afternoon light on the pristine pool stretched out in front of my toes. The flicker of the pages of the battered paperback Noah was reading, tussled by the gentle breeze. The strength of the Negroni he'd made me. The vibration of his phone on the small table between us, its octagonal top a mosaic of multicoloured tiles. Noah groaning – *why is he calling me now?* – and reluctantly answering. Sitting upright on his sun lounger. Sliding his feet to the stone floor, one and then the other. His face draining of colour.

'Noah, is everything OK?'

His eyes closing. His palm resting on top of his shuttered lids, as if the light was still too bright.

'Noah?'

His voice catching as he went to talk into the receiver. 'We'll be on the next flight.'

Tapping his screen and returning his phone to the tabletop. For a moment, neither of us speaking, neither of us moving.

Eventually, Noah turning towards me. Opening his mouth to speak, but instead of words coming out, a cry like a wounded animal's.

As my mother waned, the seascape grew in strength. I'd finally finished removing the overpaint and now it was time for the structural treatment, which I was due to carry out with Frank. We hadn't seen much of each other recently, and of course he knew I'd cut down my days. When I emailed him saying I was ready to fix the lower wood panel and asking if he was still able to help me, he said it would be his pleasure.

I must have looked as tired and weary as I felt, because when I walked into the conservation studios, his grey eyebrows lifted. I'd never thought of Frank as the hugging kind, even with me, but that morning, he walked towards me and gave my shoulder a squeeze, before telling me conspiratorially that he would be back in just a minute.

More like five minutes later, he returned with a hot chocolate. 'I won't say anything if you don't,' he said, when my mouth opened in surprise at this blatant breach of the rules.

'Thank you, Frank.'

He smiled. 'Right, get that down you and we'll make a start.'

While I sipped my hot chocolate, he set up the painting at a workstation with a sash clamp, a bridge and a handful of props for support. There was a fracture in the wood, which was widest at the edge and narrowed into a fine hairline crack in the centre. First, we had to clean and prepare the fracture for gluing, removing the old varnish and any leftover glue paste with a scalpel and solvent. Then we prepared and heated some sturgeon glue, which we fed into the split.

'OK, that should do it,' said Frank, moving the panel gently back and forth to ensure that the glue was evenly spread.

For the first hour, we regularly checked the level of the join with a straight edge, and after that we monitored the repair every hour. As we worked, I thought of my mother and how much simpler things would be if I could fix her, too. Instead, her mind was gradually crumbling, and glue wouldn't do any good.

At the end of the month, when I was with my mother in Norfolk, Anna and Theo came to visit under the pretence that it would be good for him to get out of the city and breathe in some sea air. I heard the crunch of wheels on gravel just as I was stirring some milk into two cups of coffee, the liquid turning from muddy brown to a more neutral beige. I let the teaspoon fall into the sink and went to greet her. I'd been keeping a check on my emotions in front of my mother, but now I felt a fresh wave rising. At dinner the night before, I'd asked her to pass the pepper and, mid-mouthful, she'd leant to the side and reached into her handbag. To begin with, I thought she hadn't heard me, but when she swallowed and tsked, and yanked the bag up off the floor and onto her knee to get a better look, I asked what she was doing. The look on her face when she paused then handed me the small wooden grinder standing beside the metal saltshaker in front of her plate made my chest ache.

'Cathy!' Anna called, as she got out of the car.

I breathed in and out and put on a smile, then I walked towards her and gave her a hug. When I went to let go, she wouldn't allow it. At last, relinquished and trying desperately to keep a lid on my feelings, I said, 'It's good to see you.'

'And you,' she said, brushing her fingers against my elbow. 'How are you?'

'I'm OK,' I said, blinking back the tears that had been waiting for this very question. 'Thank you for coming; you know you didn't have to.'

'I wanted to,' she said. 'We wanted to.'

'I was going to say, have you forgotten something?'

'Oh, my son is the worst fucking driving companion, let me tell you,' she said, laughing, as I peered through the window into the back of the car. Apparently, Theo had been asleep before they'd left Kentish Town.

'Do you want to wake him?' I asked, quietly hoping that the answer would be no, and I would have her to myself for a while.

'I'll leave him for a bit.'

I smiled. 'Well then, coffee?'

Back in the kitchen, my mother was on her knees on the hard tiled floor, her plaid skirt pooled around her, as she rootled in the cupboard where she kept her baking ingredients.

'Mum, is everything OK?'

'Fine, darling, I'm just looking for some sugar.'

'What for?' I asked. My voice must have risen a note or two because I felt Anna's hand rest lightly on my shoulder.

'For my coffee.'

'But you don't take sugar in your coffee?'

She reversed back from the cupboard and craned her neck to look up at me. 'Yes, I do.'

I hadn't noticed Anna's hand leave my shoulder until I heard her say, 'Here, Janey, let me help you. I for one love a spoon of sugar in any hot drink.' She held out that same hand.

My mother's eyes moved to her, then back to me, stretched wide.

'Mum, Anna's driven down from London. Remember I told you she and Theo were coming to stay for the weekend?' I could feel myself forming the words carefully in my mouth.

Instead of answering she frowned, her face creasing, the lines of her forehead multiplying to match the number on the back of her hands.

'Isn't that nice?' I tried, a little desperate now.

She ignored Anna's hand, which was still outstretched, and pushed herself up and off the floor with her palms. Then she lowered her voice as she added, 'Who did you say she was?'

'Mum.' I felt a bubbling inside me. 'It's Anna, my friend. You know Anna.'

She looked at her again, then shook her head and said, 'I'm so sorry, Anna, of course.'

Theo woke up in a grisly mood, but Anna took him straight out into the garden to play and he soon seemed happy. After a couple of weeks of cooler weather, it was as if summer had returned. Peggy had said something about it recognising the fact that we were in need of a lift. Watching them from the kitchen window, I saw Anna lying flat on her back, soaking up the sun's rays. Her arms and legs outstretched, sandaled toes pointing out, mouth moving in conversation, eyelids shut and still. Theo was crawling over and under her bare legs, using them as a climbing frame. She pushed down her skirt as he accidentally flicked up its hem. He was wearing a blue T-shirt and a pair of denim dungarees.

I turned to my mother, who was with me in the kitchen. 'How would you feel about having fish and chips for lunch, Mum?'

'Oh, I would love some,' she said, licking her lips. An old favourite.

'OK, let me go and rally the troops.'

I called out as I approached, hands cupped around my mouth for comic effect: 'Ohhhh Theo!'

Squeals.

Anna cracked one eye open and then the other. As she came to cross-legged, she smiled at me and said to him: 'Look, it's your fairy godmother!'

More squeals, followed by laps around the pair of us, his little legs moving as quickly as they could. His dungarees, previously rolled up, began to unravel and bunch around his ankles.

'Hi,' I said, joining her on the ground. 'Nice patch you got here.'

'This old thing?' she asked, tapping at the grass, playing along with my emotional charade. 'Glad you like it.'

Theo was beginning to look dizzy, his eyes glazed, but he kept on running.

'What did you give him for breakfast, sugar cubes?'

'He *is* particularly hyper after that nap,' she said, grimacing. 'Maybe he just loves Norfolk – must take after you.' While Anna had always thought of the place where we grew up as boring and a bit backward, I still felt the pull of the sea. She stood up and held out her arms, catching him and lifting him skywards. 'Got you!'

He giggled to begin with, then he started to squirm. Anna held tight and, after a moment, the smile slipped off his face like melted ice cream off a wafer cone, and he began to whine.

'Hey, Theo,' I said, standing up too, 'shall we go and get some fish and chips?'

He covered his eyes with his hands and started to cry.

I winced as I said, 'I guess it's not Norfolk, then.'

Anna laughed, then we struck a deal, or at least she and Theo did: five more minutes of playtime, then we would have lunch. Unfortunately, Theo was in the mood to play dirty. When the five minutes were up, he threw himself on the ground and wailed again.

'Maybe you two should go ahead,' said Anna, taking a deep breath and smiling apologetically at my mother as she walked towards us, coat on, handbag in hand. 'We can catch up.'

'Are you sure?'

Theo started to pummel the ground, frustrated by the lack of attention his display was garnering.

'I'm sure.' She squeezed my hand and whispered: 'Seriously, save yourself.'

I turned to my mother, but she was making a beeline for Theo.

'Now, what's all this?' she asked, bending forward to get a better look at him.

I don't know whether it was the different tone of voice, or her shadow looming over him, but Theo quickly hushed and gazed up at her, his eyes glossy and wide.

'We're all going to get fish and chips,' she said, briskly. 'Are you coming, or shall we leave you behind?'

I stretched my lips wide and whispered an apology to Anna. She shook her head quickly and smiled.

When I looked back at Theo, he was scrambling to his feet and wiping his eyes.

My mother sat up front with Anna, who asked her polite questions about things like the weather and living close to the beach. I tried to listen to my mother's responses while also reading from one of Theo's storybooks to keep him occupied.

The fish and chip shop was a little way up the coast, in a small village that for a long time had managed to slip beneath the radar of the holidaymakers who arrived in swarms every summer. On dry days, a chalkboard stood outside, bearing some batter-related pun and an aquatic illustration. A red-and-white awning extended from the whitewashed exterior over two wooden tables, the type with benches attached on either side. We used to come every other Friday to pick up a treaty dinner when I was a child. Usually, my mother would stay at home, and my father and I would drive to collect it. I remember the feeling of the warm plastic bag resting on my lap, and the temptation – rarely resisted – to taste at least one salty chip before we'd made it back.

Anna and Theo grabbed one of those outdoor tables while my mother and I joined the single-person queue behind a man who reminded me of Noah. He looked around the same age and had a similarly thick head of hair and friendly features.

'Rob?'

He whipped his head around and so did I. Behind us, a pretty woman with big eyes and a nose like a button was sitting at one of a handful of metal tables inside. She was holding a baby and gesturing towards a second child, a little girl of about Theo's height, who was making a run for it.

'Gotcha,' said her dad, picking her up just before she slipped through the door, and rubbing his nose against hers.

I looked away, the picture too bright.

While he placed his order with the skinny boy behind the counter, the little girl peered around and eventually locked eyes with me. When she did, she gave me a toothy grin.

In return, I felt my own cheeks lift.

I'd almost forgotten that my mother was standing by my side until I felt her hand knowingly clasp mine. I looked at her and she smiled with her eyes. She was her old observant self. We stayed holding hands as I ordered three portions of fish and chips, plus one kid-size scampi.

It arrived wrapped in plain white paper streaked with patches of grease.

After helping herself to some mushy peas from a polystyrene pot, my mother spooned a generous helping onto an empty spot beside Theo's pile of chips.

He looked at her uncertainly, then dipped a little finger into the bright-green mulch. After pulling a face that made both me and Anna laugh, he dipped it in again and again.

Satisfied, my mother nodded and turned her attention back to her own meal.

Despite her awareness in the queue, and the way that she understood, instinctively, how I might be feeling, it was plain to see that she was slowly fading away from me. I found myself stealing glances at her and Theo throughout lunch, watching the way both seemed to exist in their own world as well as ours, filling their mouths as Anna and I chatted, quietly content. I wondered how long it would be until he began to take part in our conversations, and equally, how long it would be until she didn't. How long it would be until his level of cognitive function surpassed hers. Though Edna had said that her deterioration so far had been fairly steady, I could sense it quickening.

'You like Janey, don't you, sweetie?' Anna asked Theo.

He smiled and pressed himself against his mum, suddenly shy.

'What about you, Mum?' I asked, shaking my head as she offered me a handful of her chips. 'What do you think of Theo here?'

She kept a straight face as she put the chips in front of me and said, 'I think he's wonderful.' On her jumper was a pea-green stain.

That night, after an afternoon of sand and sea air, Theo soon fell asleep. My mother seemed tired too and took herself off to read in bed just after nine o'clock. Anna and I, meanwhile, stayed up talking. We sat with our glasses of wine on a pair of old deck-chairs in the garden until the darkness got too much and the temperature dropped so low that our skin began to resemble gooseflesh. In the living room, in the dull yellowy light of a couple of lamps with fabric shades, we each took an end of the sofa, facing one another, our backs propped up against cushions and our legs outstretched beneath a woollen blanket.

'So,' she said, eventually, 'how are you, really?'

I wriggled my toes within my socks, and she gently steadied them. 'I'm struggling a bit,' I said, reaching for the bottle and pouring some more wine into my glass, then raising the bottle in offering.

'Please.'

'It's a lot,' I said, topping up the puddle of red at the bottom of her glass.

'I know it is.'

I returned the bottle to the coffee table, and after we'd both taken a sip, she asked if I'd had much contact with Noah.

'We talk most days, either over email or on the phone,' I said. 'I miss him.'

'He misses you, too.'

'You've heard from him?'

'I have.' When I stayed quiet, she added: 'He was worried about you and wanted me to check in.'

I rubbed at my chest.

'He loves you, Cathy – there's no doubt about that.'

'And I love him,' I said, smiling, a sad smile that wobbled before it was finished.

She smiled back, then continued. 'I know it's hard, especially with everything going on with Janey, but you're going to have to make a decision soon, for both your sakes.'

'I'm working on it.' It was true, I *was* working on it, every day.

'And how's that going?'

'It's going,' I said, with a half-hearted laugh. 'In a way, I think the situation here has helped.'

I didn't elaborate and she didn't ask me to. All she said was, 'You'll tell me if there's anything *I* can do to help?'

'I will, thank you.' For a moment, we were both quiet, and for a moment, through the quiet, I thought I could hear waves.

October

Ever since I'd removed the natural varnish resin and discovered, at the point where the sky met the sea, a floating figure and what I'd suspected to be a fin, I'd known that the apparently unremarkable Dutch painting I was working on was, in fact, quite special. There had been rumblings throughout the museum, and they were growing louder and more fervent. And so, it didn't come as much of a surprise that in November there would be a press conference and a major unveiling.

There's something magical about working on a piece you know will soon be recognised and discussed and hung in a gallery for everyone to see. For now, it was just me and the painting, which finally made sense: the crowds had gathered on Scheveningen beach on a gusty winter's day because they wanted to get a glimpse of the washed-up whale. It wasn't just a seascape; it was a spectacle. Different folks had come together to see it: a gentleman on horseback; local villagers; a homeless man begging for money. As I applied a fresh coat of varnish, I left my headphones to one side, relishing the soft scuffing of my brush on the panel and losing myself in the painterly surface, which by the time I was done had a satin-like finish, the colours saturated. When I was fully immersed, I could fool myself into believing that I was the artist, capturing the people in paint in real time as they assembled.

Next came the filling and the retouching. I plugged the small areas of damage and loss on the whale and in the sky with chalk-gelatine putty, then moved onto the deeper losses in the cluster of clouds. Once the surface was even, the creamy-white pastes acting like Polyfilla in holes and cracks on a wall, I began my retouching. Unlike the cleaning and the structural work, this part of the process is reversible. Slowly, with a fine brush, I applied fresh paint on top of the varnish, happy in the knowledge that if I wasn't sure about something I'd done, I could wipe it off and have another go, no consequences.

Together with the curator, I decided that I should touch out the pentimenti. Those wraithlike figures that had haunted me as I'd worked weren't intended to be a part of the final composition and in their half-existent state they were distracting. We'd respected Hendrick's original intention by reinserting the whale, and here we were adhering to his wishes again.

As I blocked out the clumsy grey shadow of the former carriage, I found myself yearning to do the same with my life, to erase any passing thoughts and desires – any mistakes – that didn't fit with the future self I'd had planned. I was tired of thinking and of waiting; I wanted it over and done. My mind and body had felt foggy for so long that I could barely remember what clarity felt like. I closed my eyes in an effort to focus on the feeling, and when that didn't work, I tried to picture it instead, clean and bright.

*

At the weekend, Robyn and I met for coffee. Other than the odd text, I hadn't spoken to her since everything had happened with my mother, and I wanted to see how she was. She replied right away and suggested a café off Oxford Street. Usually, I preferred to steer clear of central London when I wasn't working, but I lived north and she lived south, so meeting in the middle made sense. It was a cold but clear day, the sun shining even if it wasn't emitting any warmth, so I wrapped up and went on my bike.

The café was light and airy and tucked away on a quiet street behind the main drag. I was the first to arrive and while I waited, I ordered myself a latte. The young woman behind the counter asked if I would like the seasonal special – pumpkin spice, I think – and after a small free taster, I politely declined.

I'd just sat down and was shrugging off my coat when the door dinged and Robyn walked in looking a little red in the face.

'Sorry, delays on the Central line,' she said, shedding her own jacket and pulling up the chair opposite.

'Don't worry. I would have ordered you a coffee, but I wasn't sure what you would want.'

'Ah, no caffeine for me.' She twisted in her seat to look at the blackboard and made positive murmurings at the chalked list of juices and smoothies.

'Why's that?'

'Hm?'

'Why are you off caffeine?'

'Well,' she said, hopping back up again, 'since things didn't go to plan last time, I've decided to take every precaution known to man – or woman, I should say – with this round.'

She went to place her order and waited by the till, purse in hand, while the blender roared, drowning out the tranquil music sounding from the café's speakers. When she returned with a carrot-coloured drink, she looked less flustered, her pallor a lighter pink.

'It's good to see you,' she said, smiling.

'And you.' I smiled back. 'But wait, so you've already started your second round?'

'I have.' She exhaled as she said it. 'Three injections down. I just came from my first scan.'

I pulled in my stomach, thankful it no longer felt like a pincushion. 'How are you feeling?' I asked.

'Mm, I'm OK.' She stirred her already-separating juice up with a paper straw, then took a sip, the tidemark lowering. 'I just hope it works this time,' she said, licking her lips as they started to quiver. 'I had to take out a loan, which I really didn't want to do, at least not at this stage. You know, if I don't meet someone, and I need to have IVF, by myself . . . I just don't think it's feasible.' She went to say something else, before shaking her head and touching all ten fingertips to the wooden tabletop.

As before, I found myself wanting to tell her I was sure it would work, and as before, I stopped myself. I reached out my own hands and squeezed hers. 'I'm keeping everything crossed for you.'

'And you?' she asked. 'I'm glad your session with the counsellor went well.'

'It did, thanks again.'

'That was all you.'

I didn't know whether she could sense that I wasn't ready to talk about it, but she changed the topic of conversation, and it was only later, just before we said our goodbyes, that we returned to freezing. I noticed how her eyes glistened when, with a touch more hope, she spoke about it potentially working out for her this time, and the way she chewed her straw when she added that, of course, she understood it might not.

'I can't imagine it, though,' she said, dispensing of her straw altogether and finishing her juice straight from the glass. 'What would my life be about?'

It had been clear to me from the first time we met how much she wanted to have a child, but it was only sitting opposite her in that café that I considered what her deep and unwavering longing said about my own desire.

'Don't worry,' she added, with a sad smile, 'I don't expect you to know the answer.'

I was in the middle of a dream – a happy dream, I think – when the sound of the front door clicking off the latch stirred me. Footsteps on the stairs, then a bag being lowered to the ground. I felt my heart beat hard against my chest. I contemplated turning on all the lights and shouting out. Instead, quietly, from underneath the duvet, I reached for my phone. I'd never rung the police before, and as I dialled the number I imagined our dusky street shrieking with sirens and illuminated with blue flashing lights. I listened as whoever was down there opened and closed the fridge, which had moaned on its hinges ever since we'd moved in. They must have slipped off their shoes before going into the kitchen, because the wooden floorboards didn't creak. That was when I realised – or hoped might be more accurate. Noah. The clink of a glass knocking against its neighbours.

The glug of it being filled with cold water from a bottle. Quiet. Then, again, footsteps, approaching. My heart started to beat harder and faster.

I was returning my phone to my bedside table when I saw the bathroom light turn on through a crack in the bedroom door. I pictured him looking at himself in the mirror, hands gripped the edge of the sink, knuckles turning yellowy white. He was plucking up the courage to tell me he couldn't do this any more; he'd come back earlier than planned to put a stop to it. I moved onto my front to try to squash the butterflies fluttering around in my stomach, and I waited. I was considering rolling over to face the wall, and pretending to be asleep, when I opened one eye and saw that he was standing by the bed undressing.

'You're here?' It was more of a statement than a question, yet there was a rising note at the end.

'I am,' he said, reaching over and planting a kiss on my forehead, lingering for long enough for me to breathe in the familiar scent of him at the end of a long day. 'I'm sorry I woke you.'

Everything about him being there felt familiar, normal, like he'd been watching a game at the pub and just got in, a little late. As my heart steadied, I braced myself, ready for it to start up again, perhaps for my head to spin. Instead: 'Why didn't you tell me you were coming home?' As I asked the question, I shifted onto my side and blinked both eyes open fully.

The room was dark, but the moon was big and bright, its milky light leaking through the gap between the bottom of the blind and the window ledge.

'I wanted to surprise you.'

I propped myself up against my pillow and reached for the switch of my bedside light. The bulb flicked on and cast the room in a dull yellow glow, all highlights and shadows.

'I've missed you,' I said, instinctively bringing my knees towards my chest and wrapping my arms tight around them, steeling myself for him to say he felt differently.

'I've missed you too,' he replied. He was down to his boxers now, peeling back the duvet cover and climbing into bed to join me.

'But how are you here? Why are you here?'

'Not now, later.' He leant towards me and kissed me, properly this time, with a sense of urgency.

I unwrapped my arms from around my shins and, when I did, he parted my knees and moved in between them. He brushed the backs of his fingers over my cheek, down my neck, across my chest. My own fingers combed through his hair, which felt soft, like he'd washed it that morning. His cheeks were thick with stubble, even though it was only October and he didn't normally start growing a beard until December. He kissed me harder and pressed his body against mine. I heard myself make a noise that sounded like pleasure as I reached for the headboard and he slipped off my knickers.

I hadn't been with anyone like Noah before. I'd had boyfriends, but he was different – more a man at a time when I, in my mid-twenties, still thought of myself as a girl. He knew what he wanted in life. And once a decision had been made, there was no going back on it. We'd been dating for just a few months when he told me he was all in. I remember the feeling that spread through me at that moment, a comforting warmth, the kind you get when you wrap yourself in a towel that's spent the night on a heated rail. It was the same familiar comfort I experienced whenever I arrived home in Norfolk after an extended period away.

That night, after we had sex, we lay next to one another, my cheek on his chest, our legs interlinked. I listened as his heartbeat gradually slowed down and tried to think of nothing but the sensation of his fingertips tracing my bare skin. I noticed the weekend bag of clothes beside the bed and thought momentarily of his suitcase, which he must have left downstairs. When my mind started to race, I screwed my eyes shut and pressed my ear tighter against his chest, the volume of his heartbeat rising.

He was waiting for me to say something, I was sure of it. After all, he'd made his feelings clear. Then, shifting slightly so he could see my face, and I his, he repeated the same words he'd said all those years before: 'I'm all in, Cathy.'

I held on tight around his waist and squeezed my legs together with his.

'I've been worrying about you, with everything going on with your mum. I want you to know that I'm here for you. I want to work through this.' He noticed my tears before I did, and he sat up and lifted my chin with his fingers, trying to read me like my mother did the plants in her garden that didn't blossom when they should. 'You have to help me here, honey,' he said, his eyes flicking left and right. 'I can't tell if these are happy or sad tears.'

'Both?' I offered. 'There's just such a lot to consider, such a lot going on.'

'We can get through it, together. OK?'

I couldn't think of an adequate answer, so I simply repeated the same two letters back to him.

Noah's plane had landed on a Thursday and our wedding anniversary was that Saturday, Theo's birthday. The night before, when I told him we'd have to wait and celebrate our anniversary in the evening, he told me he understood and that he was looking forward to the little man's party. I must have raised an eyebrow because he explained that we hadn't spent time together with Anna and Caleb for a while. He also told me, with a glint in his eye, that our evening plans had been taken care of.

Just in case anyone was in doubt about the address, two buttercup-coloured balloons were tied to the front door, bobbing gently in the breeze. We climbed the stone steps and rang the buzzer, then waited, listening to the faint sound of squeals, chatter and music, muffled for the moment. Noah had taken my hand in his and was giving it a kiss when the door swung open.

'Guys, you made it, so good to see you!' Caleb was wearing a bright shirt and a smile that looked too tight, like it might be pinching.

I wondered whether it had been brought on by the presence of more than a dozen small children, or whether he'd slipped it on specially for us – no doubt Anna had filled him in on our recent comings and goings.

'Good to see you, too,' said Noah, smiling a more natural smile, shaking Caleb's hand and patting him on the arm. 'It's been a while, buddy.'

'Caleb, hi,' I said, belatedly kicking into gear myself and leaning forward to give and receive a couple of kisses.

'Well, come on in – we're all in here.' His eyes widened at the word 'all', which confirmed that it was the children who'd put him on edge and not us.

We removed our coats and followed him into the living room, which was strewn with more balloons, orange as well as yellow. Paper chains that looked too neat to be hand-made had been tacked onto the walls alongside Caleb and Anna's framed prints and photos, and there was a ball pit in the centre of the room, the coffee table relegated to a spot beneath the bay window. Above the fireplace, a banner said happy birthday in big bubble letters.

'Theo,' called Caleb, 'are you going to come and say hello to your godmother?'

Understandably, Theo was preoccupied, perched at the top of the slide that descended into the ball pit, with a tumbling queue of toddlers forming behind him.

'Come on, Theo, come down.'

'Don't worry,' I said, laughing at Caleb's attempt to coax him away from the fun and towards the grown-ups. 'I'll say hello later.' I added his present to the mounting pile by the door then scanned the room for familiar faces. It was lined with seated and standing mothers and fathers, chatting amongst themselves, instinctively glancing in the direction of their offspring every now and then.

'What can I get you two to drink?' asked Caleb, clapping his hands together, eager no doubt to escape to the kitchen. 'We've got wine, beer, champagne . . .'

'I'll take an IPA if you have one,' said Noah.

'Coming right up. Cathy?'

'White wine, please,' I said, still scanning. I recognised Anna's sister, who looked just like her, the same angular face and chestnut hair, only a few years older.

As Caleb went in search of drinks, I glanced up at Noah, expecting to catch a strained look on his own face. I was ready to apologise for subjecting him to so many children in such a small space, relatively speaking, when he turned to me and said he was glad we'd come.

'Me too!'

We spun around in sync and found Anna standing behind us, a blue-and-white plate of what she called 'adult nibbles' resting on an upturned palm. The coffee table, I'd noticed, typically topped with books and magazines, was stocked with more kiddie options: cubes of cheese, cherry tomatoes, those cold cocktail sausages with the wrinkly skin, crustless sandwiches cut into triangles, peeled carrot sticks, seedless grapes. I glanced in its direction and caught a small person with corkscrew curls dunking his entire fist into the bowl of Hula Hoops, which promptly went flying.

'Anna, hi.' I gave her a hug, careful not to tip the smoked-salmon blinis straight off the plate and onto the floor. 'Great party,' I added.

She cocked her head.

'No, really, I mean it!'

'Well, that's very kind of you to say,' she said. 'But don't worry, we have plenty of booze, and the plan is that the ball pit wears everyone out and then there's a mass nap.'

'My kind of birthday,' said Noah, accepting his bottle of beer from Caleb, who'd returned from his safe haven at the other end of the house, and passing me my wine.

'Have you seen Maz?' asked Anna, looking at me. 'I told her you were coming.'

'Yes,' I said, waving at her sister, who this time saw me too and waved back. 'Though I haven't had a chance to say hello yet.'

'Well, come on, let's leave these two to it.' She linked my arm in hers and carefully, again not to drop the nibbles, we shuffled around the perimeter of the pit, tapping runaway plastic balls aside with our toes.

I glanced over my shoulder and watched as Noah crouched down to talk to the little boy with the curly hair, who was wiggling Hula Hoops at him on his fingers.

'Maz, you remember Cathy?'

'Of course, hi!' As soon as she started speaking, she looked even more like Anna. They had matching expressions, the same habit of scrunching their noses and tilting their heads back as they laughed. 'How are you?' she asked, taking a sip of her champagne.

'I'm good, thank you,' I replied, glancing again at Noah and the boy, who was transferring Hula Hoops from his fingers to the tips of my husband's, or trying to. I smiled, shook my head, and brought my focus back to Maz. 'Happy to be here celebrating Theo's birthday.'

'Well, aren't we all!' She nudged Anna with her elbow as she added, 'And it won't be all that long until the next one comes along.'

My breath caught, but only briefly, not like before. I turned to Anna, who was staring at me with an open mouth. I lowered my voice to a whisper and asked, 'Are you pregnant?'

She handed the plate to Maz, who was belatedly holding a hand to her own open mouth, and pulled me back around the pit and out of the room.

As we passed Noah, who was still crouched down, chatting with his new friend, he looked up at me and asked, 'Everything OK?'

I smiled and nodded.

'Cathy, I'm sorry,' she said, when we were alone in the hallway, a jumble of adults' and children's coats and shoes.

'I was going to tell you, I just wanted to make sure it was the right time.' She shook her head and looked down at her empty hands, muttering something that included the words 'fucking' and 'Maz'.

'Hey,' I said, taking a breath, holding my hands to her cheeks, and lifting her face back up until her eyes met mine. 'I'm happy for you.'

'You are?'

I craned my neck as my eyes started to well and said they were tears of joy. 'Of course I am,' I said, smiling. 'You're my best friend, and you're expecting a baby!'

Her own eyes started to glisten. 'I want this to happen for you, you know, if that's what you decide you want.'

I was laughing and crying now, and she was too. 'I know that.'

'So, you're OK?'

'More than. Please don't worry about me.'

We wiped our eyes and laughed some more, then we hugged, and we were still hugging when we heard a shout from the living room.

Neither of us saw what happened, but Noah would fill me in later. Apparently, one child had started throwing plastic balls at another, gently to begin with, then harder, and not just in the stomach but also the face. The parent of the pummelled child had grabbed the other by the wrist and yanked him up and out of the pit. At this point, Noah said, dramatically, everything went dark, and chaos descended.

'Get your hands off my kid!'

'What?' Anna whipped around and so did I. 'What's going on?'

A child was crying and being scooped up by his father, who was shoving another man in the chest. I didn't recognise

263

either of them, but I had previously seen the woman who came to the affronted man's defence, a little wobbly on her feet, empty champagne flute in hand.

'Hey, cool it, guys, there are kids all around you.' Caleb was by their sides in an instant and ushering them both towards the door. 'I'm sure it was an accident.'

'Caleb, mate, he shook him!'

'I didn't shake him; I was just trying to stop him from hurting anyone.'

'Well, why the fuck is he crying?'

Anna followed the three of them down the hall and into the kitchen, and I went to find Noah, who was hastily finishing his beer. 'Time to go, perhaps?' he suggested, placing the bottle on the side.

I glanced in Theo's direction and saw that he was happily playing with Maz, who, like the other adults in the room, was trying to keep calm for the children while also peeping nervously at the door. The boy with the curly hair was back by the bowl of Hula Hoops, reloading his fingers.

'Time to go,' I said, deciding to message Anna a belated goodbye and thank you later. I felt myself relax as Noah put his arm around me and, together, we found our coats, opened the door and headed back down the stone steps.

We walked to the overground in silence, a comfortable silence, the kind you don't feel the need to fill or pierce. I thought of our flat and the quiet that awaited us there, too – the evening ahead of us, just us two. A warmth spread through me and then it settled, in the way it does after a long, hot bath. I looked out at the rooftops, red and grey against the dusky blue sky, and decided it was relief I was feeling. No, more than relief – contentment. We'd left the party because we could.

In fact, we didn't make it back to the flat until later that night. We left the party around six o'clock, and Noah told me we had a reservation in an hour.

'Where?' I asked, trying not to smile. I had a hunch, but I didn't want to say in case I was wrong.

He wrapped his arm back around my shoulder, an extra layer, and whispered in my ear, his breath tickly and warm, 'You'll find out soon enough.'

We got off the overground a few stops early, which threw me, but as we made our way through residential streets in the general direction of the restaurant we'd eaten at on our wedding day I felt my feet glide faster over the pavement. Noah steadied the pace and started asking me to pick out the house I would like to live in one day, a game we used to play when we first started dating. I waited until we hit the quiet road that swept gently uphill between two busier roads and pointed out my favourite not only in the neighbourhood but in the whole of London: a home in the city that looks like it belongs in the countryside, set back behind a well-tended hedge, with a berry-coloured door framed by potted plants.

I couldn't help but smile when we reached the stretch between the town hall and the restaurant.

He clumsily cleared his throat, trying not to smile himself. 'So, any ideas?'

'No, none.' I looked up at him and felt my face crease.

He started to tap his fingers on my shoulder, a drumroll, as we approached. When we got to the door, he turned to me and asked, sincerely, 'Are you happy with this, really?'

I leant in and up and kissed him. 'I couldn't be happier.' I meant it, I felt it.

He held the door ajar, and the red-headed woman who'd worked on front of house since the restaurant first opened greeted us warmly. 'Well, you two certainly have a lot in common, don't you?'

Noah turned to me again, this time with one eyebrow raised in question.

'Shall I tell him, or do you want to?' she asked me, noticing my smile.

I paused, wanting the moment to last, then I said to Noah, 'I also booked us a table.'

I'd started running again when Noah went away, and as soon as I had I'd remembered all the reasons why I liked it. It made me feel like life was moving forward – as my feet pounded the pavement, I could trick myself into believing that I was progressing. Of course, all I was really doing was jogging in a vague loop, along the canal and back again, which was neither progression nor regression, but simply a sort of stasis. The morning after our anniversary dinner, I caught the eye of another woman jogging in the opposite direction, and the two of us exchanged sympathetic smiles. Perhaps she felt it, too.

I expected Noah to still be in bed when I got back to the flat, and I decided to bring him a mug of coffee made with the cafetière, just as he liked it – one heaped tablespoon and a half. As I waited for the kettle to boil, I received a text from Robyn saying she'd just received her results and this time they'd retrieved even fewer eggs. I reread the message and with every word felt the wind getting knocked out of me. I started typing, then deleting, typing, deleting. Eventually, ineloquently: *Robyn, I'm sorry. Do you want to talk? I can call xx*

I could see that she'd read my message, and yet, at first, she didn't reply. The kettle clicked, steam billowing from its spout. As the seconds turned to minutes, I began to wonder why I thought she would want to be comforted by me – the hesitant woman with the husband *and* the eggs. I was casting around for something to say that would let her know I understood, that would save her from spelling it out, when my phone began to vibrate in my hand.

'Robyn, hi.'

'Hey.' The word was accompanied by an exhalation.

'I didn't think,' I said, watching the steam dissolve into the air. 'Talking is probably the last thing you want to do.' I didn't say 'talking to me'.

'No, this is good.' It sounded like she was shifting position, sitting up in bed maybe. 'I haven't spoken to anyone since I heard.'

I pictured her alone, under a duvet, with only her thoughts. 'What did Doctor Day say?'

She emitted a sad sort of 'ha'. 'He said I could try doing one more round. And I would, of course – I would do anything. Everything. But how?'

I paused, caught between encouraging and cautioning her, and ran my thumb across the droplets of condensation that had formed on the base of the cupboard above the kettle.

'I've already emptied my savings, and even if I could cobble enough together for another round, I'll never be able to afford IVF – who am I kidding?'

'What are you going to do?'

267

With audible effort, she said, 'I'll meet someone, hopefully.'

After we said our goodbyes, I brushed the back of my hand against the cooling kettle and left Noah's mug on the side, vacant.

When I tiptoed into our room, I found him showered and dressed and packing his bag. For a few seconds I stood there, the words stuck like Velcro in my throat. I could feel that my face was still red from running, and the sweat on my chest and back was turning cold.

Eventually, he looked up and asked me if I'd had a good run.

In response, I laughed.

'Is everything OK?'

'You're packing.'

He left the bag alone and held out his hands as he moved towards me. 'Classes start up again tomorrow.'

I sat on the edge of the bed, my limbs suddenly sluggish, seizing up perhaps because I hadn't taken the time to properly warm down and stretch. I thought you weren't going back, that you'd told them you couldn't finish the term. I spoke the words in my head, but not out loud. Did I really believe that? Noah would never leave his students; I'd been the one to remind him that he couldn't let them down in the first place.

He came and sat beside me. When I said I was sweaty, he told me he didn't mind.

'So, how much longer?'

'I'll have another break over Thanksgiving, next month, then I'll be home properly in December.'

I felt my eyelids closing, the energy I'd experienced first thing diluted almost to the point of disappearing. Again, I pictured Robyn alone, under the duvet. Or was it me?

'Hey,' he said, turning towards me.

I reopened my eyes.

'Can you wait?'

Those past few days, things had almost returned to the way they were before – before I'd started to feel like I was running out of time and had to take some sort of action. Really, though, when I considered what had changed, the answer was simple, staring me in the face: nothing.

'Cathy?'

'I can wait,' I said, looking him in the eye.

I hadn't realised it, but he must have been holding his breath, because he let out a sigh. He leant forward to hug me, and I repeated that I was sweaty.

He told me he didn't care.

As we embraced, I asked myself if I was lying, to him and to me, but I decided it wasn't lying if it was what we both wanted.

Finally, the date of my mother's appointment with the specialist arrived. I took the train to Norfolk and, as she had done with each of Edna's appointments, Peggy drove us to the research centre. It was starker than the surgery, a white cube with a flat roof. The car park was too big for the number of cars that would surely be present at any given time, lending it an air of unpopularity. After all my tests and scans, and with my mother's assessment process, I was getting used to spending time in waiting rooms. My senses had grown accustomed to the sights, sounds, smells. But when the automatic glass doors to the centre opened, everything seemed unfamiliar. I wondered if my mother felt the same way, and I slipped my hand into hers.

The consultant stood up and introduced himself as we walked into his office, then gestured to the seats opposite. Peggy and I sat either side, with my mother in the middle, the filling in our hastily put-together sandwich. I was so distracted by the display of framed medical achievements on the wall that I didn't catch his name. When I finally tore my eyes away from a certificate hanging wonkily on one end, and resisted reaching over and straightening it, I decided it was too late to ask him if he would mind repeating it.

'So, I'm going to examine your case in more detail,' he said, looking at my mother with eyes as glossy as marbles. 'I'll test your memory and other cognitive processes, and then I would like to do a scan.'

'And what do you hope to get from that?' asked my mother, brusquely, folding her arms across her chest.

It was out of character for her to be so irritable, and if we'd been with Edna, I might have quietly reminded her that all of this was designed to help. As it happened, I smiled, glad to hear the life in her.

Unperturbed, he told us the scan would highlight any changes in brain activity and rule out other causes for her symptoms. 'Do you have any more questions, Janey?'

Though he said it kindly, my mother must have mistakenly detected a hint of sarcasm in his voice, because she merely huffed.

This time, I mouthed an apology to him.

As he announced, 'OK then, let's get going,' the twinkle in his eye told me he'd had worse.

*

After he'd compiled all the information, including the results of the scan and the memory tests, Doctor Samuel, which I eventually gathered was his name, was ready to make the diagnosis. The night before we were due to receive it, I asked my mother over dinner if she would prefer not to know. 'I'm happy to go to the appointment alone if you would rather.'

'Of course not,' she told me, her forehead bent into a frown. After a few seconds, though, her expression softened. 'Thank you, darling.'

I put down my cutlery and reached across the table for her hand, and I told her I thought it was the right decision. That, and I'd be there beside her.

The next morning, as we piled into the car, Peggy asked if we'd like to listen to some classical music. She'd played in an orchestra as a girl and been fond of it ever since. I looked at my mother, who was wearing oddly clashing colours. She said it was fine with her, and we spent the hour-long drive listening to piano pieces so sparse they made me think of blank canvases.

In Doctor Samuel's office, we sat in the same three seats, I suppose out of habit. I glanced at the certificates on his wall and felt my fingers itch when I saw the same one was still wonky.

After a few pleasantries, he leant his elbows on his desk and clasped his hands together.

My mother jumped at the slight clapping sound.

'So, Janey, as we suspected, you're experiencing what we call the early stages of dementia,' he said. 'The cause, which is common, is Alzheimer's disease.' He paused to pass each of us a folded leaflet.

I heard Peggy turning hers over in her hands as I pressed mine down onto my fretful knees. I glanced at my mother, who was staring straight ahead, as if she didn't dare look at it, worrying her lower lip. I'd researched the various eventualities of her tests and I knew the treatment options, but still I asked the question. 'And the treatment?' I asked, forcing a smile in the hope that it might affect his answer.

'Yes, there's certainly medication we can prescribe to temporarily alleviate the symptoms,' he said, his dark eyes skipping between us, possibly trying to gauge if we understood what he meant by 'temporarily'. 'I've written to your GP, Doctor Talbot—'

'Edna,' my mother corrected.

'Edna,' he continued, 'and I've included a list of several local support services, as well as a recommended care plan.'

Like a needle, the word 'care' pierced my stomach lining.

'Do you live nearby?'

'Me?'

He nodded.

'I live in London.'

'And Janey lives alone?'

I felt the heat rising up my neck. 'Well, yes, although recently either Peggy or I have been staying with her.' I turned to my mother, still uncomfortable talking about her as if she wasn't sitting there beside me. 'Isn't that right, Mum?'

She flashed her amber eyes as she said, 'Oh yes, it's like one long sleepover.'

Peggy laughed and so did I.

'Well,' said Doctor Samuel, smiling but not laughing, 'just bear in mind that you might need to put some plans in place for when things progress.'

'You mean when things get worse,' said my mother, taking all three of us by surprise.

'I'm afraid so.'

'How long?' she asked, fixing her shining eyes on her fingers, knotted together in her lap like fishing rope.

'The speed of the progression depends on the individual, but we'll keep a close eye on things. Doctor Talbot – Edna – will be in touch about future appointments.'

She reached for her handbag.

Back when I was eleven, on the morning after my mother and I reported the washed-up sperm whale, I got up early, before either of my parents, and returned to the beach. It was quiet out, the only sounds coming from birds nesting on the marshes. I saw one or two dog walkers, their shoulders hunched up by their ears as they walked into the wind. I hadn't noticed the cold until then, and when I did, I pulled my coat tighter around my middle.

I don't know what I'd expected to find, but when I clambered over the dunes and looked down at the sand and the sea, I saw nothing. The whale was gone, disappeared. I walked up to the water and along the shore a little further in case I'd misjudged where it had been. But there was no trace – it was like someone had taken a giant brush and painted over the scene. I scoured the sand, though for what, I'm not sure. Blood, maybe.

Dumbstruck, I sat down in the middle of the empty beach. I don't know long I'd been sitting there by the time my mother arrived, but I do remember that I could barely feel my fingers.

'Cathy, thank God.' She was out of breath, her cheeks pink. When she spoke again, she sounded angry. 'You mustn't ever leave the house like that, not without telling us.'

I felt a drop in my stomach, like there had been a mistake, something was wrong. 'It's as if it was never here.'

'What are you . . .' She followed my gaze, and as she did, she let out a sigh. She sat down beside me and wrapped her arm around my shoulders, then she said, her voice softer now, 'It doesn't matter, Cathy.'

I pulled the kind of face I was prone to pulling whenever I had a bitter taste in my mouth.

'It doesn't matter that it's as if it was never here. This was the end of its life, just the very tip.' She told me not to think of it stranded on the beach. 'Think of it somewhere out there, gliding through the sea.'

I looked out at the still and glassy water beyond the froth of the waves. 'Do you think we could have done more?'

'Honestly, darling, I don't think we could have.'

She cupped my hands in hers, blew warm air onto them, and the feeling steadily returned to my fingers.

November

As autumn turned to winter, I spent most of my evenings continuing my research into my mother's condition and its inevitable progression. Noah was still in New York, and I was still dividing my time between London and Norfolk. In the city, every evening I would come home and take off my coat and boots and check the heating. It was always on, though the flat was always cold. Despite the work Noah and I had done in the bathroom and the kitchen, we hadn't got around to installing double-glazing. Whenever I touched my fingers to the window overlooking the street, already shrouded in a cloak of darkness, an icy chill would gust through me.

The day I finished retouching the seascape, I arrived home and Tom immediately began to weave in and out of my legs in figures of eight, testing my balance. One thing about living by myself was that I always knew whether he'd already been fed. After tipping some kibble into his bowl, I pulled up a chair at the dining-room table and opened my laptop. In the same way I did when I used to revise or write essays at university, I scraped my hair back from my face and up into a pile on the top of my head. I waited for the Wi-Fi to kick in, my eyes on those three little bars, then I picked up where I'd left off to the sound of Tom happily chomping pellets between his teeth.

The scan had shown that my mother's Alzheimer's had begun like most cases, with damage in the hippocampus, the structure deep inside the brain that's responsible for memory retrieval. I read that with time, the damage would get worse, making it difficult for her to remember what she'd eaten for lunch that day. Then it would spread into the cortex, stealing away her long-term memory, too. Her childhood. Her parents. Her behaviour would begin to change. Her thinking and her speaking. Her mood. I thought back to the times over the past year when she'd seemed inexplicably irritable.

As well as advising my mother to get regular exercise and drink lots of water, Doctor Samuel had prescribed a drug called Aricept, which he said would increase the levels of chemical messengers in her brain. I clicked on a link and tussled with the facts, trying to understand exactly how it would prevent an enzyme from breaking down acetylcholine, the chemical that helps to carry messages between nerve cells. It would ease at least some of the symptoms of the Alzheimer's, for a while. I kept reading. At regular intervals, I was reminded that any reprieve from the symptoms would be short-lived, and that my mother's unravelling was irretrievable.

During those evenings, when I would begin to feel the overload of scientific information pressing down on my own brain, I would pour myself a glass of wine and heat up whatever food I could find in the cupboards or the fridge. That night, I opted for leftovers from the day before: vegetable stir-fry, which had tasted surprisingly good when I'd first made it, but now looked soggy and beige.

After Doctor Samuel had brought it up at the research centre, I'd spoken to Edna about what our options would be as and when things progressed. She couldn't say for sure when my mother would need full-time care, but she did say that she wasn't far off needing someone in the house with her for at least a few hours each day. I'd always been content being an only child. I may have spent a fair amount of time by myself, but I'd learned early on how to keep myself entertained, drawing and painting. My parents were happy to take part in my make-believe games occasionally, and Anna and her family had only lived half an hour away.

Now, for the first time, I found myself longing for a sibling.

It wasn't until I was in my mid-twenties and had just started going out with Noah that I asked my mother why she and my father had never had another child. Of course, the thought had occurred to me before, but only in passing; I'd never been curious enough to formulate it in words.

We were in John Lewis, on one of our semi-regular mother-daughter shopping trips, searching for a wedding gift for a family friend, when at last I asked the question. It wasn't entirely out of the blue; we'd just been discussing the fact that this friend was one of three daughters, and that they would all no doubt want big white weddings. The parents were traditional and quite well-off, as is a certain strain of Norfolk family, which meant they would probably be picking up the bills.

My mother was still shaking her head at the prospect when I said it. She had a plain white roasting dish in her hands, and before answering she lifted it up over her head to get a look at the price tag stuck to the base. She set it back down alongside a bunch of other almost identical dishes, then she looked at me and smiled.

'You don't have to answer if you don't want to,' I said.

'Oh, it's not that,' she replied, brushing her fingers against a hand-painted serving plate with a coral design. 'I'm just surprised it's taken you this long to ask.'

She suggested we take a break from shopping and go and get some coffee, which we did at a sprawling café up on the department store's fourth floor. We rode each of the four escalators in silence and we still weren't speaking when we joined the short queue. As we sat down at a table overlooking the brightly lit atrium, a twisted intestine at the building's core, I worried something terrible might have happened.

I told her again that she needn't answer.

She blew on her cappuccino, then took a sip.

I drank some of my own and wished I'd saved this conversation for one of our walks on the beach.

'It was simple, really,' she said, still holding onto her mug. 'After we'd had you, I don't know why, but I couldn't get pregnant again.' My face must have crumpled because she told me it was all right.

'But you wanted another baby?'

'Not desperately, but yes, we thought it would be nice.'

Not desperately. I rolled the words around in my mouth and wondered if an absence of desperation would have made the absence of a child any less painful. 'I'm sorry, Mum, that must have been difficult.'

She shrugged her shoulders. 'It's in the past.' When I didn't respond, she added, 'I actually think it turned out well this way.'

'You do?'

'I do. One of your best qualities is your independence.'

'Oh, I don't know about that,' I said, thinking of the way I'd always relied on her and was already starting to rely on Noah. 'To tell you the truth, I'm not sure I'm independent at all.'

She looked at me and smiled a little harder.

When at last the painting's grand unveiling came around, I almost wished it hadn't. It had been a few weeks since I'd spent time with it one on one, alone in the conservation studios. And yet, as soon as it was secure in its frame and hanging on the wall in one of the galleries for everyone to see, I felt like I'd been cheated. I wasn't ready to say goodbye. I wanted more time with it.

It had only been framed the week before. After I'd sprayed on a final coat of protective varnish, Frank and I had got together with the curator and discussed what might work formally with the painting. In the end, we'd opted for an original from the same period. I'd accompanied it to the framing department, hidden from prying eyes in a wooden crate, and then – like a mother dropping off a child at the school gates – I'd waved it goodbye and, exercising all my efforts on not looking back, walked away.

It happens. Spending months, sometimes a year, with the same work of art can lead to a certain attachment – especially, I find, with works that contain people. But I hadn't experienced this kind of loss since the first painting I'd worked on unsupervised. If I close my eyes, I can still picture every detail on its surface. The ultramarine blue of the Virgin's gown, hanging loose in soft, fluid folds. The delicate pinpricks of light in her halo, glowing a golden yellow. The way her toes graze the edge of the canvas, as if she's testing the distance between us and capable of stepping out of her world and into mine at any moment.

There would be several unveilings of *View of Scheveningen Sands*, for patrons and other important people, the press, the public. First, though, came a slightly more informal debut for museum staff.

We gathered in the gallery to listen to a presentation by the director. The air was vibrating with chatter and excitement, and when I heard the squeak of a speaker, I realised with a jolt of surprise that the last talk I'd attended was the one Doctor Day had given at the fertility clinic's open evening. My thoughts stumbled to my frozen eggs, and then to Robyn's, less plentiful, her chances slim. I could feel my palms getting clammy when Frank slipped a cold glass of wine into one of them.

'Where did you get this?' I asked, glancing around to see if anyone else was drinking and holding my glass down low, out of sight, when I realised the answer was no.

He tapped the side of his nose.

'Frank?'

'Fine, there was a function last night.'

My eyes flashed towards my glass. 'It's the good stuff?'

There's a noticeable difference between the wine on offer at patrons' events and what the staff get.

He took a long, slow sip, then smacked his lips together. 'It is indeed.' Less than discreetly, he moved his own glass towards mine.

I coughed in an effort to drown out the clinking sound, but there was no need: just as our glasses made contact, the director began speaking.

'Thank you all for giving up your Thursday evening to be here to celebrate this truly remarkable story,' he said, smiling, his voice sounding through a small black microphone clipped onto the white collar of his shirt. 'It's not often that a painting comes into the conservation department and goes out completely transformed.'

As he gave a brief overview of Hendrick's life and career and touched on the history of seventeenth-century Dutch maritime scenes, I found myself wondering what I would be working on next. There had been talk of an oil painting from the same period, except this one was on canvas and created in Italy; a landscape, I think. The next six months or so would be taken care of, predictable and full. I was considering whether that was a good thing – it would be a nice balance, perhaps, to the unpredictability of my personal life – when I felt Frank's finger in my side.

'What?' I asked, rubbing the spot where he'd got me, just below my ribs.

'Where are you, Catherine?'

I balked. The director was talking to me.

When I didn't respond, Frank did. 'She's here,' he called, stretching up onto his tiptoes and raising a hand like a schoolboy in case anyone failed to follow the sound of his rusty voice.

Without warning, an uncompromising sea of faces turned towards me.

'Well, come on up here, Catherine.'

Frank gave me a nudge, and the sea parted.

'I want to thank you personally,' said the director, when I was standing beside him, holding my free hand over my glass in a last-ditch attempt to conceal it. 'For your hard work and your patience.'

I was blushing, I could feel it.

'For restoring this marvellous painting to its original appearance, as the artist intended it.'

I felt something else. Proud?

'Would you like to say something?'

The faces smiled encouragingly.

'Oh, yes,' I said. I smiled back and took a moment before opening my mouth. 'I would just like to say that spending the past few months with this painting has been a pleasure.' I paused, surprised to feel the sting of tears. I blinked them back and looked at the stretch of wall to the director's right where the seascape was hanging. There it was, waves rippling against the shore, clouds roiling in the thinly scumbled sky, the old church like a lighthouse in the background, and in the foreground the crowd. At the centre of it all, the whole point of the painting, the character giving it its plot: the beached whale. A portent from God, maybe, but also the thing that had brought these people together, the thing that would nourish them.

'Catherine?'

I dragged my eyes away from the painting and back towards the expectant faces before me. I felt nourished, too. 'I hope you all grow to care for Hendrick and his whale as much as I do.'

On top of the two glasses of wine he'd snuck into the unveiling, Frank, who was clearly in the mood for celebrating, had suggested a drink around the corner. So, after I'd spoken to a few colleagues, and thanked the director somewhat awkwardly for thanking me, we reconvened by the exit.

Although it was the start of winter, the air was dry and warm enough when you were wearing a coat. Frank had been rolling a cigarette when I found him, and he wasn't done smoking it when we reached the pub, which was just off Leicester Square and predictably crowded. I left him to finish it outside and squeezed through to the bar, where I finally caught the eye of the red-faced barman. I ordered Frank a pint and myself another glass of wine.

'Cheers,' said Frank, after I'd made it back out to the front. He bowed his head in thanks and clinked his glass against mine. 'How does it feel,' he asked, taking a sip, a hint of foam lining his upper lip, 'to have worked on a painting that next month is going to feature in every newspaper and magazine up and down the country?'

I smiled and told him to keep his voice down.

He tossed his head back in amusement, and I could see why – the mostly suited men around us didn't look like the sort to be keeping their ears pricked for embargoed museum announcements.

'Also, I think *every* magazine and newspaper might be a bit of an exaggeration.'

'So?' he probed.

'So, it feels good,' I said, surprising myself as I realised that it really did. Life remained full of uncertainty. Yet here I was, ringing in the end of one of my most exciting conservation projects to date, and it felt good, I felt good. More than good, I felt happy.

It was perhaps for that reason that one drink led to another, and then another, until, suddenly, we were on our fourth round. I'd switched to gin and tonic. Frank was still on beer. I watched as he took a swig and wiped his foamy lip with the back of his hand, which he then wiped on his trouser leg. I laughed, covering my mouth when I caught sight of his lifted brow. 'Sorry, Frank, it's just I don't think I've ever seen you this relaxed!'

'And you?'

'Hm?' I asked, taking a sip of my own drink.

'Are you feeling more relaxed?'

I wasn't sure whether he was referencing Noah or my frozen eggs or my mother or all of the above. Either way, I tilted my head to one side, then said, 'I think I am.'

'You think?'

'Well, it's hard to tell . . .' I waved my glass in front of his face. Too much. Clear liquid overflowed and splatted on the pavement.

He laughed.

'Can I ask you a question, Frank?'

'Depends on the question.'

'Do you and Douglas ever regret not having children?'

He blew out his cheeks. 'If I'd known that was coming, I'd have got myself another refill.'

'How have you already finished yours?!' I peered into my own glass, still half full despite the spillage, and drank some more.

He smiled, with a furrowed brow. 'Is that what you're afraid of – regret?' Before I had time to reply, he added: 'Because you don't need me to tell you that you can't live your life like that.'

I didn't need him to tell me that, but at the same time, I did. The gin was hitting me now. And the wine. 'You're a wise man, Frank.'

He nodded, gravely. 'I have heard that before.'

I watched him for a moment, noticing the way his face changed as he continued with what he was saying.

'We asked ourselves how much we wanted it.'

'Parenthood?' I asked.

'Parenthood.'

'And?'

'And we realised that we'd somehow managed to escape it – not parenthood, I mean, but that need that overwhelms some people. Maybe it's emotional or biological, I don't know. Either way, in the end, we decided not to force ourselves into it.'

'And it doesn't make you sad?' I asked, leaning my elbow on the windowsill, and my chin in the palm of my hand. 'Not wanting this thing that gives so many other people's lives meaning?'

Again, he smiled, but not in the same way. 'When I was a teenager, I never imagined I would ever get married, let alone have children.'

'And?'

'There's no one definition of family, Cathy, remember that.'

I nodded. I would.

He peered into his glass then nodded his head towards mine to ask if I wanted another.

'Yes.'

He eyed me suspiciously. 'And maybe some chips.'

'Chips, yes. Brilliant. And ketchup.'

He laughed again and turned to go inside. Before he did, though, he turned back around and said, 'You know, meaning comes from all sorts of things – take getting drunk with a friend.'

I couldn't remember the last time I'd been out two nights in a row, but the next day Anna suggested we meet for cocktails

– real for me, pretend for her. I'd been seeing what I could of her between work, my research rabbit holes, and regular visits to Norfolk. Though my mother's confidence in my ability to spend time alone was unerring, my best friend clearly worried about me being in the flat by myself. The couple of times when she came out and said just that, I reminded her that I wasn't by myself: I had Tom. She said that was her point exactly.

I tried to ignore the pounding headache that I'd woken up with, and washed and blow-dried my hair. I put on a silky black dress with long sleeves and a scooped back, and even took time to run a mascara wand through my eyelashes and draw some liquid eyeliner across my upper lids. I spritzed the insides of my wrists with a bottle of perfume Noah had given me, and as I did so, I wondered if he was going out much in New York. He hadn't mentioned it, but then again, would he? I shook my head and put a mental stop to my speculation. With Noah, there was no need for it.

Anna had suggested a bar between my place and hers, tucked away on a side street on the fringes of Islington. It was small and dimly lit, with just a handful of tables and chairs.

'Can we sit there?' Anna asked a bartender with overly tended-to stubble as she pointed to a piano in the corner.

I laughed, then raised my eyebrows when he said yes.

'This is great,' I said, peeling off my coat and hooking it onto one arm of a wooden stand by the door.

Anna wolf-whistled and, in a phoney accent, told me I scrubbed up good.

I told her to shush. 'Well, I'm hungover, and I thought I should at least try to hide it.'

We sat side by side on two stools where a piano stool should have been, our knees touching. Anna was dressed up, too, a less unusual sight, in a blue velvet shirt and a matching pair of trousers. Whenever she moved, the velvet caught the light and the shade of blue brightened. Watching it felt like being at sea. I brushed my fingers against the material, which was soft to touch.

'Here are your menus, ladies.'

I looked again at the bartender's stubble and tried to picture what kind of state Noah's would be in by now.

'See, I knew this place had more than a couple of mocktails.'

I smiled and quickly skimmed the menu, recognising only a few names. 'An almond Bellini for me, I think.'

After we'd ordered and watched the initial mixing of our drinks, I asked her how she was feeling. 'You don't seem to be as nauseous this time?'

'No, this one's being good to me,' she said, stroking the palm of her hand across her barely visible belly.

'How long has it been?'

She took a sharp intake of air before she said, 'Almost eighteen weeks.'

I reached out my hand and rested it on hers.

'I am vaguely starting to relax,' she said, breathing out a long, slow breath, then exclaiming happily as our drinks arrived, along with a shallow ceramic bowl of salted almonds.

We clinked glasses.

'And you?' she asked.

'Hm, what about me?' I took a sip, and in an instant, felt my headache fade. 'Oh, this is delicious.'

'So is this,' she said, wiggling her non-alcoholic drink in front of my face.

I laughed. 'Sorry.'

'So?'

I took another sip, then I told her what I'd told Frank – that I was feeling more relaxed, too.

Now it was her turn to touch my hand. 'How's your mum?'

'Up and down,' I said, quickly. I paused, then added, 'Sometimes she has moments of total lucidity, and not just in terms of what she says and remembers. I can actually see it in her eyes; it's like they're brighter somehow. At other times, there's no way of getting through to her or making her understand. It's as if she isn't in the room with me.' I thought but didn't say that, when that happened, it was as if I wasn't in the room either.

'How's she doing living-wise? Do you think you'll need to get someone in full-time?'

'At some point, yes.' I told her that, for now, Peggy and I were managing between the two of us. I smiled as I said, 'I think Peggy quite likes having someone to take care of again.'

'But at some point, it will get too much for her, no?'

'It will, but not yet.'

'Well, if there's anything I can do to help,' she said, her eyes squinting into a smile. 'You just want to have a plan in place.'

'Thank you,' I said. 'I know, I'm working on it.'

The waiter was hovering by our sides. 'Another?' he asked.

I hadn't realised that I was already down to the dregs of my Bellini. My eyes flashed towards Anna's glass, and I felt myself blush when I saw that it was still half full of yellow liquid.

'Hey, I would be drinking a lot quicker if there was booze in this.'

I laughed and turned to the waiter, whose own lips were curving upwards. 'I'll have the same again.'

I could tell that Anna wanted to ask me something else but was trying to work out if now was the right time. Her mouth opened, more than once. Both times, she closed it again and bit down onto her lower lip with her two front teeth. When it happened for a third time, I asked what was on her mind.

'I'm sorry, I feel like I'm interrogating you.'

As the waiter handed me my second almond Bellini of the night, I said, 'Don't worry, keep these coming and I won't even notice.'

She laughed.

Noah would be laughing, too, if he were here. He always drank more than I did and found it funny when I tried to keep up.

As if she'd read my mind, Anna asked after him. 'Have the two of you managed to talk more this time?' When he first left, and I'd told her the five-hour time difference made lengthy phone calls tricky, she'd said that was a crappy excuse and I knew it.

'We have.'

She smiled, visibly relieved.

I popped an almond into my mouth and crunched it down between my molars.

'When's he next coming home?'

'Quite soon, actually,' I said, sensing a coil unfurling inside me. 'He gets a few days off around Thanksgiving, which is in a couple of weeks.' I drank some of my drink, trying to focus on the feeling of it slipping down my throat. 'And then it will be December and he'll be back for good.'

'And that makes you happy?'

It was such a straightforward question, and yet my answer was in knots. I tried to untangle it, then realised doing so would require that I also untangle the fate of my frozen eggs.

'Have you made a decision, Cathy?' With her eyes, she indicated towards my stomach.

I sucked it in and glanced around the room. The bar had filled up since we'd arrived, mostly with couples, which I assumed was partly down to space limitations. In one corner, two small tables had been pushed together to accommodate a party of four, but other than that, the space was set up for intimate encounters. Closest to us were a man and a woman, both of whom looked around Noah's age. They leant towards one another as they talked, closing the already narrow gap between their faces. At one point, he reached forward and brushed some hair away from her eyes. I looked away like I'd seen something I shouldn't.

Anna must have followed my gaze, because when I turned back to her, she was still watching them.

'Do you think they have children?' I asked.

I half expected her to whip her head around and ask why I cared. Instead, she kept watching, then she slowly turned to me and said, 'It's hard to tell.'

'They look happy,' I said, feeling the emotion rising within me, like a wave.

She agreed. 'They do.' After a moment, she asked, 'And you?'

I swivelled my legs around and under the piano, as if I was about to spread my fingers and play.

Anna did the same, a silent duet.

I looked down at the keys and wished my life was as black and white, then I bristled at the cliché. I thought back to how I'd felt the night before, how I'd felt happy, and why.

Anna touched her toes to mine. 'Cathy, I know it's hard, but you have to find a way to move forward, one way or the other.'

Gently, with my index finger, I pressed down on one key. It made a pleasing sound, and I craned my neck to see if anyone had noticed. As before, they were drinking and chatting, enjoying an evening out, carefree. 'I know,' I said, touching the same finger to the same key, but this time not exerting any pressure. 'I know what I want, what I need.'

The last time I'd been on a plane was when Noah and I went to Florence in the spring. I'm not exactly a nervous flyer, but I do prefer to have someone with me when I'm up in the sky, especially when the metal chamber starts to tremble.

On the plane to New York, passengers were getting settled before take-off and flight attendants were sweeping up and down the aisles. I angled my head to the left and watched as the woman beside me bent forward over her knees to unlace and remove her trainers. With long manicured nails, she tore into the polythene bag that contained her in-flight blanket, and after shaking it loose pulled it up to her chin. She slipped on an eye mask that replaced the features of her own face with those of a reptile. The shiny scales shifted slightly as she ran her tongue over a crack in her lower lip. That was the last movement I would see from her until the wheels hit the tarmac with a bump at JFK.

On my right was a man who was spilling over his own seat into mine. When he'd first sat down, he'd given me the kind of smile that contained an apology within its creases. The less-than-smiley flight attendant, whose arm he'd tapped as she was passing by, had brought him an extension for his belt. He shuffled in his seat as he attached it. Thankfully, my own slight build meant that even with his overspill our unfamiliar bodies didn't need to come into contact. Once he was comfortable, he turned his attention to the small screen built into the back of the seat in front of him. I stared at my own version of a home cinema, which was pitch black, dormant.

Can't it wait? That was Anna's response when I'd messaged her first thing and told her I was on my way to the airport. I was on the Tube at the time, another metal chamber, with limited access to Wi-Fi, so the conversation had been stilted. It had gone something like this:

Me: *I'm going to New York*

Anna: *What????*

Me: *To see Noah*

Me: *To talk*

Anna: *Didn't you say he's coming back in a couple of weeks?*

Me: *I need to tell him I've made up my mind*

Anna: *Can't it wait?*

Me: *It can't wait*

I'd bought a plane ticket on my way back to the flat from the bar – and not because I'd drunk too many almond Bellinis. I'd decided to walk rather than take the overground, and after five minutes or so on a busy stretch I found myself winding through quieter streets. The view into most houses was blocked off with curtains, shutters, blinds. The shadowy pavements were pricked with rays of artificial light beaming down from tall lamp-posts. When I looked up at the sky, I could see smoke-like clouds drifting with the current through the dark.

As I walked, I turned over in my mind the questions that, over the past few months, almost the past year, had made me feel unthinkably stuck. Whether or not I wanted to have a baby. What would happen if I decided I didn't and then later came to regret it. Whether Noah would ever change his mind. What would happen if he didn't. What it all meant for our marriage.

Like a hoover, these questions had been sucking up my time. Time I no longer wanted to toss away. Time that wasn't, as my mother's condition had reminded me, in endless supply. I was rounding the bend onto our street when I considered the one thing we all know for certain: at some point, we will die.

It wasn't a dramatic thought, accompanied by crashing waves; it didn't make me feel like I was drowning, short of breath, desperate for air. Instead, it came to me calmly and rationally, and as it sank in, I felt like I was being released from a vice.

The flight attendants did one final sweep, and the plane began to roll across the tarmac, slowly at first, then faster. I felt an invisible force press my body back against my seat. I heard the rumble of the engine. A voiceover talking about safety.

Either way, there was going to be a loss. But I knew what I wanted, and I was going to tell him.

Epilogue

I wanted her bedroom to be just right. I leafed through my sketchbooks and teased out my favourite charcoal and pencil drawings of strands of seaweed that twisted like ribbons, seagulls with bracket-like wings, lumpy sand dunes, the vast and open sea. I took them to my local framer, then I arranged them on the carpet and one by one hung them all on the same yellow wall, an ode to Norfolk and our very own stretch of the beach. I dotted the windowsill with shells and pebbles I'd collected over the years and brought back to the house, my coat pockets clattering. On the chest of drawers is a small ceramic vase that I keep filled with flowers: pink and red tulips, honey-sweet freesias, creamy anemones. Occasionally I leave them too long and the petals begin to fade and lose their grip.

My mother always told me not to look too far ahead, to live in the present. For a while I forgot to heed her advice. But I wasn't the only one forgetting. Christmas came and went and one year rolled seamlessly into the next. By mid-January I was spending more than half my time in Norfolk. I'd heard friends talk about babyproofing their homes and now I felt I was doing the same, in a way.

I replaced her house phone with one with extra-large pads and speed dial, writing my name, along with Peggy's and Edna's, in block capitals on the programmable buttons. With the remote, I taped up every button except for the soft red nodule that turned the TV on and off. I tucked away any electric cords and cables that might cause her to trip and bought first a non-slip mat with tentacle-like suckers, and later wall handles and a small white stool, for the shower. I replaced her lace-up shoes with Velcro ones. All the while, she watched me with eyes that grew more and more narrow.

By the spring she had a professional carer with her five days a week. She was struggling to focus on any given task, to stay connected. She would start reading a book and a few pages in forget what had happened and go back to the beginning, two, three, four times before sending the book flying. One week she went flying herself; the carer didn't see what happened, and my mother didn't tell anyone, but when I visited her next, I noticed that her wrist was bruised and swollen. I asked her if it hurt, and she looked at me with vacant eyes and asked, What, darling? The sky was an azure blue and the fields glowing gold with rape when Peggy and I finally sat down together at the kitchen table and made the decision we'd both known was coming all along: it was time to move my mother into a nursing home.

Her bedroom overlooks a garden that's small and plain in comparison with the one she so lovingly planted at home, but tidy and inviting, nonetheless. The lawn is mown every other week by the same friendly man who comes to water the flower beds and the hanging baskets in the days in between. If the weather is nice, my mother is encouraged to walk around or sit for a while on one of the wooden benches. When the temperature drops and she refuses to come back inside, a kind woman brings her a mug of milky tea and a soft woollen blanket.

For the first few weeks, she would pack her bag every night in anticipation of returning home the following morning. To ease the transition, we'd been advised to tell her that her house needed some building work and it would be best for her to move out temporarily. A month in and any thoughts of home were forgotten, like an item of clothing that had slipped down the back of the sofa and begun to gather dust. My nerves quietened when I saw her settled, but a part of me also willed her to keep fighting.

Her body has become a plaster cast – a copy of her former self. Her mind is torn with holes, more recent memories muddled with those from long ago. Frayed recollections of my father and me are interspersed with those of her own parents and herself as a child, the whole lot jumbled up. Hers is a static sort of half-presence.

'There you are.' Noah finds me sitting on the wooden bench my father installed in that awkward corner at the top of the stairs, facing the narrow, arched window.

'Here I am.' I watch as he walks barefoot towards me. Against his linen shirt, a pale grey, his skin is a light brown, fresh from spending the day on the beach. I feel my cheeks lift when I see he's still wearing his shorts. The summer air is hot and thick, even though it's evening.

'I brought you a nightcap,' he says, handing me a small glass of something honey-coloured.

I crane my neck to look up at him, and I smile.

He leans down to plant a kiss on the crown of my head, then slots in behind me, the two of us facing towards the window now, which is open a crack, overlooking the sea.

Apart from birdsong and the gentle rumble of a farm vehicle still hard at work in the next-door field, there's no sound. The sky is dark, with a hazy yellow strip running like gold leaf along the horizon.

'What time are we expecting the storm tomorrow?' he asks.

I laugh. 'Anna said they'd be here around midday.'

Noah has an unofficial goddaughter now, a sister to my unofficial godson. Anna's pregnancy continued without complications, and she gave birth to a baby girl called Camille. We asked if they were sure that they wanted us both to be godparents, and Caleb told us yes, and that in fact they also wanted us to be the children's legal guardians. He said there was no one else they would trust more to take care of them if anything happened to him and Anna. When he said it, my heart swelled.

'Then we'll probably all head back to London on Sunday evening, if that works?'

'That works.'

Noah slips an arm around my waist, and I lean back until my body is resting against his. I stretch out my legs and gently push the window open wider with my toes. He remarks on how dextrous I am.

The marshes stretch out like a dozy animal beneath the night sky. I can no longer make out details, just vague shapes, highlights and shadows. I squint at the sea, just for a moment, then I blink and, like a camera lens, readjust my focus to what's there right in front of my face.

It was a year of asking questions. A year of indecision. And now? The questions remain, but there's no longer just one option.

I look down at my hand, in Noah's.

I see clearly now.

Acknowledgements

Thank you to Emma Finn, for her encouragement and guidance, and to all at C&W. To Zoe Yang and Carina Bryan, for their thoughtful edits, and to Serena Arthur, Sareeta Domingo and the entire team at Trapeze for nudging my manuscript (and me) through to publication. To Alex Layt, Helena Fouracre and Virginia Woolstencroft for getting the word out.

I'm grateful to everyone who read earlier drafts, especially Steph Siddall, Daisy Watt, Sally Foreman and Sonia Zhuravlyova. To the women in my life with whom I've had conversations about bodies and blood tests and babies, and to the women who started those conversations in the first place.

To the galleries and museums for inspiring me. Cathy's discovery of the beached whale in Hendrick's painting is, as they say, based on a true story. I encourage you to seek out *View of Scheveningen Sands* at the Fitzwilliam Museum in Cambridge. Thanks to Shan Kuang, for speaking with me about peeling back the layers of oil paint and uncovering a hidden history.

To the writers, readers and booksellers with whom I've come into contact online and in person since the publication of *Wet Paint*. Your ongoing support means everything.

To the whole extended Ashby/Cotton/Begley family. To Tristan and Fran, and Granny Jane and Poppa, for their cheerleading. To my dad, Charlie, for talking to me about what it's like to care for a parent who's forgetting. To my mum, Anne, and stepdad, Adam, for doing all they do, and doing it so well and so generously.

And to Ollie, for giving me the change of scene I was craving to help me write my second novel. For talking and for listening. For always meeting me in the middle.

Credits

Trapeze would like to thank everyone at Orion who worked on the publication of *Second Self*.

Agent
Emma Finn

Editorial
Serena Arthur
Zoe Yang
Carina Bryan

Copy-editor
Donna Hillyer

Proofreader
Kim Bishop

Audio
Paul Stark
Jake Alderson

Editorial Management
Charlie Panayiotou
Jane Hughes
Bartley Shaw
Tamara Morriss
Claire Boyle

Contracts
Anne Goddard
Dan Herron
Ellie Bowker

Design
Tomas Almeida
Nick Shah
Joanna Ridley
Nick May
Helen Ewing

Picture Research
Natalie Dawkins

Finance
Nick Gibson
Jasdip Nandra
Sue Baker
Tom Costello

Inventory
Jo Jacobs
Dan Stevens

Marketing
Helena Fouracre

Production
Claire Keep
Katie Horrocks

Publicity
Alex Layt
Virginia Woolstencroft

Sales
Jen Wilson
Victoria Laws
Esther Waters

Group Sales teams across Digital, Field Sales, International and Non-Trade
Georgina Cutler

Group Sales Operations team
Sharon Willis

Rights
Rebecca Folland
Barney Duly
Ruth Blakemore
Flora McMichael
Ayesha Kinley
Marie Henckel